ELVIS IN KABUL

ELVIS
IN
KABUL

DS MACDONALD

The Book Guild Ltd

First published in Great Britain in 2021 by
The Book Guild Ltd
9 Priory Business Park
Wistow Road, Kibworth
Leicestershire, LE8 0RX
Freephone: 0800 999 2982
www.bookguild.co.uk
Email: info@bookguild.co.uk
Twitter: @bookguild

This book includes references to actual places, people and events,
but it should be read as a work of fiction. All dialogue is invented and any real
incidents have been altered or reimagined.

Typeset in 11pt Baskerville

Printed and bound in the UK by TJ Books LTD, Padstow, Cornwall

ISBN 978 1913913 717

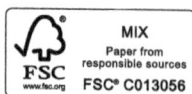

MIX
Paper from
responsible sources
FSC® C013056

For Liz, Lucy and Roseanna
with love

Security is like oxygen. You tend not to notice it until you begin to lose it, but once that occurs there is nothing else that you will think about.

Joseph S. Nye Jnr,
Harvard University *Foreign Affairs*, July/August 2005

We keep cruising down this road
trying to be Elvis, looking for mercy and a
shoulder to cry on tonight.

Willy Clay Band,
Trying to Be Elvis, 2006

ONE

AT THE SCENE, IN KABUL,

Thursday 19 October 2005

The one-armed Elvis dangled from the vehicle's mirror, its hand clutching a silver microphone held close to a mouth baring tiny white teeth. The other arm, wrenched from its socket leaving a sharp metal spring exposed, looked dangerous. The arm itself lay stiff and abandoned in the well below the ashtray.

Elvis was dressed for Las Vegas. Tight white trousers with red flared inserts topped by a bolero adorned with rhinestones in the design of an eagle. The bird glinted in the last rays of the early evening sun. Dark sunglasses and a fixed sneer on the singer's curled lips gave nothing away.

The small figure slowly spun on its twisted cord surrounded by a shattered windscreen and doors perforated with bullet holes. The vehicle had the look of a giant colander rather than a smart new Toyota Land

1

Cruiser. A pool of dark brown blood lay congealed on the front seat, its sharp metallic odour lingering. There was no other sign that anyone had ever been inside the vehicle's plush leather interior.

By the time Gil and Mario arrived at the scene it was dusk, the street quiet. Olivier declined to come with them even though he was the agency boss. Apart from the office and guesthouse, he was reluctant to drive anywhere in the city, especially as darkness approached.

Elvis was still there, now suspended motionless in the silent vehicle. Who could have done such a thing to Waheed, a mild-mannered and well-respected agency driver? The signs of carnage produced a stunned look on Mario's face. Gil looked grim as he surveyed the scene but his mind was elsewhere. He hardly noticed the small plastic figure hanging from the mirror, distinctively bright against the vehicle's darkening interior.

The figure of Elvis was economically worthless, a plastic icon of otherness in such a foreign land. In the spring of 1999 it had come free with a pair of Kef B400 loudspeakers proudly purchased by Danny Lawson, a social worker from Castlemilk housing estate on the south side of Glasgow.

Along with a white coffee mug with 'Richer Sounds' emblazoned on its side in bold red and black letters, it was taken home and left in a cupboard drawer. There was no way that Mary Lawson would entertain a plastic Elvis hanging from the windscreen of their three-year-old Ford Fiesta. No way. Displaying hoi polloi kitsch in public was anathema to her east coast aspirations.

Elvis languished in the drawer for a year until Mary's annual spring clear-out when he was donated to an Oxfam shop up Byres Road along with other unwanted gifts and sundry household junk. Within a few days he had been snapped up by ten-year-old Ahmed Shinwari, the son of a Pakistani greengrocer resident in Glasgow for over thirty years. Elvis was a bargain at only forty pence, plastically perfect with both arms still intact.

Mr Shinwari was a doting father. He was relaxed enough to allow Ahmed to hang Elvis from his van's mirror where he happily dangled for the next six months. As the old Transit stuttered down the road it caused Ahmed no end of delight as the figure swayed and danced to the sounds of his father's qawwali cassette tapes. His eldest brother Shiraz, brown suede winklepicker boots poking from cream-coloured shalwar, feigned disinterest but was even more delighted.

It was a few months later that Ahmed's paternal grandfather unexpectedly died at the family compound in a village outside Peshawar on the tight winding road leading to the Khyber Pass. Immediately Ahmed, his father, mother and three brothers made plans to return to Pakistan for the funeral – accompanied by Elvis. It was a long journey and the boy felt exhausted when they finally reached his grandfather's house.

The next day many relatives, and there were many, came to the house to say their salaams and pay respects. These included Ahmed's first cousin Hassan, who had spent his childhood in the wild hills of the North West Frontier Province learning to shoot an old .22 bore rifle before his sixth birthday and an AK-47 Kalashnikov assault rifle to celebrate his eleventh, although it knocked him off his feet the first time he fired it. His shoulder had been proudly bruised to a deep purple for weeks. The two boys bonded immediately and when Hassan departed for his village a few days later the only thing of worth that Ahmed could give him was the Elvis figure.

It was early September when Hassan accompanied his father on a business trip to Afghanistan, taking Elvis along for the ride, although he was forbidden from hanging the plastic figure on the windscreen. The Taliban forbade any public display of effigies, replicas or any other representations of human or animal form. They were heathens as far as Hassan's father was concerned.

The fifty kilometres of road from Peshawar to the Torkham border post passed through lawless tribal lands as it snaked its way up the mountainous pass through endless hairpin bends before being sucked into the black hole of Afghanistan. Hassan, trying to avoid throwing-up, concentrated on watching the armed tribesman from his village sitting in the back of the bouncing truck, shining slits of eyes never fully closed even as he snored loudly.

The old Pajero soon passed a walled compound belonging to one of Pakistan's better-known drug traffickers. The walls were twenty feet high marking a one-kilometre perimeter. Inside, so it was said by those who claimed to know, lay a near-Olympic size swimming pool, two houses posing as mini-palaces, a mosque, two chained monkeys and a flock of strutting peacocks. Not to mention an armoury that would have made the Pakistan military proud. Drugs were a lucrative business.

The border at the pass was dominated by a set of high thick wooden gates imposingly set between brick walls that stopped abruptly as they reached the near-vertical mountains cradling the pass. Bustling, jostling crowds and impatient lines of vehicles squeezed past each other and through to the other side. Even minor Pakistani border officials paid over a thousand dollars for a job at the gate. Juicy bribes were easily extracted from paperless people.

Today the area round the gate was chaotic. A flood of would-be refugees was trying to forge its way into Pakistan, but the long-time tide was turning. The government wanted no more drug traffickers, carpetbaggers, economic migrants – no more Afghans. The country was saturated with them. Even after twenty-five years of war most of the two million Afghan refugees left embedded in the cities and refugee camps of Pakistan were resolute in their attempts not to return to the Taliban, whatever their reasons for arriving in the first place. The border stretched for over two thousand miles, a faint line on the map, porous for all and a well-oiled revolving door for those with business on either side.

Hassan's father knew one of the gate guards, a grinning Pashtun with teeth stained red from chewing betel nuts. A fifty-dollar handshake and their passports were soon stamped, the gates edged open, and they drove through and into Afghanistan.

The dilapidated shed that passed for an immigration

hall was smoke-filled and windowless apart from a small square hole chiselled high in the wall facing the door. The white flag of the Taliban hung listlessly on a flagpole above the shed. Inside, the stern black-turbaned officials sat cross-legged on the packed earth floor next to a battered old wooden desk. One of them jumped to his feet and took the offered passports, swiftly handing them over to his seated companions.

Another older Talib, a closed enigmatic look on his face, languidly perused the documents, stamped them with a hand stamp that left little impression on the paper, and invited Hassan and his father to 'stay for tea and biscuits'. A selection of guns and RPGs, the rocket-propelled grenades second only to Kalashnikovs as the Afghan weapon of choice, sat casually propped against the wall as if they were old walking sticks.

The Talib laughed, his dark eyes transforming in the sole shaft of sunlight that entered the room. Hassan's father politely declined the offer and they quickly made their way back to the vehicle.

Hassan's eyes stayed glued to the window as they passed the container city lining both sides of the road immediately after the border. He had never seen anything so vast. The containers were shipped from Bandar Abbas in Iran then driven through Afghanistan to Torkham, where most of the goods sat waiting to be smuggled into Pakistan. Each container functioned as a shop, the back peeled off as if it were a sardine tin, its wares immediately and invitingly on display.

The turbaned merchants sat in front of their steel-lined

emporiums, drinking tea and gossiping. Car parts, fridges, televisions, video recorders, stereo systems, boxes of soap, thick multi-coloured Korean blankets, power tools plus assorted pots and pans and other domestic goods whizzed by in a kaleidoscopic blur as they settled onto the road to Jalalabad.

Most of the road still had a reasonable tarred surface as it cut a swathe through a countryside littered with the debris of war, the scatterings of Soviet failure. A matt green tank, still rust-free and fresh-looking in the dry climate, sat on the roadside at a rakish angle. Even its scrap value had not tempted anyone to test the cruelty of Soviet ingenuity. Faded Cyrillic writing was visible on its side. Hassan wanted to stop and remove a small red metal star attached to the turret.

His father laughed. 'Hassan, my son, this tank has been lying here for over ten years. Why do you think it remains? It is mined. Do you see the stones painted red that surround it? They are a warning. It has killed many of our people in the past. Even now it could kill you.'

As the tank receded into the distance, Hassan glanced back over his shoulder. The small red star embellishing its turret would have made a great souvenir to show his friends, better even than Elvis.

The passing countryside served as a lush oasis that enveloped the road running along the south bank of the river Kabul. Such greenery lay in stark contrast to the dun rock-bound mountains rising from the north side of the river towards the snow-capped peaks of the Hindu Kush. Further to the south lay the famed white mountains of the Spin Ghar and the cave complex of Tora Bora.

Much of Nangarhar's fertile plain was poppy territory, but now the fields lay fallow; only a few were planted in wheat. Mullah Omar's ban on poppy cultivation proved ruthlessly effective. The value of the Taliban's stockpiles of opium had risen as cultivation fell, leaving farmers even poorer and their families suffering. Children went hungry. Sons were taken out of school. Daughters sold to pay debts. Raw opium gum fetched ten times the price of wheat.

Hassan's father knew the Taliban banned opium so prices would increase and the profit from the sale of their own considerable stocks would soar. Hassan's father knew a lot about opium; it was his business, the reason for visiting Kabul.

Soon thousands of olive trees appeared standing in long straight lines, an endless grove stretching along the roadside and off to the horizon where the mountains began. The trees were thick and bushy, resembling old English oaks, their branches gnarled and wizened-looking, never pruned since the olives were picked and canned in a nearby Soviet-run factory now lying derelict and broken.

Soon they were driving through Jalalabad, capital of the province. A place frequented by rich Kabuli families escaping the biting winter cold of the capital. Now it was late summer and still baking hot in the plains. Hassan squashed a fat malarial mosquito against the side window of the Pajero and watched its tiny blood-flecked innards dribble down the glass.

Deciding not to stop in the city, they opted for a short break at Sarobi some miles to the west before the paved road to Kabul gave way to little more than a potholed track. War

8

had claimed it; there was little serviceable paved surface left. It was difficult to avoid the occasional shell or mortar hole that pockmarked the road. Hassan's teeth crunched together as the Pajero rattled over the surface. Nevertheless, this was a busy main artery, a commercial lifeline with a never-ending stream of vehicles plying their trade to and from Kabul.

Brightly painted Pakistani trucks, old dented Peugeot 504s and dusty yellow and white Corolla taxis all bounced along, swerving wildly to avoid each other as well as the odd donkey cart or pedestrian. A motley collection of SUVs prevailed, including a white Toyota double cab full of black-turbaned Talibs on their way to the frontline against the Northern Alliance only twenty-five miles to the north, their bedrolls and weapons slung in the back, the RPG heads painted in vibrant metallic blues and greens.

Soon the road started to climb through rolling foothills and past the dilapidated headquarters of a commander from the dark anarchic days of the early nineties when mujahideen factions were locked in mortal combat. The headquarters included a restaurant where passing vehicles were invited by the commander and his men to stop for lunch.

'An expensive lunch,' Hassan overheard his father tell their guard, a distant cousin who had never visited Afghanistan before. 'Any goods being transported were taxed by the commander. There was a television in my friend's brother's car and he was asked to pay ten dollars' tax.' "*That's too much, it's old!*" the brother protested. "*Twenty dollars*" the commander replied. "*I can't pay that much,*" said the brother. "*Then thirty dollars…*"

'The man finally understood and at fifty dollars paid up,' Hassan's father explained.

'What would have happened if he hadn't paid?' Hassan eagerly questioned.

'For those who wouldn't pay the commander called on his lieutenant, a man called Dog. He was a huge man known for his strong teeth. He was a madman. He would bite the arms of those who refused lunch. The biting would continue until he drew blood and flesh was torn from the bone. Really, this is true. Eventually they paid. You can see the graves next to the building. Those who refused to pay lie there.' Small mounds of grey rocks next to the deserted restaurant were testament to what lay beneath.

Hassan was glad they were not stopping at this grim place. For the next few nights he would dream of a giant man with no eyes and blood dripping from rotten teeth onto a large silver plate of raw meat. The plate lay on a smooth white marble gravestone with a tattered green prayer flag fluttering high above it, a flag carrying an outline of Elvis's head in its centre surrounded by a burning flame.

As they drove on, the road turned a blind bend and swooped into a narrow gorge rising steeply to a plateau at six thousand feet and Kabul city. Screeching to a halt they saw a container lorry laying on its side blocking the road at the foot of the gorge. Already there were twenty or more trucks and other vehicles lining the steep hill waiting to descend and travel eastwards towards the Khyber and Pakistan.

A cast of what appeared to be a thousand onlookers

materialised from the static vehicles, if not the bare jagged rock itself. They stood huddled together in small groups staring at the scene, arms folded across chests or hands stuck deep into the pockets of their kameez.

At once Hassan's father leapt from the Pajero onto the downed container and shouted orders to the crowd to move the fallen rocks and rubble caused by the blocked lorry. Within minutes a narrow passage was cleared and the Pajero edged its way uphill between the steep rock face and the sides of the long line of gaily painted trucks. The trucks would have to wait much longer before the gap was wide enough to allow their precipitous descent onto the flatter Jalalabad road.

The gorge itself had been the site of some of Afghanistan's fiercest fighting over the centuries. It was still heavily mined and littered with the detritus of war. But as they rounded the final bend the gorge widened, the road opening onto a fertile plain that felt much cooler, a welcome change from the heat and dust of Jalalabad.

Another thirty minutes and they were driving through the scattered suburbs of Kabul itself. On his left Hassan could make out the dark outline of Pul-i-Charkhi Prison, torture rack and burial chamber for countless thousands. Its vast cellars lay bottled up below the earth as still as giants' coffins, its image quickly passing in the cracked glass of the wing mirror as they entered the city itself.

The day was sunny and bright. It was the 11th of September 2001. Elvis had arrived in Kabul. Another four years would pass before he would be found gently spinning above the blood-soaked seats of a bullet-holed Toyota Land

Cruiser sitting casually, two wheels on the pavement of a residential side street in the central Shahr-e-Naw district of the city.

TWO

AT THE WORKSHOP, IN KABUL,

Early September 2005

Gil was worn out. The bile still settled in his stomach. The one-hour flight from Islamabad had been bumpy. Flying below puffy white cumulus clouds that greedily sucked up the small plane along with the thermal air rising from the baked hills was gut-wrenching. The pilot struggled to fly low enough to the ground to avoid the ominous banks of lightning-streaked black cloud rolling in from the rapidly approaching horizon. The small plane bucked up and down following the contours of the ground as if it was some weightless fairground ride.

Settling into the JDL Land Cruiser sent to pick him up at the airport, Gil's stomach was still doing barrel rolls. The drive into the city from the airport hadn't changed. They soon passed a huge smiling poster of President Karzai erected on the traffic circle adjacent to a graveyard of dead aircraft, their rotting blue and white hulks intertwined like lovers. Not that the airport itself was dead. On the contrary, it was a hive of activity. Lumbering grey cargo planes were taking off and landing with alarming regularity. The fleet of new helicopter gunships sitting in rows looked decidedly American. Several other planes lay scattered around, distinguishable by their lack of markings.

Gil tightened the seat belt round his chest as the driver braked hard to avoid a cyclist. The bicycle, carrying three men, swerved across the road and into their path. The driver, who had introduced himself with 'I am Abdul Qabir. Welcome to Kabul, Mr Gil. Are you fine?' muttered an oath under his breath, gave a blast on the horn and accelerated away. In return the cyclist and his two passengers gave cheery waves and wobbled off.

It was typical. Instead of driving straight to the office, Gil was instructed to attend a workshop run by the Ministry of Women's Affairs in the old German Club in Shahr-e-Naw. He didn't know which guesthouse he was staying in, but this could wait until after the workshop.

Standing outside the large studded wooden door guarding the entrance to the club compound, an old long-bearded chowkidar greeted people in halting English with a handshake and a jovial, '*Salaam aleikum.* Good mourning!'

Once inside the compound the ambience changed. Gil walked past an empty swimming pool with ragged strips of blue paint flaking from its sides. In an adjacent dusty tennis court two men knocked around a brown ball that had once been yellow.

Lounging in the registration area, a contingent of

sullen-faced young Turkish ISAF soldiers dressed in casual gear and black flak jackets slung their snub-nosed automatic rifles over their shoulders. Three vigilant Afghans in plain clothes stood around the doorway, Kalashnikovs held by their sides pointing at the floor with fingers on triggers. Her Excellency the Minister was already in the building along with her entourage.

The workshop opened with a short speech in halting Dari from one of the legions of female UN staff in attendance. Introduced by an energetic woman with a pronounced eastern European accent, the minister proceeded to give a brief speech in regal fashion as befitted her recently appointed status. As a cheery aide-de-camp completed the translation into English, the minister left the workshop with a promise she would return later for the roundup session.

Luckily Gil had arrived in sufficient time to claim one of the comfier seats making up the first four rows. As he sank into the green plush, sticking his feet onto the bar of the chair in front, he felt more relaxed, content to lazily cast his eyes round the room. Late arrivals were still finding seats and there was a quiet flurry of activity directly behind the speakers table where three women sat, each getting ready to spell out her enthusiastic vision of what the workshop would accomplish.

He marvelled at the sartorial style of many of the Afghan women present. A few reminded him of 1940s Hollywood, a cinematic period he loved. One woman, a Lana Turner lookalike whose strained war-etched face could not mask her beauty, allowed her long headscarf to slip onto her shoulders, revealing a hairstyle clasped with an oval-shaped silver pin that let the hair cascade down her back. He imagined that several other women in the room would like to wear a similar style, but the bulges under their headscarves holding hair in buns could only be released in more intimate settings.

Several of the Afghan women wore long dresses of a similar style complimented by high tight-waisted jackets. This outfit was covered with an open chador, Iranian style, which a few women had removed, feeling comfortable in the company of so many foreign women and the few men attending. Several of the more conservatively dressed allowed black fishnet stockings with intricate designs to peek from below their long buttoned-up cloaks. Such clothing was in marked contrast to the predominantly loose kaftan-style tops, denim jeans and Scholl-type sandals favoured by the few non-Afghan women present, most with colourful pashmina shawls draped casually over their head and shoulders.

During the tea break Gil found himself standing next to a tall elegant woman slowly sipping green tea from one of the few cups without a crack. She exuded a subtle musky perfume that wafted gently in his direction. Her pale grey chador rippled as she tossed a shock of jet-black hair over her shoulder, narrowly avoiding the tea cup. A necklace of pure blue lapis lazuli adorned her neck.

Still feeling tired from the flight, he was thinking about summoning enough energy to introduce himself when she pre-empted him in a softly inflected voice: 'Hello, I'm Mena. I'm a doctor in the Ministry of Women's Affairs. So what do you think of the workshop so far?'

Gil was surprised by the slight American inflection in her voice, the abruptness of the introduction. It sounded so, well, Californian, just as the aquiline nose framed by high cheekbones and startling brown eyes flecked with green appeared local in origin. Perhaps she'd studied in the States? He would find out soon enough.

Replying in his mild Scottish burr, he smiled. 'Hello, Mena, pleased to meet you. I'm Gil Moncrief. I arrived in Kabul a few hours ago and I've no idea why I was sent to this workshop!'

'You only arrived today?'

'Earlier this morning, actually, I came straight from the airport.'

'And before that?'

'I arrived in Islamabad from the UK on Monday then flew into Kabul on the next available flight. I've worked here before, back in January. It was freezing at the time, a lot of snow. Only for a month, but this is going to be a one-year contract. This time I'm employed by JDL, a corporate development organisation, as a full-time strategy advisor seconded to a UN agency.'

'Good luck with that!' Mena replied. A knowing look revealed she'd dealt with the bureaucratic behemoth before. 'You know what the assistant UN secretary general who resigned recently said?'

'No, tell me.'

'The UN is a Remington typewriter in a smartphone world!'

They both laughed. It was an auspicious start. Gil could sense the chemistry. He was already attracted to this woman, although his heart knew any relationship could only be platonic. He was reminded of a line from a poem: *Love bade me welcome yet my soul drew back.*

The words were all too apposite. As they returned to their seats to listen to the next speaker he could already feel himself drawing away from her. It was all he could do to stop the sadness enveloping him.

After sitting through the morning sessions they headed to the lunch buffet, collected their food and made their way to one of the tables. Mena looked at Gil, her eyes questioning. 'So you're from Scotland, Gil, I've always wanted to go there. A friend told me it's a melancholic land of mists and mountains. Is that true?'

Gil laughed. 'Well, that's one way of describing it. Certainly rains a lot. I grew up in the Highlands and there was a lot of misty mountains and grey cloud about for sure, but when I was sixteen we moved to Namibia and the edge of the Kalahari desert. My father took up a post at the university in Windhoek and we all went with him. Quite a contrast, the sand and the clear blue sky, not to mention the heat.'

As the lunch and their searching conversation finished, they made ready to join small groups for the afternoon session.

'Look, Gil, in case we don't meet up later I've been invited to a party tomorrow night,' Mena started. 'Would you like to come along? It's a leaving do for one of my colleagues at the ministry.'

'Thanks, Mena, that'd be great. I'll know where I'm

staying by tonight hopefully. Give me your mobile number and I'll be in contact to confirm.'

There could be no harm. At least it meant his social life was already picking up and he'd been in the country less than a day.

THREE

ON THE ROAD, IN KABUL,
Wednesday 26 October 2005

The three sparrows sat shivering on the windowsill, feathers plumped against the early-morning chill. It was mid-autumn and the descent into winter already noticeable after the searing summer heat. Two of the birds sat with heads nestled under mottled brown wings, the other more alert to the breadcrumbs Gil spread on the sill in a daily morning ritual. Looking through the glass he could see the little birds slowly awakening to another Kabul day. He had been awake since six. Images of Stella disturbed his dreams and woke him early. It was still happening three years after her disappearance.

The sparrows' vulnerability reminded him of a family trip to Florida. After the obligatory visit to Disneyland they had visited the Ornithology Collection at the Florida Museum of National History. It was difficult to console his daughter Mhairi as she gazed in horror at the last dusky seaside sparrow pickled in a small glass jar, its feathers ruffled and fluffed by the alcohol, its hooded eyes as extinct as its species.

The chemicals sprayed over the salt marshes to control mosquitoes, along with rows of brash new condominiums, ensured the disappearance of the sparrows' cord grass habitat. Now the dusky seaside sparrow was no more, it had disappeared from the face of the earth.

Gil wondered if a similar fate awaited the sparrows outside his window. He loved the little birds. They were the most unassuming of creatures, passing unnoticed as if they were some type of feathered wallpaper. The excited cry that went up at the snowbound airport back in January when they were waiting for the vehicles to arrive and Big William had spotted a red-beaked green parrot squawking its way across the cold grey Kabul skies!

The bird seemed an aberration in such a dark and sombre place. Was it someone's pet released to fend for itself or was it an escapee from the Ka Farushi bird market or the city's dilapidated zoo? Perhaps it had flown to Kabul, alone, from some far-off place?

Questions and theories were excitedly exchanged, but none of them apart from Gil noticed the flock of scrawny chirping sparrows trying to scavenge a living from the strip of frozen ground next to the terminal building.

As Gil straightened his well-worn cord jacket and tugged a comb through a mass of unruly hair the sparrows flew off, disturbed by the growing sounds filtering up from the street. Through the blast-filmed window he could see the rubbish collectors arriving at the large putrefying mound lying at the edge of the pot-holed dirt road opposite the house. A dog sniffed around while large brown beetles scuttled in and out. A flash of black cat disappeared into a culvert.

The scene appeared as if shot on grainy 35mm film, the cheap blast proof coating on the windows causing a lined ripple effect on the glass. A small herd of goats were already munching their way through rotting vegetable peelings and decayed fruit, the odd plastic bag slipping down unnoticed. The goatherd, an old man with a wide striped turban and grey wool tunic belted at the waist, leant impassively on a long stick as the goats fulfilled their function as refuse collectors.

A teenage boy approached on an ancient battered bicycle wearing a ragged North Face anorak, a scarf wrapped tightly round his mouth. Slowly he began to collect bits of plastic, cloth and metal ensnared among the accumulated detritus. Anything that could be salvaged was stuffed into a large burlap sack attached to a rickety pannier on the back of his bicycle.

Gil watched until the sack ballooned into a bundle so bulky the boy had difficulty lifting it, never mind attaching it to the pannier. As the boy wobbled off, invisible behind his load, the goatherd came to life, whacked a couple of goats with his stick and they all ambled off down the road together. By this time a few young children had appeared and were rummaging through the remnants of the tip, straining their imaginations to find anything resembling a toy.

Looking at his watch Gil realised he was late for breakfast. It was seven thirty. Most of his fellow housemates had already eaten and were now scrambling to see if they could find Ahmed or Khalilullah to take them to work. Anyone except Abdul Qabir, commonly referred to in the house as *The Demon*, a driver who was absolutely fearless even by Kabul's normal standards of road anarchy.

Gil liked Abdul Qabir. His driving abilities appeared to be an expression of some inner focus that enabled a vision of himself as the only driver on the road safely cocooned from the seething mass of other road users surrounding his vehicle. The way Abdul Qabir could weave in and out of traffic finding the tiniest gap to slip the old Land Cruiser through was sheer magic but considered far too reckless by most of the house residents.

Unlike the other drivers who came to the city seeking jobs and security, two of them teachers and another a doctor, driving was Abdul Qabir's vocation. He was streetwise, a Kabuli who knew the city and its secrets. His family had lived deep in the old part of the city for generations. They were embedded in its history.

He was proud that during the Soviet invasion and later in the early 1990s when mujahideen factions fought over Kabul, destroying large parts of the city's south-west, his family stayed while others fled. Packs of ravenous dogs roamed the city, scavenging uncollected corpses. His cousin Fatima had been abducted and raped. His uncle had lost his home, thrown out by some mujahideen faction. He hated them all: Masood, Dostum, Sayyaf and all the other warlords who had ravaged his city.

Even the destruction of Kabul by Genghis Khan and his marauding armies seven centuries earlier wove its way through his dreams. The razing to the ground of the great

Char Chatta bazaar, a wonder of Mughal architecture and one of the greatest buildings in Central Asia, by the British Army of Retribution in 1843, was a frequent visitor. Yet what was time but a breath of Allah? Now it was his job to chauffeur these outsiders, these *kharaji*, round *his* city.

While he also hated the Taliban and their petty rules and restrictions, at least they'd never destroyed the city's buildings. This was his home. He would give way to no one. Driving in Kabul was a contact sport. He was in competition with every other driver for the accolade of being first past some imaginary winning post. None had ever sat a driving test, held a bona fide driving licence or given a centimetre to any other road user. Gil wondered where they were all rushing to, driving lemming-like to some unknown fatal destination.

At least Abdul Qabir saved him from having to share breakfast with Brock. Six feet plus of West Virginian redneck, Brock was a self-proclaimed veteran of what passed for post-conflict development in Bosnia and East Timor.

To Gil, he appeared like some craggy-faced 1950s movie star, Victor Mature or Robert Mitchum, perhaps. The square tanned face, pockmarked with acne scars round the jaw, held a knowing if cynical gaze. A shambling gait belied the hours he spent in the House gym. The other housemates, apart from Cheryl the scouser and Irish Mickey, seemed to admire his razor-sharp sense of humour and wry one-liners, but Gil recognised the barbs behind the bonhomie.

Brock was an accountant, a profession he had come to later in life after a brief career in the military. In his JDL incarnation he was an advisor to the Ministry of Finance, showing the Afghans how to balance their books, how to account the vast amounts of aid and development money flooding into the country.

Observing American verbal sandpaper rubbing against the Afghan mind, Gil was aware of the looks between the house boys and the drivers when they took the opportunity to silently witness Brock deliver his one-liners. Thursday's house party would no doubt provide the perfect opportunity for them to observe the action.

Cheryl seethed constantly at Brock's comments, the other two women in the house too intent on fawning over his outmoded machismo. After entering the house in April, Gil soon realised he had been identified as a pliable butt for Brock's one-liners, a soft target, frequently referred to as a *yoghurt knitter*, whatever the hell that meant.

Initially trading shaded insults, Gil's growing silence and refusal to engage had eventually diverted Brock's attention onto Rufus, a gregarious twenty-six-year-old with an Oxford college insouciance and pleasant demeanour that spoke of an easy Home Counties upbringing. Gil liked Rufus; he was a young man who seemed completely unaware of what Brock was throwing at him or didn't care in the slightest if he did.

Gulping down a plate of cornflakes laced with honey and chopped banana, Gil had little time to peruse the day's local English-language newspapers strewn across the table.

Every day the papers would arrive, sitting mostly unread next to a large collection of condiments stacked on a rattan mat in the middle of the dining table. He wondered if there would be anything in the papers about Waheed, but it was unlikely; he was only a driver. His was only another killing in Kabul, one of many.

Gil couldn't get the image of the vehicle out of his mind, the congealed blood on the seats and the somehow familiar little figure dangling from the mirror. He had accompanied Mario to assess whether the Land Cruiser could be repaired, but with several bullets piercing the engine cowling and the bodywork so lacerated it was headed for the scrapyard. Even if it were repaired none of the other drivers would want to drive it, a vehicle tarred with the lingering smell of another's death. Gil had liked Waheed. He was such a composed and well-mannered man as well as a careful driver.

Grabbing a banana and a small bag of almonds, Gil stuffed them into his jacket pocket for later. Nobody could fault JTD in providing for the house residents. The cupboards were packed with cereals, biscuits, breads and fruit juices. Jars of peanut butter, jam and honey, bags of sultanas, dried figs, and various nuts lined the cupboard tops. The large fridge that sat next to the flat-screen TV in the lounge acted as an overspill to the even bigger fridge in the kitchen.

Another cupboard held the house's generous supply of alcohol: cases of red and white wine; bottles of whisky, gin, and vodka; several six-packs of Heineken beer in their green and silver metallic cans. Two magnums of champagne and a litre of Courvoisier brandy lay unopened in a side cupboard. Tea and coffee were constantly on tap, and Habib the cook didn't mind if the residents went into the kitchen and cooked for themselves. They didn't even have to clear up afterwards, although they usually did.

'*Salaam aleikum*, Mr Gil. Are you fine this morning?' Abdul Qabir stood at the entrance to the lounge, black leather mitts already fitted, left leg pumping impatiently up and down as if trying to escape from his impossibly tight blue jeans.

He'll have some private business to attend to after he's dropped me, Gil thought, finishing his last mouthful of tea before heading for the door.

'*Waleikum a salaam*, Abdul Qabir. I'm fine, thank you, how are you?'

'I am fine, very fine. Let us go.'

Gil climbed into the front passenger seat of the old Land Cruiser and clicked the frayed safety belt into place. Abdul Qabir proceeded to wrap his belt across his chest but refrained from clicking it into the metal holder. While JTD insisted seat belts be worn, they were anathema to Abdul Qabir and the other drivers. Their fate was not in their hands, Insha'Allah. A belt was irrelevant as well as a source of derision from fellow drivers, who viewed wearing one a sign of weakness, their own driving skills being naturally infallible.

The two Gurkha guards, grins on their faces and guns loosely cradled in their arms, opened the high metal gates, checked the road left and right, and waved them through as Abdul Qabir eased the vehicle out of the yard and onto the muddy potholed street.

Gil would have loved to just ride round Kabul all day, soaking up the sights and sounds. A variety of sweet and not so sweet smells were already wafting their way through the permitted inch of open window on the passenger side. Nobody could squeeze a grenade through a one-inch gap.

In such a dull environment the vibrancy of colour flashing by at the most unexpected of moments was always welcome: two women hurriedly walking past in bright blue burqas; the balloon vendor with his helium-filled orbs straining at their strings; a shadow of red carpet in a shop window; piles of green striped watermelons on the roadside stretched out under a tattered pink awning.

Most enticing was the achingly blue sky, even if filtered through a layer of thick polluted air that hovered above the city on windless days. For the old and young and those with respiratory problems it was a silent killer. The air, more dust and smoke than anything else, held dangerous microorganisms including what official reports primly described as 'human faecal matter'.

Gil wondered about breathing in this windblown dust, finer than talcum powder, its origin millions of decaying turds lying scattered all over the city. He laughed. For all the shit masking the blue sky he still preferred it to the uncertainties of Scotland's bipolar weather, but that was no comfort for those living under it.

As they turned onto the main road they entered the stream of rush-hour traffic. At the roadblocks boy soldiers in dark khaki uniforms and peaked military caps had been replaced by armed police. When Karzai and his dignitaries moved through the city the roadside was lined with green-bereted Afghan Special Forces looking serious and professional.

Since the chaotic days of early 2002 just after the Taliban evacuated the city, a semblance of order on the roads had been slowly established. The white-capped traffic police tasked with controlling the major roundabouts and junctions were beginning to take some control. Now the traffic crept forward, cyclists on Chinese-built bicycles threading their way through the mass of slow-moving vehicles.

A boy wearing a sequined waistcoat that flickered brightly against the stark backdrop disappeared down a side street. Neat rows of skinned sheep's heads, matt black with vacuous staring eyes and surrounded by clouds of buzzing flies, lay on a small table outside a butcher's shop. A man pulled a small handcart loaded with a blue-velvet three-piece lounge suite perilously tied on with string. Grubby snot-nosed children at the traffic lights sold matches, maps, newspapers, chewing gum, anything to scrape a living for their families. The glove box of the Land Cruiser was jammed with packets of unopened gum.

As the traffic thinned, they cruised down a tree-lined street that passed by the Ministry of Public Health. Windblown dust streaked across the urban landscape, leaves on the remaining trees were filmed a drab listless green, some already tinged with the oranges and browns of autumn.

Dust in the mouth, in the ears, up the nose, stinging the eyes. Gil hoped there would soon be rain to wash the trees giving the city the brief illusion of a clean bright place lingering under that relentless blue sky.

The same rain could be merciless, leaving mud everywhere, causing landslides and washing away the tents of the displaced camped on the hillside north of the airport. Earlier in the year the city's titanic market had vanished under the waves of the Kabul river, taking with it over two hundred stalls and three stallholders. The first time for years there was any water in the river and a flash flood simply swept away the market built up on its shallow banks.

The market had stood precariously alongside the few fetid pools and trickles of water still running between high stone walls bounding the wide flat-bottomed channel that allowed the river to pass through the centre of the city. Gil loved visiting it, the sheer optimism and bravado, or perhaps desperation, needed to set up market stalls on the dried bed of an unpredictable river flowing down from high snow-clad mountains. It was admirable and foolhardy in equal measure.

Some stalls were no more than rickety tables covered with a cloth awning, often a tattered UNHCR tarpaulin designated for the displaced hordes descending on the city. Others were more sophisticated structures with a permanent yet risky air about them. Most sold cheap plastic and tin household goods, second-hand clothes or newly imported Chinese shoes, sandals, teapots, anything to turn a profit, however meagre.

He recalled seeing sandals and T-shirts, and even a woman's handbag, imprinted with the word *Titanic* etched in different colours and designs. The *Titanic* movie had become an iconic symbol for Kabulis, the most popular

DVD passed clandestinely from household to household during the time of the Taliban, its epic romance and disaster-laden footage striking a chord with a people who were as trapped as those about to be hit by a ship-shredding iceberg.

But now as they approached the agency building Gil perused the agenda for yet another frustrating meeting chaired by Mario with Olivier hiding in his office, something he did more frequently since the killing. There would be too much irrelevant talk, little discussion and much grandstanding. The room would be littered with cold dusty mirrors and smoke trails weaving their way through the proceedings. Would Waheed's tragic death even be mentioned? He doubted it.

FOUR

AT THE MEETING, IN KABUL,
Wednesday 26 October 2005

The man spoke briefly, his face impassive. Elegant hands expressed the finer points of his argument yet trembled when resting at his sides. After finishing his speech he quickly sat down. The fingers of his left hand played with a black biro pen lying on a spiral notebook placed precisely in front of him on the broad inlaid table. The other hand stayed firmly hidden from view.

Click-click, click-click, click-click… The noise irritated the woman seated diagonally across the table. Her hand also played with a pen, a dark blue Chinese-made counterfeit Parker, but she refrained from clicking the point in and out. Instead the pen was noiselessly rolled round and round in her hand.

She shifted restlessly as the furrows of annoyance on her brow grew deeper. Her dark lidded eyes discreetly flashed towards the man but were ignored even as he stared at her. While the pair were irrevocably bonded by memory, they were separated by more than the width of a polished wooden table.

Mahdi and Samira shared a history, one not easily forgotten. They had intuitively known they were innocent until that one defining moment even though their early childhoods had been hard, forged as they were in the vicissitudes of an unforgiving rural life.

It was over twenty years since the Soviets arrived in their village. High in the mountains of southern Nangarhar, the village had been mercifully spared war until that moment. Painfully seared into their memories, the images still infiltrated their thoughts and dreams like howling ghosts.

Hard-faced men in grey uniforms, some no older than boys with fear etched on their faces. With small red stars embroidered on their dirty fur-lined hats, the soldiers came into the village riding on huge rumbling machines. Samira remembered the stars. They looked like small jagged spots of blood. Mahdi never forgot the machines, creatures from another world belching smoke, noise and a death that still haunted him.

Some years later when he was a teenager, Ahmed his cousin gave him the small black balls of opium to take with tea each morning. It had helped although the opium made him so constipated Dr Saif at the German clinic prescribed small blue pills that helped him sleep better. All these years later and he was still taking them, his dreams still disturbed but more diluted as if viewed through a lens clouded by warm water.

Mohammad Gul had been the village headman. An old man stooped with age, a long neatly trimmed white beard hanging over the front of his spotless kameez. Kind eyes and a sense of justice marked him out as the chosen leader of the local *jirga*.

The whole village watched as the soldiers tied a stout rope round his ankles and roughly dragged him to the line of tanks. They tied the rope to a metallic bar at the rear of the first tank and drove round the village several times. Endlessly round and round until the tank stopped in front of the villagers who were all herded together, corralled like goats in front of the Guls' small earthen-floored house.

All that was left tied to the bloody rope were the lower legs, the rest of the body torn to shreds on the stony ground by the sharp serrated tracks of a second tank driving too close to the first and crunching over the body. The tank commander was furious with the driver and slapped him hard across his flushed cheeks. At the time Mahdi found this incomprehensible. The commander had been angry with the soldier yet laughed as Mohammad Gul was dragged helplessly through the village.

Most disturbing of all was the soldiers then cut down the old mulberry tree that stood for centuries in the middle of the village, its vast leafy branches providing shade, comfort and food for generations, as well as a sense of security. Mohammad Gul could be replaced, but the mulberry tree was gone forever.

The clipped high-pitched voice readily took over as Mahdi sat down. 'Colleagues, we are saddened and sorry to hear

34

about Waheed's passing – he was a good man. Please give our commiserations to his family. We will miss him.'

Mahdi and Samira heard the chairman's words without emotion. They were both long inured to death. The souls of the dead littered their inner landscapes like flies dancing on a bloated corpse.

'We will make a collection and give it to the family. Samira, can you please arrange this? Now let us move to the next item on the agenda.'

Typical Mario, Gil silently fumed. *Passing!* What the fuck was that about? There was not even a cursory acknowledgement that Waheed's had been a violent death, a ruthless murder, his blood-torn body punctured by a hail of bullets from an AK-47.

Mario was a bureaucratic martinet who would go to any lengths to maintain protocol. It appeared difficult for him to drop petty formalities and display any modicum of basic human feeling. Perhaps he was scared, the killing too close to home, a reminder of where his train was currently stationed.

Or was Gil becoming more cynical the longer he worked with Mario, a supercilious and effete version of a younger Berlusconi with receding swept-back black hair, immaculately tailored suits, La Croix silk ties and a penchant, according to office *gup-shup*, for his younger male assistant.

Mario sat erect in his chair, an assumed regal pose, peering over the top of rimless glasses at the subdued room. A portrait of the equally sartorially clad President Karzai looked down on the proceedings from a large gilt-framed painting positioned on the wall directly behind Mario. There was no doubt Mario Morelli's star was ascendant as he was carried inexorably up the track on the UN gravy train.

Gil had met others like Mario, young bureaucrats smart enough to assuage their bosses, keep the books balanced, smile the diplomat's smile and act like their next contract was assured. Peters the management guru was right. '*In a bureaucracy a person is promoted to their level of inefficiency.*' And the UN was the leviathan of all bureaucracies.

Staffers like Mario kept neat paperwork, reams of it, but this only served to obscure the waste and ineptitude strung out along a well-camouflaged paper trail. The mediocrity of it all infuriated Gil.

Mario knew it would be difficult to find a job outside a system that provided him with a generous tax-free salary plus other financial benefits merited neither by ability nor experience. Not to mention the prestige of a blue UN passport. He had been lucky and smart enough to take the opportunity when a cousin introduced him to a senior UN official in Rome who knowingly enquired whether Mario ever considered applying for a post with the UN.

With a minor degree in Economics and Business Studies from Bologna University and fluent in English and French, as well as his native Italian, he quickly managed to assert himself as someone who wouldn't rock the boat or ask too many questions – especially when faced with questionable decision-making and a trail of squandered resources. Now here he was, in his early thirties and a P5 already, head of a key section in a UN agency in frontline Afghanistan.

Most of Gil's UN friends had been harassed, bullied or squeezed out of the organisation, cast as bit players, mere technicians in a well-oiled yet rusty machine. They were nuts and bolts specialists, pragmatic realists doing good work but who posed a threat to bureaucratic minds like Mario's shackled by endless rules and regulations.

'Zalmei, have you prepared the papers for the next item? Please distribute them if you do not mind.' Gil watched as Mario's eyes bored into the face of the elderly admin assistant. The heavily bearded man looked down at his feet and shuffled the few papers lying on the table in front of him.

'Zalmei, the papers, please… do you have them?'

Even from across the table Gil could see Zalmei's downcast look, his voice slowing as he replied, 'No… sorry, sir… I had no chance to copy them…the photocopier was—'

Mario's face was impassive as he peered even further over his glasses and shouted, 'Zalmei, you have done this before. It is not acceptable. Once more and you are out, *out*! Do you understand?'

Looking ashen-faced, Zalmei nodded briefly before lowering his head, ashamed at such a public dressing-down. Although incensed, he said nothing. Mr Morelli's signature on his next contract was all that stood between a regular income and the excruciating inability to feed and clothe an extended family of over twenty people.

Gil wondered how far Mario's cultural ineptitude actually stretched. He had insulted Zalmei in front of his colleagues. The man had been in Afghanistan for little over a few months but had learned little. Just another instant expert on Afghanistan and its woes.

As Mario abruptly closed the meeting, people eagerly shuffled their chairs back and began to leave. Gil could hear muffled sighs of 'Mash'Allah! Mash'Allah!' as they filed out the door, but it was doubtful God had willed it. It was a human being made of flesh and blood that pulled the trigger of the gun pumping the bullets into Waheed's body.

After leaving the building and walking across the car park to meet Abdul Qabir, Gil noticed a young man leaning against the bonnet of the Land Cruiser. The man stared in his direction. He looked familiar, yet Gil was sure they'd never met before.

'Ah, Mr Gil, this is Asidullah, he waits to talk to you.' Lounging in the driver's seat, one leg leaning out of the open door, Abdul Qabir indicated towards the front of the Land Cruiser with a nonchalant flick of his gloved hand.

The young man quickly levered himself off the bonnet and stood in front of Gil. He was tall and wore a faded navy blazer with shiny brass buttons over a pair of baggy black shalwar. His solemn eyes were wide and luminescent and creased by old laughter lines. Eyes that had witnessed better days.

'*Salaam aleikum*, Mr Gil. I am Asidullah, youngest son of Waheed. You knew my father.'

It was a statement not a question. Gil noticed the resemblance to Waheed: the cock of the head, the brief yet deliberate words spoken in a clear voice.

'*Waleikum salaam*, Asidullah. Yes, I knew your father. He was a good man. I was so sorry to hear of his death.'

'My family is in trouble, Mr Gil. You are the only *kharaji* we can trust.'

'Me? What do you mean?' Gil's surprise was all too apparent to the ever-watchful Abdul Qabir.

'My father said if we ever needed help we should come to you.'

'Me? Why, what's happened?'

Asidullah moved away from the vehicle. Turning his back to Abdul Qabir he talked in a much quieter voice. 'There is a bag.'

'What do you mean a bag, Asidullah?'

'Men came to our house. They threatened my mother. We must give them the bag, but we know of no bag. There was no bag in the vehicle when my father was killed and there is no bag in our house.'

'Who were these men? Did they say why they wanted this bag?' Gil felt he was interviewing the young man yet was unsure how else to respond.

'There were four men. Two Afghans, dark-skinned from the south, and two foreigners. One resembled a man I saw in a movie. He wore dark glasses and had small scars on his right cheek.'

'Did they say what was in the bag?'

'I heard one say there was dollars in the bag. They spoke in English. They thought we couldn't understand.'

'American dollars?'

'Yes, I overheard him say two million dollars.'

'Two million dollars in a bag!' Gil pondered for a

moment. 'Asidullah, have you reported this to the police?'

The young man smiled, looking quizzically at Gil. 'There are many men in Kabul with guns and uniforms, Mr Gil, but there are few police. This is Afghanistan.'

Realising his faux pas Gil could only reply, 'Look, Asidullah, I'd like to help but I'm not sure I can.'

'Please, Mr Gil. We cannot trust other family members. My brothers do not live with us. You know my father had two wives?'

'No, I didn't. He never talked much about himself.'

'At home he also spoke little. We loved my father and we miss him, but he had secrets never shared with us. This is a country of secrets, Mr Gil. His elder brother left Kabul for Australia in 1980 and never returned. We never hear from him. My other uncles were killed in the fighting. There is no one else we can trust.'

This brief exchange made Gil uneasy. The last thing he needed was another mystery. He suspected there would be no end to it, only the unravelling of secrets compelling him down a path he would prefer not to tread.

Much against his better judgement Gil reached into his pocket. 'Look, Asidullah, here's my card. Call me in a few days. I have a friend who might be able to help.'

With a quick, 'Thank you, Mr Gil,' the young man placed his right hand over his heart, gave a brief bow, and walked quickly away towards the guarded exit of the car park and the waiting street.

FIVE

ON THE BEACH, IN GOA, INDIA,
December 2002

M emory is a fickle thing. What it remembers is often far from any truth. But what is the truth? Gil remembered his father's words as he approached old age. *'When the wee box in my head goes, that's it. Just hit me on the back of the head with a spade and bury me in the garden.'*

No more truth, only the hallucinated dreams and con tricks of an addled old mind. Gil recalled the words of a Harvard professor. *'You don't need to worry about memory loss until you look in the mirror and don't know the name of the person staring back at you.'*

It would be hard living without the memories responsible for forging the contours that mapped your face. It wasn't a face he would like to look at in a mirror. It would be a face hard to recognise.

While he was blessed with a good memory, that

41

fateful day on the beach was becoming increasingly blurred. Memories of the day kept fading into shadow. Mhairi and Jamie had been sitting at a table under the striped awning of Ram's beach shack sipping fresh lime sodas engrossed in some board game picked up from the pile behind the bar. He could remember, sometimes with stunning clarity, the tiny bubbles rising from the bottom of their glasses popping alongside the lemon wedges floating on the surface.

But of Stella no sharp image remained in his mind. Only a blurred memory of the last view he ever had of her – a trim bikinied bottom walking slowly over the sun-bleached sand and into the sparkling waters of the Arabian sea. Dark blue cotton briefs adorned with small silver stars and a matching top with ties dropping loosely down her tanned back. He could almost see her. Like a bright evening sky that kept fading into the impenetrable darkness of night.

She hadn't turned and waved, although he desperately wanted to believe she had. As usual she was too engrossed in checking her swimming goggles, eyes already gazing towards the lure of the ocean.

That was his last image of Stella. She had simply disappeared. Some sea monster had taken her to its lair. A gang further up the beach had abducted her. A band of aliens had whisked her away to some far-off galaxy. Who knew what happened to her? It was still a mystery. All he knew was she was missing and had stayed that way for almost three years.

Later, when he could think more rationally, he accepted that for whatever reason the warm sea had welcomed her into its comforting bosom. Stella the swimmer, his wife and confidante.

They were on vacation in Goa, two weeks of sand, sea and sun over the Christmas period of 2002, an ideal escape from the festive celebrations with Stella's sisters and the other members of her family back in Scotland.

While Gil had never considered Stella a particularly challenging partner, on occasion he had seen her with a feral look in her eyes staring out at him. Only ever a fleeting glance, yet it made him wonder whether it was a reflection of something in himself and nothing to do with her or her family at all. Ah yes, her family.

As soon as the alcohol started flowing they would become unbridled, the bickering would start and they would be at each other's throats throwing insults, gouging out past slights from febrile minds and killing off any bright future they might scrape together.

Inevitably it ended in tears – or worse. One Christmas when the kids were much younger the celebrations prematurely ended on Christmas Eve after dinner finished. During a heated argument with their brother Colin, Stella's elder sister Joan had pulled the step ladders from under the stairs, pushed them up against the tree draped with glistening fairy lights and started ripping down the decorations, loudly proclaiming in a rapidly slurring voice, *'That's fuckin' it, that's the last Christmas we're having in this fuckin' house!'*

In her drunken state Joan had fallen off the ladder, ending up in hospital with concussion and a fractured shoulder. Gil remembered how Jamie looked up at Stella, his voice small and shaking, and said, '*Is that the end of Christmas, Mummy?*'

But here they were in Goa, a safe place, an easy place, a place highly recommended by his friend Robbie, a passing hippy there in the sixties. Compared to life in Pakistan it was easy and secure. It was a comparatively short distance from Islamabad, although it took two days of travel and an overnight in Karachi to get there.

It had been a difficult year for Stella, he understood that. All of them were affected after the planes crashed into the Twin Towers leaving a traumatised and unpredictable America. He should never have taken them to live in Pakistan in the first place, although they all loved being there.

Before 9/11 Islamabad had been a safe secure city with its modern buildings and broad spacious boulevards, light years away from the real Pakistan that began ten miles down the highway in the teeming bazaars of Rawalpindi. The city's northern hinterland was perfect for exploring, their house a veritable marble palace overlooking the green-wooded Margalla hills with its networks of jungle paths and roaming bands of monkeys and wild boars.

After that fateful day, however, they were given two days to pack and go leaving behind the kids' bicycles, schools, friends and the house that was their home for three years. Not to mention Blackie the dog.

Landing back in Scotland had been a shock for them all. A few months later Stella returned to Islamabad to pack up the house. It was hard for her, harder than Gil realised at the time.

When Gil's contract came up for renewal they made the decision to return to Islamabad, never imagining that within the year fate would cast its net on a day when they all felt so carefree. On holiday on a beach, a hot sun blazing overhead, a cooling breeze on their backs, palm trees swaying in the background.

Stella was usually gone for about an hour. The time it took to swim as far as the concrete plinth that bedded the tall pole with a spotlight on top marking the start of Calangute beach. Then back to Candolim. Not a leisurely swim, not Stella. Her powerful fluid strokes were fast enough to catch the endorphin buzz she loved so much.

After an hour and twenty minutes he became concerned. Not overly, for she had been away longer than that before. Once she misjudged the rip and was forced to tack along the coast before being able to beach herself. On another occasion she was approached by a large fish that swam between her legs, bumping itself suggestively against her crotch, or so she claimed.

He felt uneasy. The kids were still playing their game at the shack. He had finished his gin and tonic and another chapter of Ian Rankin's latest book, his mind absorbed in Edinburgh's criminal underbelly.

Putting the book down and easing himself off the rickety sunbed with the stuffing oozing out of the old mattress, he walked slowly up the beach looking for Stella's head bobbing up and down at the end of each breaststroke. She was usually easy to spot, swimming fifty metres further out to sea than anybody else.

As he walked up the beach, possible scenarios began to

play out in his mind. She'd gone further than intended and was taking longer than usual to return. She'd taken time to stop for a rest. She'd met her swimming buddy Marty and gone to some beach shack for a drink. Once she and Marty had staggered back down the beach half cut two hours after she left for her swim. He was furious.

After thirty minutes walking up the beach, such hopeful scenarios began to fade. There was no sign of her. Where was she? The increased heartbeat and the rush of blood to his head were not due to the afternoon heat and the alcohol. The signs of panic were already apparent.

He noticed the tide was on the turn, the waters slowly ebbing from the beach, each wave leaving a marker, a faint line on the sand where tiny dead crabs and shells lay carried there by the last wave. With an increasing sense of resignation and dread, he realised his life had changed. It had crossed a line in the sand. There could be no going back.

SIX

THE HOUSE PARTY, IN KABUL,
Thursday 27 October 2005

I t was Thursday night, the end of the working week. Friday functioned as the weekend, with work resuming on Saturday morning when the government returned to work. Most expats also resumed work then, apart from those not involved with government or still nursing a hangover.

Friday was the day for rest and recovery, for taking it easy, going to the ISAF market, watching DVDs, going out for lunch or just hanging out with friends. For the fitness freaks there was always a tempting run up Telegraph Hill with H3, the Hash House Harriers, Kabul chapter.

Thursday night functioned as expat Saturday night – party time. Mobiles buzzed with whispers of where the latest parties were going to be held: a guesthouse, a club, at the launch of some new restaurant or bar.

It was the only night when NGO staff were officially permitted to use the UNICA club, its bar often serving as a clearing house for party locations. NGO staff seemed to be younger with fewer restrictions than UN or embassy staff, their own parties more raucous and less exclusive. Some parties were themed – a toga party or tarts and vicars; others were booze-fuelled raucous bacchanalias. A few even managed to be sedate affairs.

Gil's last party invitation came from Lucinda and Bob back in January. A young couple from New York who were leaving Afghanistan after a two-year stint with an aid agency, their invitation card read:

The Ministry for the
Promotion of Vice and Prevention of Virtue
requests the pleasure of the company of
Mr Gil Moncrief
for a final evening of Sin
with Lucinda and Bob
at eight o'clock on
Thursday 27 January 2005
for dinner and light revelry.

It was a far cry from the 1970s when the city's establishment was replete with embassy balls, sophisticated dances, soirees and cocktail lounges frequented by the Kabul elite dressed in the latest European fashions. Expat Italians even produced local wines and brandy from the country's abundant grape harvest.

Now the new glossy monthly magazine *Afghan Scene*

had started a feature called *What's On: Be Scene*, requesting readers to submit event or party pics. These typically portrayed groups of people drinking, dancing and generally having fun, with the younger ones grinning inanely into the camera lens, arms slung around each other's shoulders, wine glasses firmly in hand. More than anything they resembled a scene from the pages of *The Tatler* or Mhairi's Facebook page.

While Gil had no problem with parties, this insistent capturing of the moment to share with the outside world irked him. For some, the memory was not enough. And in Kabul there was always an excuse for a party. Welcome to a new colleague, farewell to a departing one, the launch of a restaurant, a club or a new bar, or just a regular guesthouse Thursday-night do.

Tonight the house was having its own party. Mena was not able to attend; she had urgent work to attend to at the ministry, even if it was a Thursday night. This left Gil feeling less than cheerful.

He didn't particularly enjoy these house parties but felt obliged to attend. There was a colonial fin de siècle air about them. The sahibs and memsahibs getting plastered, letting their hair down and making fools of themselves while the local staff sneaked a look, later telling their friends how 'that blonde woman had been dancing on the table, pulling her dress up beyond the knee'.

In this case it happened to be Sarah who had worked as a development advisor in Westminster before arriving in Kabul. She had taken little persuasion to join Brock as he climbed onto the main lounge table, now shorn of food and stripped of its white linen tablecloth. Proceeding to gyrate to the music, hips locked together, the whoops and hollers of the other party-goers egged them on.

On his head Brock wore what appeared to be a Viking helmet, or at least one modified by an Afghan Hells Angel. Two thick pointed horns sprouted from a domed metal helmet, giving it a definitive don't-mess-with-me look. It was adorned with small rusted chains, old coins, beads and other artefacts, plus a string of spent AK-47 shells trailing from its green metallic back like some fiendish pigtail.

The music was terrible: eighties disco bump and grind. Sarah and Cheryl resisted Gil's attempts to introduce more danceable sounds, early Stones or Township jive. Music that would hit the groove. Perhaps they wanted to relive the music of their 1980s youth spent somewhere in middle England. There would always be a part of them stuck in such a bland cultural time warp.

The disco beat seemed to suit Brock as he waved his accompanying spear, another relic from Chicken Street, and continued to gyrate ever closer to Sarah's swaying body. Wearing a grin like a drunken Cheshire cat, Sarah tossed back her mane of blonde hair as she lurched towards Brock, her tight black diamante studded dress riding further and further up her legs.

Gil could see not all of the invited guests approved. An Iranian woman from UNICEF turned to her partner and mouthed words that he knew were disapproving. An official from the Indian embassy looked embarrassed while his eyes remained glued to the table, his hand tightly clasped round a large glass of whisky. Abdul Qabir and two other drivers stood half-hidden in the kitchen doorway intently watching the proceedings with folded arms and impassive faces.

Then the crash happened, causing smirks and smiles among the Afghans present. Sarah had lost her footing, tripped and fallen off the table right into the arms of Big William, the most portly of the house's residents. He tried to catch her, but she simply bounced off his enormous stomach and landed on the floor at the feet of the Iranian woman. Producing a glare that would have sunk a thousand battleships the woman turned abruptly and gestured to her companion that it was time to leave.

The Indian diplomat quickly poured himself another glass of whisky. Downing it in one gulp, he watched as some of the younger guests, seeing Sarah pick herself up with no more than a glazed smile on her face, clapped loudly then doubled up in hysterical laughter.

The party had certainly ended with a bang. Guests began to drift off, mobiles busy summoning drivers. Sarah, Brock and Big William, clutching a bottle of gin and giggling, made their way upstairs to continue a more private party.

Now it was getting late. Only three of the housemates remained in the lounge. Stretched out in comfortable easy chairs with their night caps, the talk was light-hearted. They were already reminiscing about the party and the evening's entertainment.

Then the door opened and Mickey staggered into the room fresh from some other howff. Waving his beer can in greeting he collapsed onto one of the free chairs. It took him less than thirty seconds to start. It was as if he could conjure up a topic and everybody would silently acquiesce. Gil wasn't even sure what had set him off as the young man took a swig from his can, hawked his throat, and began one of his interminable tirades.

'Aye, they all want a slice of Afghanistan, so they do. The Iranians, the Paks, the Indians. The old Soviet states lurkin' on the northern borders. And let's not forget the Americans. Have you seen the size of their fucken embassy?! They're going to be here for a while. Lookit Rumsfeld's visit in April, lobbying for permanent US military bases. Mind you, it's the Chinese that have it taped, signing a deal with Karzai for the copper mine south of Kabul plus a railroad to the Pak border. Fucken brilliant, so it is. Good luck to them, all I say.'

Mickey was on a roll. Gil wondered if he took some type of stimulant. Or was it the natural exuberance of youth, the trusting self-belief signalling he was never wrong? The boy was certainly sharp and never missed a trick, but his breezy jauntiness was a shade off tactlessness, never mind downright vulgarity. He was extremely gregarious and voluble, letting it all out in lengthy staccato bursts. '*Verbal diarrhoea*,' Brock invariably sneered, but it was noticeable he never engaged with Mickey. The American seemed wary of him and was derogatory, frequently referring to him as an oxygen thief.

Mickey flicked back his mane of thick black hair, lit up a cigarette, popped a fresh can of Heineken and rolled on.

'See, everybody's at it. Lookit the Friday ISAF market. A secure military base in the middle of Kabul and anybody with a foreign passport can get in! Ye'll have seen them selling all the usual fucken crap, the pirated CDs and DVDs, the electronic gizmos, the jewellery, the souvenir trinkets. Then you get the carpets, the guns, the fur coats. They're buying them up like sweeties, so they are. I saw a Polish soldier buy six fur coats from that Afghan stallholder that wears the red fez. D'ye think he has six girlfriends? Come on! Jeezus! They have wolf, fox, chinchilla, mink, and cheap at that and all fucken genuine. You should feel them. Soft as silk. There was even one made from a snow leopard pelt.'

Mickey waxed on in his singular way, by this time visibly the worse for wear. He was more than happy to recount how he had already downed nine cans at the other party, plus several 'wee chasers' held in a small personal glass with a Bavarian castle stencilled on the side usually kept topped up with a solid pouring of Stolichnaya but now drained empty.

But he's right, Gil mused, *his old friend Alex had told him about the guns*. They had been laid out on display on the one occasion they visited the market together. All types of guns. Old Afghan *jezails* with their intricately carved stocks and long smoothbore barrels. Accurate at long range, they were dubbed the sniper rifle of the nineteenth century responsible for the slaughter of the retreating British army at the infamous Bolan Pass.

Most of the guns were fakes from the weapons bazaar in Darra Adam Khel over the border in Pakistan, although the Remingtons and Lee Enfields looked genuine, their detail declaring age and provenance. Taken from the retreating British armies that failed to hold their slice of the Afghan landscape since the Imperial sortie in 1873, one had the date '1878' clearly etched on the metal along with 'Enfield' and a 'VR' topped with an imperial crown, on which sat a conspicuous little cross. They were in decent condition given their active service, with well-oiled deep-blued barrels. Some displayed dark grooves and hacks in their brass-butted stocks, evidence of wood clashing with razor sharp steel.

It was no coincidence there was so many bayonets in faded brown leather sheaths for sale in the market. Hand-to-hand fighting had been common. The Afghan tribesmen with their sabres and the British, apart from the sword-wielding officers, with bayonets stuck on the end of their rifles.

Many of the Enfields on display had been etched with a small Islamic seal, plainly visible on the metal, before being taken to a government armoury and locked away for over a hundred years. It was only the dark anarchic days of the early 1990s that allowed mujahideen groups to release them from their captivity.

Here they were now, swamping the Kabul souvenir market, ready to be bought up, de-commissioned and shipped off to America and Europe. They would fetch a good price on the antique arms market, gun collectors would be happy to have a genuine one in their collection…

'…and ye see, some of them have never set foot on Afghan soil since arrivin'. I know a girl in the British embassy, she's never been out of the fucken place for three months. That's the God's honest truth, so it is.'

After a short trip to the toilet Mickey had returned to the lounge, eased himself back into his chair and fired up again.

'Does everything in there. Eats, works, sleeps, goes to the gym. Probably shags one of those public-school wankers the place is full of. When she gets her next posting they'll look at her CV, see "Afghanistan" and she'll be off to Paris or New York or some other plum posting. It's not only the bragging rights of spending a year in Afghanistan they come here for, ye know.

'And she's never really been in the fucken country, just sat at her desk in a concrete block surrounded by high walls and coils of razor wire. What a scam! They're all the same, the Brits, off on their fortnight breather breaks every six weeks. I mean, their whole fucken embassy is never even here.'

Gil was intrigued by Mickey. He liked him despite the brashness. With his dark Irish looks and flashing white teeth showing through the half-grin etched on his face, he held the air of some nineteenth-century swashbuckler. Diplomat he was not. He was reckless in a way Gil could never imagine himself to be.

While Mickey was a thinker – he had been the youngest doctoral student at MIT for twenty years – he was no academic. He was primarily a doer, and unlike most of the other housemates was constantly looking for opportunities to explore Kabul and its environs. His job as IT Advisor in the Ministry of Finance was certainly hands-on. Setting up a new LAN system that would power and protect Afghanistan's state coffers was no small task, and not without its risks.

He would also occasionally disappear for a few days. Rumour had it he was flown down to Helmand to help the Brits with an IT system for a new military base they were building. JTD were fine with this; they would be charging an astronomical sum and Mickey would be happy with his £500 a day consultancy fee plus the opportunity to get out of town, if only to some military outpost stuck in the remote southern desert near Qandahar.

Gil could see Cheryl was trying her best to move the conversation on to another subject, although it was hardly a conversation. Mickey was still intent on holding court.

Cheryl was an advisor at the Ministry of Education, helping to develop a national strategy for teacher training. She regarded Mickey as little more than a mountebank while he meanwhile concentrated on re-filling his jug from a vodka bottle he had miracled from the cupboard.

'You see, it's a big problem for us. Teachers receive these night letters from the Taliban warning that if they turn up at school they'll be killed… *schloop*. They're so brave. Last week a male teacher in Oruzgan was beheaded. Can you imagine? It's horrible, just horrible. These people are worse than medieval barbarians… *schloop*.'

Cheryl had an unfortunate habit of making a *schlooping* noise each time she paused, sucked air into her mouth, and swallowed saliva. As she became more visibly upset, this noise seemed to increase in frequency and volume while Mickey, in typical fashion, appeared quite oblivious to her feelings.

'Away with you, you're wrong. That's shite,' he

announced, a dribble of vodka running down his chin. 'The Taliban are at least out front. They're happy to put their beheadings on the internet for the world to see, but they're fucken stupid. People are afraid of them already – they don't need to publicise rolling heads. Anyhow, they've all been at the old beheading game. Look at the eighties, those Contra bastards in Nicaragua backed and resourced by the CIA and all. They beheaded the Sandinistas left and right, maimed young kids, dismembered them, bayoneted pregnant women in the stomach. Jeezus, they even crucified people!'

Mickey paused, took another swig of beer, burped loudly and resumed his unstoppable monologue. 'You wouldn't find the Taliban doing that, now would ye!' He laughed loudly at the irony and Gil couldn't resist a quiet chuckle.

'And then there's the fucken English! Don't get me started on them. They had the Gurkhas lop the heads off young Argie recruits during the British war on those Malvinas islands. They'd hunker down in their bunkers, cook their curries, then when it was dark draw their kukris, creep behind the Argie lines and take a few scalps. Then they'd stick the heads on tall poles above the bunkers to put the fear of living God into any young Argie soldier looking at them through binoculars from across the moor. Jeezus, I'd prefer facin' the Taliban meself! And anyway, look at the fucken Saudis. They behead people all the time and the Brits still cosy up to them, sell them weapons and buy their oil.'

With this Mickey slugged down the last of his beer,

stubbed out what was left of his cigarette, gave a loud belch and declared, 'See youse tomorrow then. I'm off to me bed, night all.'

As he staggered up the stairs clutching his empty glass jug, the three remaining housemates looked at each other, raising their eyes in mutual exasperation, silently declaring, '*We just have to put up with him, he's young, he'll learn but somebody will have to bloody well tell him.*' But nobody ever did.

SEVEN

AT THE DOGFIGHT, IN PAGHMAN,
Friday 28 October 2005

ena had never been without a dog in her life. Why start now just because she was living in Kabul? She knew the Afghans had no time for dogs except the brute variety trained as guards or fighters. It seemed each house in her neighbourhood had a dog, although she'd never actually seen one. Only the tips of snarling black muzzles poking through small gaps in tightly padlocked gates. Their continuous growling and ferocious barking made her grateful to be separated from them by high compound walls.

During the night she frequently woke up to a cacophony of dog noise. One mutt would start barking then howling, perhaps a bad dream, a hint of nighttime intruder, one flea bite too many, an impending full moon. Then the rest would start, one by one, until it seemed the whole canine population of the city had joined in.

They barked in stereo, in surround sound with base lines and descants, their howling echoes carrying off into the far distance until the crescendo faded and she fell back to sleep.

Mena looked at the dog lying at her feet. It looked grateful. She had saved its life. It was a scrawny little thing abandoned in the doorway of a fruit shop up a side street close to her house when she found him. You wouldn't think it now. Tazi was a purebred Afghan hound. The long pointed face, intelligent eyes, sleek athletic build, the long sable brown coat matted with mud from the riverbank.

Tazi was dignified, but with a warm nature so unlike the Afghan hounds on TV dog shows in California, coats too long and feathery with their loping prancing gaits, heads held high and aloof. They were too cool for Mena's comfort.

The Afghan hound might be closer to the wolf than any other breed of dog, but Tazi was just a friendly hound dog that loved to chase rabbits up by the dam and collect any object light enough to be returned to the thrower.

Mena left him curled up at the foot of the chair and moved to the kitchen to make a cup of tea. How she loved this house. It had been in the family for over a hundred years, her surrogate home until she was nine and left for America.

While she lived with her parents and two brothers in a smaller house in Khair Khana, she spent as much time as possible in the large rambling house with its gaily painted shutters, red corrugated tin roof and tall fir trees dotted around the green expanse of the garden. Her grandfather lived in the house alone apart from his old housekeeper

Suraya. Mena had spent many happy weekends listening to his stories of life in Kabul before the Soviets insinuated their way into the country.

After the family left for America the house remained empty until the mujahideen began battling for control of the city. A commander belonging to Massoud's faction simply demanded the key from old Abdul the caretaker and billeted eight of his men in the house. There was no threat: Massoud's name was enough.

When the Taliban took over the city in 1995 and the mujahideen retreated, a young Talib commander, Mullah Dadullah, moved into the house with his men. Then after the Taliban fled Kabul in November 2001 another commander from the Northern Alliance brought his family from the Shomali plains north of the city and moved in.

When she arrived in Kabul a year later Mena was shocked to find strangers living in the family home. She was resolute: the house belonged to her family and she was determined to claim it back. Incensed, she had asked Dr Salazar, the highest placed official in the UN she knew, to help her reclaim the house. His reply was kindly if terse. *'Leave it for now, Mena. Wait for some time before you attempt this. I'll help you then.'* She knew from his tone that *then* would never come.

Her initial reaction was one of anger and frustration. Her parents had instilled a strong sense of right and wrong in her and this was so unjust. Yet she recognised this was Afghanistan, as foreign now to her as America had been when she first arrived in that vast land.

After biding time for nearly six months, she contacted

her father's youngest brother in Mazar-i-Sharif and asked for his help. *'Yes Mena, I will sort this out for you, but please wait, be patient, take time,'* he told her. Frustrating though it was she had no choice but to wait; there were no other avenues left open to her.

Two long months later her uncle arrived in Kabul, made contact with the commander and explained the situation to him. The meetings and negotiations lasted for three days. After many cups of green tea the commander agreed to move his family out of the house and into another house in Kabul owned by her uncle.

Not only that, the commander was persuaded to pay a small rental for the property, something to do with its location on the hill near the Intercontinental Hotel and its stunning views to the north and the Hindu Kush. The velvet green grapevines growing in swathes over the long white metal pergola leading from the door of the house to the high wooden gates of the compound wall also helped.

Mena was happy and grateful to her uncle, as well as relieved. Afghans were skilled negotiators. They could spend days or even weeks sitting round in polite discussion, amiably arguing back and forth, drinking endless cups of tea before an agreement was reached. If there was no agreement they were likely to fight it out to a bloody conclusion.

Such feuds could last for years, some for decades and some even lifetimes. They were the spark lighting a fire of revenge that could burn through the centuries. This was the Afghan way, the other side of her countrymen's hospitable nature. It made her feel sad; the whole country was a memento mori, a reminder death lurked constantly, even in the shadow of a cup of tea.

On moving into the house what surprised Mena most was the old carpets she played on as a child remained so familiar. Even the oil painting of Darul Aman Palace hung on the wall above the old hall table was still there. The table itself looked none the worse for wear except one of its thick round wooden legs was now broken and roughly bound together with garden twine. Most of the original furniture and fittings also remained, although the walls looked dingy and badly needed repainting.

Laying her cup on the table she moved through to the bedroom and collected her coat and boots before making her way to the front door. She didn't particularly want to go to a dogfight on her day off but Gil had been persuasive. They'd seen quite a lot of each other since meeting at the workshop back in April. Their relationship, while platonic, felt like it was growing ever closer.

She could see him outside sitting in the Land Cruiser waiting to drive the thirty minutes that would take them west of the city towards Paghman, once famous as a holiday retreat complete with marble villas and chalets. Its European-style gardens now lay overgrown and derelict, although the grand arch, modelled on the Arc de Triomphe in Paris, still stood at the entrance to the village. The dogfights were held every Friday morning on a flat parched area of wasteland before the road ascended to Paghman and the foothills of the Hindu Kush.

Mena knew that Gil wouldn't sound the horn. He

was too polite. During their phone call he had seemed particularly impatient, insisting she be ready to go as soon as he arrived. For once he was driving himself; most of the house drivers had taken the day off.

'Coming, I'm coming!' she gesticulated with a smile and wave of her gloved hand. He waved back, opening the passenger door for her as soon as she'd locked the house and made her way down the path to the vehicle.

He looked as good as ever. He was a handsome man despite the unkempt appearance and the short straggly beard, but for a few days now he'd seemed preoccupied, even more so than usual. She understood that Waheed's death had touched him deeply.

During the ride he didn't say much, exchanging little more than a few pleasantries. Acknowledging his mood, Mena settled into the seat and watched the passing countryside as they headed towards Paghman.

By the time they drew close to the site there were already many spectators huddled together in a wide circle. Aware she was the only woman present, Mena drew her dupatta tighter round her head and shoulders while Gil parked the Land Cruiser alongside several other 4x4s.

Walking along the dusty track to the arena, they passed a man selling hot beans scooped into paper cones made out of old newspaper. A young boy carried a huge basket filled with cakes of dubious quality. Several snot-nosed urchins, one no more than four years old, were busily trying to sell small plastic bottles of even more dubious-looking water.

She could hear growling and barking that became

louder as they approached the edge of the arena. An old man holding a long stick with a white rag tied to the end proceeded to swish it towards the spectators as he walked round the circle shouting, 'Who wants to fight! Bring your dogs! Bring your dogs!'

Two other men standing in the centre of the arena stretched a wide green cloth between them so the two dogs preparing to fight were unable to see each other. Each dog was held back by its handler, their ferocious snarling leaving no doubt they already sensed their opponent on the other side of the cloth. One was a great bear of a beast, sable brown with clipped ears flattened against its head and a short stubby tail. The other was a smaller mastiff, brindled black and white but with massive shoulders and a head that looked too big for its body.

The cloth was hurriedly pulled away and the two unleashed dogs flew at each other, rearing up on their hind legs to lock muscular bodies as if they were wrestlers beginning a bout. Their heads collided, their bodies jostling for control until one was able to sink its fangs into the other's shoulder and bring it tumbling to the ground.

While the dog underneath valiantly tried to turn the heavier dog, it only succeeded in having the grip on its shoulder shift upwards to its neck. Mena could see the blood ooze from the wound even as the two animals rolled back and forward on the dusty ground.

As quickly as the fight started it ended, the owners rushing in to pull the dogs apart, one by the tail, the other lifted bodily and carried off with the man's arms clamped round the dog's shoulders as he struggled to hold its weight.

How they never turned on their handlers Mena had no idea. They seemed to change from ferocious beasts into docile animals in a split second. Maybe they intuited they were fighting dogs and what was expected of them. This was not a fight to the death, only for domination. The care and attention lavished on such dogs made them too precious a commodity to die in the arena. Perhaps the dogs sensed this.

As they waited for the next fight to begin a tall man dressed in a dark blue shalwar kameez, the loose trousers and long shirt favoured by most Afghans, approached them. A ponytail flowed down the back of his beaten brown leather jacket and an untrimmed grey-flecked beard covered most of a high-boned, almost regal, face.

The man placed his right hand lightly on Gil's left shoulder, Gil reciprocating before the two men embraced while giving each other a warm handshake. Mena knew in Islamic teaching this signified both men's sins had been washed away. It was strange. The other man was definitely a westerner and Gil not a Muslim.

'*Salaam aleikum*, Alex, how are you? Haven't seen you for ages.'

The man smiled warmly. '*Waleikum*, Gil, what brings you to the dogfight? But first please introduce me to your friend.'

Mena smiled at the man, told him her name and was met with a quick appraising look before a deep sonorous voice said, 'Pleased to meet you. I am Alex de Wolfe.'

Gil looked a little irked at being slow in making the introductions but was soon animatedly recounting his meeting with Asidullah in the car park. He knew the dogfight was the most likely place to find Alex on a Friday morning. As Gil spoke, Mena could see the furrows on his tanned brow undulate like waves coming in from a storm bound sea.

So this is the legendary Alex de Wolfe, she thought. He was reputed to be a private person who rarely attended any expat functions or parties, although he occasionally ate in the Delhi Durbar according to her friend Giselle who claimed to have seen him there a few weeks previously.

At fifty, Alex was older than Gil by a decade and had lived in Kabul during the 1970s, the last of the peaceful days before the Soviets invaded. His parents worked with a Canadian aid agency and were overjoyed he chose to accompany them rather than opting for high school in Toronto.

The few remaining people who knew him during those years remembered how he and his friends rode round Kabul on clapped-out old motorcycles frequently stoned on hashish, Alex with an old revolver tucked into the back of his Levi jeans.

Mena could see he was a careful man. He took his time before replying to Gil. It impressed her.

'Hard to know. It could be drug money or diverted aid, maybe a bribe. The men involved could be anybody. If they are American that's a problem for sure, most likely military. It's risky for you to be involved, Gil, people are killed here for much smaller sums than two million dollars.' Alex looked thoughtful as Gil listened intently to his words. 'It's a small amount compared to some of the illicit caches

67

moving round this city, but it's important for somebody.'

'Can you help?' replied Gil, his brow working harder.

'I'll ask around and let you know. You need to be careful – this city is full of intrigue and suspicion. The truth can be hard to decipher for us foreigners.'

Gil understood completely. Machiavelli had nothing on the Afghans. Throwing some expat carpetbaggers into the mix upped the stakes. Such men were likely to be unpredictable. That they were dangerous was a given.

EIGHT

DOWN BY THE POOL, IN KABUL,
Friday 28 October 2005

A few months earlier it could have been a scene from a Club Med brochure. Lithe tanned bodies in tight swimsuits chatting and laughing together as they sat round the pool. Now it had cooled down too much for serious swimming. Only a few intrepid souls dared to continue their early-morning dip, at least until ice covered the pool. Winter was coming.

The UK Embassy Babes, beloved of the club barflies, would sit in a huddle stretching long bare legs, sipping drinks and gossiping while Samiullah the barman stood impassively in the centre of the circular bar preparing his lethally amateurish cocktails. The other Afghans working at the club were banned from going near the pool during the summer, any ogling of western flesh severely sanctioned.

A few tattoos were proudly on display at the

poolside but no yakuza bodysuits, only small discrete signs of a drunken trip to the tattoo parlour. Butterflies and chrysanthemums, green dragons, a couple of grim reapers dressed in black hooded capes holding long scythes. A poorly executed figure that looked like a smiling Yogi Bear adorned the right shoulder of a young man wearing thick-lensed horn-rimmed spectacles.

Gil once spotted a couple of off-duty marines who had wangled their way into the club, at the poolside with their regimental insignia stippled on their backs, the letters etched around life sized images of daggers. One NGO worker with 'Carpe diem' tattooed on his inner forearm sat at the bar cradling a cocktail. Where had this vogue for replacing traditional anchors and bluebirds with words originated? Maybe the Beckham effect, or some sailor forgot to have a red heart encase 'Mother' on his forearm.

Now it was a bleaker scene. A few souls still sat by the pool, but most were in small groups eating a late lunch, their plates lying on slatted wooden tables arranged haphazardly on the grass. Two workers wheeled out a large umbrella-shaped gas heater ready for the evening chill.

The salsa classes in the garden had finished for the season, replaced by indoor socialising, drinking and the odd dance display in the club bar from the salsa experts. Like expat bars everywhere it provided a lubricated camaraderie that fostered the fleeting illusion of familiarity, a temporary respite from the foreign.

Gil had decided to come to the club on his own after saying goodbye to Alex and dropping Mena and her friend Giselle at the Serena Hotel. Built at a cost of over thirty-five million dollars by the Agha Khan Fund for Economic Development, the Serena's opulence sat uneasily alongside the motley collection of maimed beggars sitting in abject poverty outside its fortress walls. The blind, the limbless, the mentally ill, thin women shrouded in faded blue burqas with malnourished children tugging at their hems.

Like Nero's imperial Rome, Karzai and his many advisors held court and fiddled (the accounts, according to Abdul Qabir), while many of Kabul's citizens burned in the fires of squalor. Sushi for lunch and rooms at two hundred and fifty dollars a night with the presidential suite going for over a thousand. In Kabul! The Serena was an attack waiting to happen. A heartbreak hotel in the making.

Gil stopped off at the bar to see if there was anyone he knew. It already held a healthy Friday lunchtime clientele, some nursing hangovers with a hair of the dog, others regulars who always seemed to be in attendance, serious drinkers serially dependent on booze.

There was no alcometer, no vetting system for the many expats arriving in Afghanistan. Mickey had told him about the Australian advisor recruited to the ministry who missed his Kabul flight in Dubai. When the man phoned to say when he would be arriving he was obviously still under the influence so was told in no uncertain terms to go back to Melbourne. The guy broke down in tears.

For those who slipped through, Gil wondered what baggage they brought with them. What problems they might leave for the Afghans to clear up. The maths was easy. For every thousand civilian aid and development workers (not to mention diplomatic staff) who were drinkers, you would expect around forty to have some type of alcohol-related problem. With thousands of expats already in Kabul that meant a fair number you wouldn't want to rely on to make judgments about their own safety and security, never mind yours. It was ironic – in AA parlance somebody trying to escape something is called 'pulling a geographic'. Coming all the way to Afghanistan seemed to Gil an excessive geographic.

There were exceptions, however. German Frank was propping up the corner of the bar, thin frame balanced on his usual stool as he cradled a beer and gesticulated to an American colleague. Gil liked Frank, misnamed as he had been born and raised in South Africa. As he frequently told people, '*I've never been to Germany in my life!*' He might be a serious drinker, but he was an old hand who had worked in Afghanistan for several years as a demining specialist and could speak Pashto and Dari fluently.

'Hi, Frank, how are you?'

'Hi, Gil. Howzit! What you doing here?'

'About to have lunch. You heard about Waheed, Frank?'

'Indeed I did. What a way to go, mown down like that. I liked the guy, he was solid. He was my driver when I worked for the AMCAD Trust.'

'I never knew Waheed was your driver? I'm trying to help his family out but there are problems.'

'I guess with Waheed there'd always be problems.'

'What do you mean?' Gil was taken aback by Frank's words. Waheed never gave the impression of a man with problems. His life appeared settled, or as settled as any life could be in a war-torn city like Kabul.

'He was constantly looking for ways to make money. Never knew why he wanted it. His family lived a frugal life and he'd no debts. I know because he told me. He never asked for a penny from me.'

'He never opened up to me like that – he was usually quiet, quite reserved.'

'Ah, it's a funny old world being a deminer. You're in a nerve-shredding business. When people see you going out to the field they think you might get the wrong wires crossed. *Kaboom!* You might never come back. They might never see you again, so they open up. Happens all the time.' Frank laughed. 'Thing is, Old Frank always returns! So far so good, heh, but it's coming to an end. I'm resigning and going home. I've had it. Put in for promotion, but they say I'm not eligible because I've no paper qualifications. More experience than all of them put together, heh. C'est la fucking vie.'

Gil's face displayed his indignation. Frank deserved better. He had saved more lives in Afghanistan than anyone else still living, but lacking paper qualifications meant he wasn't entitled to be paid more even though he was on a low salary rating.

'Bloody typical, Frank. You know what the bureaucrats are like. I'll see you before you go, make sure of it. When are you off?'

'Next month, I'm handing in my resignation Monday.'

'Alright. Take care of yourself.'

'Always.'

Gil left Frank sitting at the bar resuming conversation with his colleague, arms soon waving all over the place, his body still as a corpse. Frank was a popular man, permanently cheerful. Gil would miss him.

Moving into the restaurant he noticed Lars Berggren sitting by himself at a corner table fighting his way through a gargantuan plate of roast chicken, a rack of carrots and a substantial wedge of potato salad. As usual he was attired in local garb, off-white shalwar kameez with fawn waistcoat covering his rotund figure and a flat-topped brown *pakol* rakishly set on his head. A long well-trimmed beard flowed down his chest.

He looked like some misplaced tribal chief who had ended up in the club restaurant happily munching away alongside the mostly be-denimed sweat-shirted diners. Lars was a fixture in the club and ate most of his meals there. As he'd explained to Gil on a previous occasion, '*It's not the best food in Kabul but there is an elegant sufficiency and it's convenient. I have few complaints.*'

Although the food was passable, Gil wasn't too fond of the place. Its dingy dark brown décor and poor lighting reminded him of bars he frequented as a student.

'Hey, Gil! Good to see you, please join me.'

'Thanks, Lars, I will.'

'I wanted to have a word about the agency. They're doing a lot of work but seem to have no sense of where they're headed. We're concerned.'

'I'm not surprised.'

'No strategy, eh?'

'Exactly, not a clue. They keep building at all costs. It provides lots of glossy pics for headquarters reports, though!'

Lars laughed. He had been long enough in Afghanistan and understood Gil's cynicism for the reality it held. As a respected senior UN staffer his was the level head trying to keep the dreams and schemes of newcomers in check.

'I know. I've sat in a couple of reps meetings with Olivier until he started sending that pompous little twat Mario. His hands are too heavy for his wrists, if you know what I mean. Mind you, I wouldn't trust Olivier – he's a hard man to pin down.'

'Olivier is alright but ineffectual. Mario has more drive but little sense of the country and what's going on here. He acts like a martinet. Thinks he's still in Geneva. At least he's well read. He has the information if not the understanding.'

'Exactly. I know the type. Not much to choose between them. Diplomats they're not. I love Churchill's definition of diplomacy, "*the art of telling people to go to hell in such a way that they ask for directions*"!'

Gil chuckled, although he'd heard Lars repeat the same quote on several occasions. 'Well, no point in asking either of them for directions – they don't know where they are or where they're going, they need directions themselves. First principle, Lars – know where you are.'

Lars laughed heartily at this and nodded in agreement, a stray morsel of chicken toppling onto his waistcoat. After laying his fork and knife at the side of the plate, he looked at Gil with a more serious expression. 'And what about your enquiries into Waheed's death, Gil? Where are you with that? Do you have a direction there?'

Gil was surprised. On Alex's advice he'd kept their enquiries low-key, only telling a few people. 'How do you know about Waheed, Lars? I just feel obliged to help the family. The UN seems useless in a situation like this.'

'Look, Gil, you know we have our hands tied. It's a local police matter – we have no jurisdiction. The family are given compensation money, that's as far as we can go.'

'What price for a life, eh? Is it enough, Lars? If it was an international staff member you would have been right on top of it, putting pressure on the authorities.'

'You're right, but we have to play the game. There's nothing else we can do. You don't know what's behind this killing or who's involved. I've seen expats like us get sucked into local affairs before and it seldom ends well. Be careful.'

'I feel we owe it to the family. You know Alex de Wolfe? He's going to contact a friend in the local police. He speaks the language and knows his way round Kabul much better than me.'

While Gil prided himself on taking a professional approach to his work, trying to unravel a murder made him feel like a rank amateur. He was no detective, although he knew that he and Alex desperately needed some sort of strategy to take their enquiries forward.

'We're not approaching this in a haphazard way, Lars, we're trying to take a strategic view of the situation and moving slowly. We're aware of the risks.'

Lars laughed. 'You're sounding like the UN now, Gil. We're always developing strategies for this and that, but they don't always pan out. Quite often we're reduced to short-term quick-impact measures when what they really need here is flick and turn.'

'What?'

'The flick of the switch and the turn of the tap. Providing people with electricity and potable water, the type of amenities we westerners take for granted.'

Gil would have laughed if Lars hadn't looked so serious.

'Sometimes I think we're all shooting for the moon here, Gil. When we pull out, and I'll give it a decade at best, you'd need a big crystal ball to predict what'll remain sustainable. It's the old illusion of validity. The Americans know Afghanistan can never be truly democratic in the western sense yet they continue with ideas and policies that suggest it can.'

From previous experience Gil knew Lars was an expert in diverting from any issue he didn't want to discuss further. He had flicked the switch very effectively. Gil could only shrug in agreement as the waiter brought a plate of pasta and salad and placed it in front of him.

'Okay, Gil, sorry, I'll have to leave you to it, I'm off to Chicken Street to look for a present for Jane. It's her birthday next week. See you soon, I hope. Good luck and be safe.'

Lars pulled out his chair, stood up, shook Gil's hand and waddled off through the garden exit.

Jane. Gil liked her on the one occasion they'd met. She'd been in Kabul en route to Herat to assess some gender project or other. She reminded him so much of Stella. The same intense blue eyes, the open laugh. Meeting her had unsettled him, eliciting a feeling of unease but little semblance of joy in meeting a beautiful woman.

He was too easily reminded of Stella. Even seeing a young woman in a blue bikini at the UN pool back in

July set his heart racing. Emails from the kids sometimes disturbed him, although recently they seldom mentioned their mother. Phone calls with Stella's sister, whose voice was eerily similar to Stella's, were the worst of all.

Sometimes he felt he had been born a lost soul, destined to wander the earth with no peace. Maybe it was just ennui, that most self-indulgent of emotions, one he tried to resist at all costs. *Snap out of it*, he thought. *Focus on Waheed's family. You have things to do.* He drained the last mouthful of water from the fluted glass, pushed his half-finished plate aside, pulled his mobile from his jacket pocket and called Abdul Qabir.

NINE

THE CAGE, IN BAGRAM BASE,
Friday 28 October 2005

As Gil sat back from the table and made ready to leave the club, forty miles north of Kabul another lunch was also finishing. It consisted of a lump of bread and a bowl of lukewarm meat and vegetable stew – but with no meat.

Hassan pushed the bowl away and stared at the filthy grey walls of the room beyond his cage. The cage itself was no more than a chicken coop, a six square metre wood and wire cell. He could feel himself shivering yet it wasn't particularly cold.

He had no idea how long he'd been in this place or whether it was day or night. There were no windows in the room. He didn't know where he was being held yet was sure it was somewhere near Kabul. Apart from the permanent odours of urine, faeces and stale sweat laced with disinfectant, occasionally a familiar smell wafted its way through the small blacked-out slatted vents high in the wall. Cooking spices or the faint pungent smell of burning hashish.

He had no way of knowing he was in the dungeons of America's Bagram facility close to the old brick factory housing the infamous CIA black site prison and interrogation centre, code-named the Salt Pit.

But this was of no concern to Hassan. One of the guards kept telling him he would soon be transferred to Guantanamo Bay. *A place far from here*, the guard emphasised. *You'll never see your family again.*

Several of the older prisoners had already disappeared. He overheard a guard laughing, saying they had 'gone on holiday' to this Bay place. Through the guard's mask of harsh laughter Hassan knew it would be no holiday.

He was young and strong but was resigned. One day soon he too would be going to the Bay. They had told him. Then they said he would be staying in his cell. Then a few days later that he would be leaving the next day. He didn't. He stayed.

This was the worst part, the not knowing. The terror of uncertainty and what might happen to him next. When would he leave this prison? Would he ever leave? Alive or dead? His shivering continued, try as he might he could not control it.

When he thought about Farnood the shivering intensified. His body shook. Why pretend. It was fear. Hassan was scared. He could admit it now. He had seen what these men could do.

They had taken Farnood from his cage and chained

him to the ceiling by his wrists, leaving only the toes of his feet tipping frantically at the ground. Then they had beaten him. Not on the head or body; there were no marks left there, only on the legs. The clinical peroneal strikes, the severe numbing blows to the sides of the legs above the knees, his body slumped forward held up only by the chains. Hassan saw them beating the poor man every day for over a week. His bloody legs looked like a truck had run over them.

For Farnood sleep was impossible, the pain too excruciating. The rest of the men caged in the room managed only fitful sleep as he moaned and groaned, his body writhing against the chains. It was, of course, all proper and in keeping with the declaration made by President Bush's head of counter-terrorism two days after the Twin Towers collapsed: *'The country's enemies must be left with flies walking across their eyeballs.'*

It would be years before the media was able to disclose the two thousand-page United States Army report on the homicides of two unarmed civilian Afghan prisoners by US armed forces at Bagram, too late for Farnood or any of the men in the room who might embrace a similar fate.

Hassan had witnessed Farnood being kicked, punched, slapped, shackled to the wall like an animal and deprived of sleep. More than that even, the shame of being stripped of his clothes, naked in front of these infidels. Worse, they'd put a filthy dog collar round his neck and led him round the room on a chain.

Hassan felt continuously threatened. Yet he himself wasn't some terrorist or a threat or a danger to anyone. He knew he hadn't just been in the wrong place at the wrong time like some of the others. He'd been targeted. He knew why he was here and what the two guards wanted from him. There was little doubt. They had told him. It was information about the madrassah where he worked since his father returned to Peshawar four years earlier.

'*Hadji Zarak is a good man,*' his father told him. '*He will look after you. Work hard for him, it will help our business. You must learn from him.*' Then his father left and returned to Pakistan, leaving his young son in a strange city without family or friends.

Hassan had never been in a madrassah before, only attending a small village school near the family home in the mountains north of Peshawar learning to read and write and recite a few passages from the Holy Koran. This school was different, however. The boys in the madrassah spent much of the day memorising the Koran while sitting cross-legged on small floor cushions rocking rhythmically back and forth, back and forth, endlessly back and forth.

Meanwhile his job was to run errands for Hadji Zarak, usually in the form of sealed letters to be delivered to various houses throughout the city. He was given a mobile with explicit instructions to only use it if stopped at a checkpoint, which was unlikely. Hassan was inconspicuous on the streets. He looked like any other bright-eyed youth wearing a more or less clean shalwar kameez.

He was a clever boy. It didn't take long for him to figure out that behind the façade of pious learning Hadji Zarak was coordinating a drugs empire from the madrassah. He was the middleman between the traders and those who arranged to take the *taryak* and the *poder* out of the country. He was the banker who brokered the deals, the man who held a million-dollar bank account in Dubai. Hassan knew this, for he had sneaked a look at a bank statement lying on the hadji's desk, carelessly left there by the official head of the madrassah, a small bespectacled mullah from Logar province who happened to be the hadji's second cousin.

'Give 'em somethin' light to begin with. Wake 'em up, for Christ's sake.' It was the voice of the tall guard with the faint scars running across his cheek. Hassan could see the man's name badge sewn on the front pocket of his green army uniform – 'COLLINS'. The guards knew most of the prisoners couldn't read so made no pretence about hiding their names. Thankfully they would soon be out of this godforsaken country, no chance of reprisals.

Then it started. A blasting grating noise exploded from the four speakers mounted high up in the corners of the room. The room itself seemed to act as a natural amplifier as the noise swirled and echoed, bouncing off the bare concrete walls. Each of the twelve men penned in their cages wrapped their head in a blanket, but it didn't stop the noise. It could begin at any time, usually on the few occasions when they had settled down to a fitful sleep with only Farnood's muted moaning to contend with.

'Crank it up, Frank,' shouted the other guard. 'Give 'em "The Star-Spangled Banner". Might help the cocky little motherfucker to remember what we need to know. He'll talk sooner or later. I'll make sure of it.'

'Yea, Chucky, but it'll need to be soon – we're off home in a week, thank the good Lord.'

With that the two guards replaced their headphones, adjusted them to a snug fit and sat down behind the green metal desk to drink black coffee and flick through old *Guns and Ammo* magazines. The noise was deafening. Jimi Hendrix had never sounded so bad. They were playing the disc at three times its normal speed, preferring it to the death metal the relief guards played.

Hassan desperately wanted to forget the continuous crashing sounds that made his brain throb. He covered his head with a blanket and tried to remember the time before he entered the room, the time when he was alive.

He never saw the black SUV with the dark tinted windows slowly drawing to a halt beside him as he walked back to the madrassah late one afternoon. Two men quickly opened the back door, jumped out and grabbed him. They were big men, fast for their size. He could see the look in their eyes. One of them was smiling as he whispered, his face creased in a mocking grin, '*Inside the car, motherfucker, now.*'

He could do nothing as he watched in slow motion the small white plastic Elvis topple from his shalwar pocket and land in the dusty road. It was the last thing Hassan saw before a coarse cloth bag was rammed over his head and he was pushed into the back seat of the vehicle.

TEN

THE HOLE-IN-THE-WALL, IN KABUL,
Friday 28 October 2005

There was no shortage of restaurants in Kabul: Afghan food at the Sufi, Italian at the Boccaccio, French at L'Atmosphere, Lebanese at the Taverna du Liban, Indian at the Jaisalmer, the old Turkish restaurant with the waiters wearing black bow ties, several Chinese eateries and the popular Lai Thai in Wazir Akbar Khan.

It was a freezing night back in February when Gil arranged to go to the Lai Thai with Farooq, a journalist friend. As they approached the restaurant their headlights picked up two sparkling orbs slowly gyrating down the street in front of them. Drawing closer, they saw it was two young Thai women walking arm in arm, one on her mobile, the other tucked into tight purple spandex trousers, her bottom continuing to gyrate as they climbed into a car with two men, rendezvous successful, nocturnal mission still to be completed.

There were many more restaurants and clubs, no reason for Gil to know them all. New ones opened all the time. There was an ever-increasing number of expat workers in Kabul with money to spend and limited ways of spending it.

But tonight they would go to the Hole-in-the-Wall, his favourite. A small Chinese restaurant in a residential house tucked up a narrow side street in Shahr-e-Naw. The only indication it even existed was a small red Chinese lantern hanging from the gateway arch. No sign, no other indication there was a restaurant hidden behind the compound walls. Gil didn't even know its official name.

The other Chinese restaurants in town had garish fronts with large imperial dragons lacquered in red and gold sitting outside. Wide doorways, their elaborate name signs carved in wood, were festooned with swinging paper lanterns. One restaurant had young, and some not so young, short-skirted waitresses who delivered, so it was alleged, off-the-menu services.

Each evening several new and expensive SUVs could be seen parked outside the entrance, their drivers and guards standing around in the street smoking and chatting while their bosses lingered inside. Gil had no interest in frequenting such a louche establishment, although he knew a few expats who utilised its services on a regular basis.

There were no vehicles parked outside the Hole-in-the-Wall as Abdul Qabir dropped them off at seven. Gil and Mena, Farooq and Charlotte, a young Australian doctor recently arrived at the agency to take up a post as gender advisor. Her relationship with Mario was already strained and being with a fellow doctor might help her to ease into the work.

After introductions, the group quickly established an amiable atmosphere and settled down to chat about the exigencies of living and working in Kabul. Gil wanted to talk with Farooq about his meeting with Asidullah, but it would have to wait until later when they were alone.

The restaurant was small and only held seven tables. Choosing to sit in an alcove partly obscured from other diners, their nearest neighbour was a circular table seating eight Chinese, six men and two women. Clashing their cans of Heineken together the eight laughed and joked, toasting each other with cries of 'Banzai! Banzai!' It was strange to hear them using a cheer derived from an ancient Japanese battle cry. May you indeed live for ten thousand years.

Gil placed their order. Four cans of beer, a bottle of mineral water, steamed rice, baked fish, lemon chicken and his favourite, spinach in a garlic and black bean sauce.

While they waited for the food, Mena recounted having to deal with a man brought by his sister to the ministry for help. Although he was called Mohammad, everybody referred to him as the-man-with-no-mouth. It was unusual for the ministry to deal with men's issues; the staff had enough problems trying to deal with the flood of women seeking help with a myriad of complaints, frequently concerning the violence they experienced at the hands of men.

As Mena began to explain Mohammad's situation they

87

became aware that the loud chatter from the Chinese table had died away. Their own table was the only one still talking. The door of the restaurant lay open, a senior police officer standing in its doorway, his uniform festooned with gold braid, broad white-topped cap still perched on his head.

When they first arrived at the restaurant Gil had noticed several young Afghans sitting at other tables, green and silver cans in hand. These tables were now rigid in silence as they watched the policeman remove his cap, nod curtly to them and make his way over to the bar counter where four waitresses stood with expressionless faces, forearms languidly draped on the bar top.

The words of the latest JDL security advice came flooding into Gil's mind. 'DO NOT *drink alcohol with Afghan colleagues – if you are present in a restaurant when it is raided, contact the OPS room immediately and comply with any reasonable request.* DO NOT *put up a battle to save your drink/meal, or attempt to think you could influence the situation – compliance is the way to proceed.*'

Gil was quite prepared to be compliant. He wasn't ready to have a confrontation with Kabul's finest. However, after talking to the restaurant's owner, a tall Han woman dressed in a red Cheongsam with slits to the waist, one of the waitresses took the officer by the arm and led him out a side door to the stairs and the upper part of the building where bedrooms were located.

The young Afghans looked extremely relieved and resumed their chat, beer cans re-appearing from under the table. The officer wasn't there to arrest them for drinking; his visit was for services about to be rendered. The Chinese table erupted with noise and laughter. He could only guess at what secrets they might want kept from the Afghan police.

In seeming celebration, two of the young Chinese men, already quite drunk, lurched behind the bar, returning with a set of large speakers while the owner wheeled a TV and stand to the front of the bar and plugged in a karaoke machine.

Soon the members of the Chinese table, sometimes on their own but mostly in pairs, stood up, selected a song from the programme and began to sing. In one case this produced a discordant wailing noise that sounded neither English nor Cantonese. Meanwhile, one of the women, so drunk she was having difficulty standing, was lurching between the tables handing out fresh cans of beer to the other diners.

Arriving at Gil's table she appeared excited, grabbed his hand and gesticulated to the karaoke machine. Shooing away the two young Chinese men clinging to the microphone, by this time on their third song, she hauled him up to the low stage.

While he was no singer and had never sung karaoke before, Gil knew it would be impolite to refuse. The two cans of beer he had already consumed, plus the wine at the house before he left, provided just enough courage for him to proceed with this most unexpected of tasks.

Flashing a sheepish grin towards his companions and apologising to Mena, he walked over to the karaoke machine where the woman thrust the microphone into his hand. Looking down the long list of available songs he found it difficult to choose. Most were American soft-rock numbers, the Byrds or the Eagles, others popular Chinese songs with misspelt English sub-titles.

As he perused the list, his companions began a chant of 'Gil! Gil! Gil!' soon taken up by the Chinese table but sounding like 'Kill! Kill! Kill!' He had been purposely slow in making a choice in the hope someone might come up and grab the microphone from him. Now it was too late. He had to choose a song.

Of the few numbers he considered, he finally settled on Elvis Presley's 'Blue Suede Shoes'. It was a simple enough song with a good beat and all too apposite. You wouldn't want to step on someone's shoes, blue suede or not, in Kabul; it was the wrong kind of city for that. Not that it bothered him – his own shoes were neither blue nor suede, just scuffed brown leather. It wouldn't be the first time they had been stepped on.

ELEVEN

AT THE OFFICE, IN KABUL,
Saturday 29 October 2005

Farhad was twenty-eight years of age. He'd returned to Kabul nine months earlier with his mother, father, two brothers and two sisters. It was the first time he set foot in the city since the family escaped to Pakistan over twenty years previously. It had been a frightening journey fleeing the safety of their home to a foreign land. His mother was left crippled trying to struggle over the impossibly high snow-clad mountain passes. His brother Said, aged three at the time, died in a howling snowstorm. There was no medical help as they trudged through the freezing conditions.

His father left for the office that day as usual. Kabul was tense. The Kalkh and Parcham factions of the People's Democratic Party of Afghanistan continued to argue and fight with each other. One of his uncles, also called Farhad, had already disappeared.

They came for his father in the late morning, two thickset men from the Ministry of Interior. Wearing crumpled woollen suits, their faces stern and set like stone, there was no doubt they were from the feared Khad. They were state intelligence agents, lawless secret policemen backed by their KGB handlers.

The secretary had been able to stall them while a colleague slipped into his father's office to warn him. His father had nothing to hide, nothing to feel guilty about. He wanted to stay and confront these men but knew there was only two doors leading from his office. Through one lay a chance of escape, through the other lay death, or worse, in Pul-i-Charkhi's dungeons.

Farhad remembered how his father had hurriedly arrived home, not even eaten lunch, just scooped them all up, bundled them into a friend's old van and driven to the mountains where their journey into Pakistan continued on foot. He thought of this gruelling journey often, of his dead brother, of how it still affected his mother's health.

But the journey was not his most vivid memory of that time. Two days before they fled, he and Aman, his best friend, along with several other boys from the neighbourhood, were playing football in the street at the bottom of the hill that rose up to the Soviet-built Intercontinental Hotel, a great rectangular concrete block nestled in its eyrie surveying the north and east of the city like some hooded raptor.

The street was quiet, in those days mostly devoid of traffic. Their ball was an old bundle of rags bound tightly with string. They were proud of it, smooth and round and soft enough to kick with their dirty bare feet.

The sudden explosion came from further up the hill towards the hotel. It didn't faze them particularly. They were young and were used to hearing explosions. Safi from the house next door had lost part of his right hand when he lived in Jalalabad. He knew more than any of them about explosions. But this explosion was closer than they had ever experienced, although not close enough to stop their game. It was two goals apiece and a decider needed to be played out. A cup final couldn't have been more tense.

Out of the corner of his eye Farhad was first to see the ball rolling down the hill towards them. '*Look, look*,' he cried out, '*here is a big football for us to play with!*'

The ball continued to bounce its way towards them, careening off a wall before it slowly came to rest at their feet. They stared at it without saying a word. Two sightless brown eyes stared back up at them, one peeking through a matted lock of black hair and a forehead plastered with dust.

Now here he was again, driving down the same hill past the heavily secured Intercontinental in a welter of honking morning traffic. But not so early morning. He had been delayed and was late for the office. Reaching his desk well after nine was an hour later than usual and he knew Mr Gil would be waiting for him.

There were several reports needing to be finalised and they were relying on him to make sure the LAN system was operating smoothly. The foreign staff were always sending email reports to each other, checking and re-checking before they were forwarded to Geneva or New York. It made him feel important. If the LAN went down it was a crisis. Usually it didn't. He had been well trained in IT at the college in Peshawar.

It was one benefit of spending his teenage years in Pakistan. That and being able to go out with his friends to the Fun Park to ride the dodgem cars, eat huge whirls of sickly yellow candy floss and sneak glances at the groups of giggling young girls with hands over mouths carefully guarding the words that might spill from them. The girls slowly walked round the park arm in arm, their colourful dupattas trailing behind them along with their parents.

The girls would sometimes glance back, giggle even louder and sometimes smile in their direction. Not exactly flirting yet it made them feel good, their young hearts beating faster with each smile.

Here in Kabul there was nothing for a young man to do of an evening, nowhere to walk or stroll where he could see girls his own age. Only flocks of schoolgirls in their blue and white uniforms clutching school bags as they hurriedly made their way home before dark. Only the occasional furtive glance was possible and even that could be considered inappropriate incurring a father's wrath, or worse.

Anyway, most places shut as soon as darkness descended. Only car headlights and a glimmer of light from the few streetlamps broke the gloom. Most evenings he and his friend Hashmat would sit in the compound of Hashmat's father's guesthouse drinking Heineken beer bought from a friend in Shashdarak.

Farhad liked his evening drink; it made him feel mellow.

His problems seemed to drift away, clearing his mind at least for a while. Last night they'd drunk six cans each, more than usual, and today his head felt fuzzy, although this wasn't why he was late. He had risen at the usual time of six o'clock, carefully bathed, then completed his morning prayers and eaten breakfast. It was only then he was delayed.

'Good morning, Farhad, *salaam aleikum*. How are you today? What happened? It's not like you to be late – we've a lot on, you know.'

Gil detected the sour hint of yesterday's alcohol wafting from the young man who had a more serious look on his face than usual. Having a slight headache himself from the previous night at the Hole-in-the-Wall he decided not to mention it.

'*Waleikum salaam*, Mr Gil. Sorry, it was our house. It was on fire this morning and I stayed to help put out the flames.'

'Again, Farhad! This is the third time in six months there's been a fire in your house. Was it a gas leak? Has it been checked? Are you cooking on an open fire, or what?'

'No, it is my youngest sister.'

'Your sister?'

'The fire always starts in her room.'

'She sets fire to her room?! I thought she was only fourteen? Do you allow her to have matches or a lighter?'

'No, no, nothing like that. After the first fire we made sure.'

'What's going on then, Farhad? How do these fires start?'

'It is a djinn, Mr Gil. We have sent for the mullah.

He will say a prayer and give her a *tawiz*. All will be well, Insha'Allah.'

Somehow a djinn was appropriate. Gil knew it referred to an invisible presence making itself manifest through fire. He recalled the Koran's definition, that djinns were made of a smokeless scorching fire. Along with humans and angels, they made up the three sentient creations of God and, like humans, could be good, evil or neutrally benevolent. Most importantly, they induced fear and were to be appeased at all costs. Gil hoped the mullah knew his business.

He remembered Bill Johnson from WFP telling him that when he'd been in Rwanda during the genocide, the rampaging killer mobs of Hutus and Tutsis gave Muslim neighbourhoods, especially mosques, a wide berth, fearing the wrath of their protective djinns.

When Gil spent a month in Liberia interviewing ex-child soldiers, Dr Bernice, head of the UNICEF rehabilitation centre, recounted that during the civil war the most feared cadre of child soldiers was composed entirely of young women. Carrying AK-47s they went into battle naked in the belief they were immune to bullets. Adorned only with a mass of protective amulets round their necks, their temples were slit and a potent cocktail of drugs rubbed into the wounds.

Magic in Africa. Magic in Afghanistan. Another impenetrable layer for the *kharaji* to decipher. Here was Farhad with his western-styled suits tailored in Pakistan, the current one a lime green cotton and linen mix, and his modern high-tech education yet with a firm belief in djinns. A young Afghan brought up and schooled within the relative freedoms that Pakistan's cities afforded yet with one foot in another more ancient culture.

Djinns were no different from poltergeists in the West, Gil mused. Funny how all these spirits were usually associated with teenage girls. What power did these sub-adult females hold? If only they were allowed to harness and wield it perhaps the world would become a better place.

Farhad's family would be able to assuage the djinn problem with a mullah and a *taweez*. Lucky them. Gil sometimes felt his own genie had been released from the bottle with no indication it would ever return. Even Afghanistan had burst from its bottle, its warlike genies with no intention of ever being cooped up together again behind glass walls. The country had lain for centuries like some broken bottle on the map of south Asia, its jagged contents lying in wait for any unsuspecting invader, and there had been many.

Gil realised Farhad was standing waiting for him to say something while he had been musing over the djinn, his mind not quite present. These lapses of thought were becoming all too frequent. Perhaps it was his increasing alcohol use – or maybe he wasn't drinking enough?

'Okay, fine, Farhad, go and check the LAN and please have a cup of tea. I'll see you later when you've finished.'

Farhad looked relieved and went over to his desk in the corner while Gil prepared the papers for the meeting with Olivier. Battle was about to commence.

TWELVE

OFFICE NEGOTIATIONS, IN KABUL,
Saturday 29 October 2005

Olivier Levasseur looked out on a prim and exceedingly clean office as he sat behind his broad polished wooden desk. Apart from a desktop computer, a small vase of neatly arranged yellow flowers and an orderly pile of paper files, its surface was empty. In one corner of the room a printer sat next to a flat-screen TV standing on a dark mahogany table. They were seldom switched on. In the corner opposite, a large pile of box files was neatly stacked against a tall grey metal filing cabinet.

Three expensive off-white leather chairs, imported from Dubai on Olivier's instructions and charged to the agency, sat in formation in front of the desk ready to receive visitors, although there were few. The floor carpet was an old Turkman of excellent quality. It had cost a small fortune, again purchased with agency money.

Olivier happily bought it on one of the few occasions he'd been persuaded by Mario to accompany him to the bazaar. Not the city bazaar teeming with a ragged assortment of people all crushed together, but the shops in Chicken Street catering for the many expats staying in Kabul as they had once done for young western travellers in the sixties and seventies.

Olivier didn't want to stay in Kabul; he hated the place. He longed for the clean smooth streets of Geneva, the civilised people, the cocktail bars where he spent many happy hours with friends. It was Toichiev! The bastard had sent him to Afghanistan as a punishment for some perceived slight or other. The two had never seen eye to eye and clashed on several occasions, their cultural obstinacies to the fore.

The look on the Russian's face festered for months before he was able to put his get-rid-of-Olivier plan into action. The new policy from the Executive Director provided the opening, the perfect opportunity. It proclaimed that those desk-bound officers who had been in HQ for several years (in Olivier's case over twenty) should now do a minimum one-year tour of duty in a field station so they could reacquaint themselves with development issues in situ.

'*You will enjoy your time there, Olivier, Afghanistan is an interesting and challenging post!*' Toichiev cheerily told him as he outlined the travel details, his bland features a mask of smugness. As if in situ mattered; admin was admin and there was no way he would be venturing out of Kabul to any other situ if he could help it. In fact he rarely left his office or his room in the guesthouse except to attend essential meetings and functions, although if possible he sent Mario, ruthlessly ambitious but always biddable.

Olivier's connection with Kabul was limited to the view seen through the windows of the car ferrying him between guesthouse and office. What he saw was enough. The city was filthy, piles of rubbish everywhere, buildings collapsed or pockmarked with bullet holes. Beggars and cripples abounded, blue-burqaed women scuttled along the roadside like ants and the traffic was a nightmare.

When they slowed down for the inevitable traffic jam, dark eyes set in lined swarthy faces stared at him through the window. He tried to keep a dignified appearance. It was hard. All he wanted to do was hunker down, curl up on the seat and disappear. If he left the safety of the Land Cruiser there was every chance he would be attacked. These were wild unpredictable people; their violent history was a testament to that, wasn't it? His safety and security were a thing of the past and he was afraid. He was like a fish removed from the cocoon of its watery world left stranded and gasping for air.

Olivier reached down and unlocked the bottom drawer of the desk. Removing the bottle, the drawer's sole occupant apart from a well-used crystal tumbler, he poured himself three fingers. Gulping down the amber liquid – after all, he was drinking it for medicinal purposes – he savoured the lingering peaty aftertaste.

The availability of Lagavulin was the only real highlight of living in Kabul. Mario was pleased to purchase it for him at the PX. It was a military exchange, yet anybody with a foreign passport could gain access to its seemingly unlimited supply of duty-free alcohol. Its selection of Scotch whisky was particularly good and he tended to favour the peaty malts like Laphroaig, Bowmore or Lagavulin. There was always a bottle stashed in the bottom of his underwear drawer back at the guesthouse.

But he'd much preferred the Intercontinental Hotel to the agency guesthouse. Although a bit rundown and a concrete monstrosity typical of the Soviets (how he missed old Geneva's architectural charms), it was quieter and had none of the agency staff milling around wanting to chat. Despite the creaking rickety lift and the tin basins placed in the lobby when it rained, his room on the hotel's fifth floor was acceptable.

He had insisted on a deluxe room. It was comfortable enough, if a bit drab. At night its panoramic views over the north and east of the city looked as if a myriad of fireflies were twinkling across the plains. When darkness fell it could have been anywhere. The food in the dining room was edible and a small band played music during dinner. Not exactly a string quartet, but the rabab player was talented and had a strong voice. Backed by a harmonium and tabla, their playing was a pleasant backdrop to dinner.

Then that Thursday evening he received the phone call from UN security. '*The Taliban are threatening a strike against the Intercon, sir. You can't stay. You'll have to leave.*'

'*Thank you,*' he replied. '*I'll pack this evening and the car can collect me in the morning.*'

'*No, sir, you have to leave now. We're sending a car for you. It'll be there in twenty minutes. Be in the lobby.*'

The caller abruptly hung up and he was left to pack

his bags as best he could, taking a last hurried look at the fireflies in the process. It was most inconvenient, but what if the Taliban attacked within the next twenty minutes?

He frantically moved round the room collecting suits, shirts, ties, underwear. The new two hundred-dollar python skin shoes he bought on his last trip to Manila were quickly pulled from the bottom of the wardrobe. Everything was then crammed into the hard-shell Antler case. Most of his paperwork was kept at the office; the rest easily fitted into a briefcase. He had no time to do a final check, panic rising in his chest. Something of importance in the room perhaps left behind? He didn't care. He had to leave – fast.

Into the lift, then across the lobby where security was already waiting and into the UN Land Cruiser parked outside the hotel entrance with its engine running. A quick nod to the red-capped uniformed doorman and they were on their way. As they left he glanced back and saw the large white wooden sign standing outside the main hotel door. It displayed a drawing of an AK-47 with a bold red cross painted over it. Underneath in both English and Dari the black print stated a futile 'No Weapons'.

Then the co-driver, a serious look on his face, gun hidden at his side under a white and black chequered scarf, turned to look at Olivier. 'Sorry about the short notice, Mr Levasseur. Our intel is good. We're evacuating all UN staff staying at the hotel. Any embassy staff are also being moved out. We'll take you to UNICA Guesthouse for tonight.'

Oh God, he thought. UNICA was too busy and noisy with its dreadful gloomy bar and restaurant. He would inevitably meet colleagues he would have to talk to. It would be difficult staying in his room. The place was habitually overcrowded, there was a shortage of rooms, most were doubled up, even trebled, and some not very clean. He winced. One night was enough. He would have to phone Mario and arrange a room in the agency's main guesthouse; there was little choice. At least there were only twelve of them staying there and the food was supposedly good, the cook being trained in Rome or so he claimed.

His mobile abruptly rang, bringing him back to the world outside his thoughts, a world he studiously tried to avoid. He quickly wiped the empty glass and returned it to the drawer. It was Mario. They were ready to start the meeting. Not the whole staff, only Julia his admin assistant, Mario of course, plus Mahdi and Zalmei, and that irksome Moncrief.

He didn't like the man, always asking for clarifications and scruffy-looking for an international advisor. It offended his Parisian sensibilities. Why couldn't the man wear a tie and comb his hair properly? It resembled a bird's nest, tufts sticking out everywhere. His shoes were never polished, anathema to Olivier, who took great pride in his shoe collection, each pair with its own made-to-measure trees to avoid stretching the leather.

Popping a mint into his mouth, he tucked the folder under his arm and went into the adjoining bathroom to check himself in the mirror before locking the office door and making his way to the meeting room.

They were already seated. After greeting each one personally – good manners had to be maintained, after all

– he sat at the head of the small table, extracted a pair of gold-rimmed spectacles from their case, popped them on his nose and opened a burgundy leather folder.

'Welcome, colleagues. There are two important items on the agenda today: the new bridge and the school. We have committed pledges for both. The work will proceed as soon as possible.'

The school was to be built in Wardak province – for girls only. The bridge was a two-tonne load-bearing road bridge over a narrow and strategic river in Nangarhar province. A river whose source was in the White Mountains of the Spin Ghar, its waters rushing down from the snow-capped peaks before smoothing out over Nangarhar's fertile plains and irrigating its acres of wheat fields laced with opium poppies.

Olivier continued to outline the details of both projects: how the local NGOs were selected for building work, who would be tasked with monitoring progress, when the tranches of funding would be released and so on.

After he finished speaking, he looked round the table for approval. Mario and Julia nodded vigorously while Zalmei sat immobile, consent already evident in his eyes. Mahdi was his usual inscrutable self, observing everything, saying little. Gil looked quizzical. Olivier knew there was a question coming.

'Olivier, do we have funding for teachers' salaries and resources for books and desks, not to mention security? This is a school for girls, after all.'

'Yes, yes, this will be arranged, Mr Moncrief. Do not be concerned.'

'Are these funds already in the agency's account or are they only pledged?' Gil queried, his challenging stare fixed on Olivier.

Olivier paused, the exasperation clear on his face as he answered. 'Pledged, of course. The funds will come eventually, we are confident. We have a deadline for the building work. It must begin soon.'

'Please remember the *shabnamas* sent by the Taliban to teachers in Wardak province saying if they went into school they would be killed. As you know, two of them were killed, resulting in the school being closed.'

'Yes, Gil, but you know many of these so-called night letters are only a bluff,' Mario chipped in, revealing yet again his well of ignorance.

'Maybe, Mario, but not a bluff I'd like to call. Would you?'

Mario gave one of his famous pouts, re-arranged the papers lying in front of him and sat back in his chair.

Gil was pleased to see Julia taking minutes, although it didn't assuage his frustration fuelled by Olivier not even mentioning Waheed's murder. There was little else he could do to delay the start of the building before all the necessary funding was in the bank. He didn't want to see yet another ghost school created. There was no guarantee with new buildings either; they were often substandard due to under-funding and poor construction.

The bright-yellow health clinic recently completed in the village of Qalai Qazi near Kabul was a good example. Built by American contractor the Louis Berger Group, the clinic was meant to function as a prime example of

American engineering and serve as a model for the eighty-one clinics the group was hired to construct. The problem was that this so-called model clinic was already falling apart, much of the ceiling had rotted, the plumbing leaked, the place smelled of sewage and the chimney, made of flimsy metal, threatened to set the roof on fire.

'Are we finished?' Olivier declared, scanning the room with a look that said 'yes, we are'.

'One other thing,' Gil interjected. 'What about the bridge? Has a full assessment been carried out to see if it's absolutely necessary?'

'Of course,' Mario chipped in. 'An assessment has been carried out by the NGO building the bridge. It's a reputable organisation. There was a competitive bidding process. They were selected from a short list of three and we've contracted them before.'

Gil's face masked his annoyance. What about an independent assessment, and why contract an organisation recommended by one of the agency's Afghan staff, most likely Mahdi? Gil was never clear about Mahdi's role in the agency. As the designated National Programme Officer, much of his time was spent ensconced in meetings with Olivier and Mario; he rarely interacted with other staff members and at meetings usually kept his own counsel.

The Afghans were good at this game and who could blame them? Give the project to a relative or friend and then take your cut. If it was a paper-only project, more difficult to arrange in these post-Taliban times, then split the money fifty-fifty. A profitable venture all round yet preferable to the misspent reconstruction money that ended up in the coffers of Kellog, Brown and Root or DynCorp without ever leaving the US. At least the agency's money stayed in Afghanistan, whoever it was paid to.

Gil looked directly at a stony-faced Mario. 'You'll recall the Nuristan bridge project? It was finally completed the month after you arrived in Kabul.'

There was an awkward silence in the room before he continued.

'After building the bridge it was discovered there was a better one already built by USAID a mile upstream. Then the Deputy Governor came to Kabul to see Karzai demanding to know who authorised the building of these bridges. They didn't even need one in the valley; they needed it much further upstream.'

With that Gil sat back in his chair and waited for a response from Olivier or Mario. There was none. Mario's sidelong glance at Olivier, signalling he was going to say nothing in reply, gave Olivier the cue to finish the meeting.

'Thank you, Mr Moncrief, point noted, but this bridge will be built. We have committed funding and an approaching deadline. If there is no more business the meeting is now closed. At the next meeting we will discuss the new project to the east of Kabul. Thank you all.

As they moved their chairs back and stood to leave, Gil could feel his mobile vibrating. Flipping it open, he looked at the message blinking on the screen. It was from Asidullah suggesting a meeting at 7.00pm with a man called Mirwais.

According to Asidullah, he had been Waheed's best friend and might have some useful information. While it would probably be of little help in finding out who killed

Waheed, at the moment there were few other leads. Gil texted back his consent to the visit, then escaped the meeting as quickly as possible.

THIRTEEN

AT THE MACRORAYAN COMPLEX, IN KABUL,

Saturday 29 October 2005

The Land Cruiser eased its way through lingering clouds of exhaust fumes, past a congested roundabout and turned a sharp right onto the Jalalabad road. Dusk was approaching. It would soon be dark. On the left side of the road a wide paving area gave way to rows of Macrorayan, monotonous grey Soviet-built five-storey apartment blocks stretching into the distance.

Although several of the blocks appeared a bit dilapidated, their upkeep uncertain since the Soviets left in 1989, they were still highly prized. In an earthquake-prone country these were solid chunks of real estate. Several still displayed the pockmarks from gun and rocket fire.

Similar blocks along the Airport Road were mostly

bombed out but their concrete frames still stood. From a distance they looked like ragged new-build skeletons. The families camped out on each floor continued to rig up tarpaulins and plastic sheets against remnants of concrete walls, little comfort against the coming winter.

In the fading light Gil could see washing slung over balconies. Multi-coloured lines of garments stretched out on makeshift pulleys ran from the balconies to the few tall trees still standing between the blocks. He wondered who shinned up these light-limbed trees to fix the pulleys.

The apartment blocks reminded him of sink estates in Glasgow designed for the hoi polloi. Here in Kabul they had been built for the middle-class heralding in a false dawn of Soviet-inspired progress. Similar blocks stretched throughout the old Soviet lands of central Asia and Eastern Europe, from Tajikistan all the way to East Germany. Substantial accommodation for the communist masses yet now faded as their empire.

As they pulled off the road and approached block 2A, satellite dishes, some fixed to the roof, others to balconies, appeared silhouetted against the building. Mirwais's apartment was on the third floor facing away from the road and towards the north of the city.

So this was Waheed's closest friend. Asidullah's message had been brief and to the point. '*Salaam aleikum, Mr Gil. My father's best friend Mirwais will help. He would like to meet you. He lives in apartment 32, Block 2A Macrorayan on Jalalabad Road. At 7.00 this evening please. Thank you.*'

Asidullah's mobile was then conveniently shut off, denying any opportunity to respond. Despite some misgivings, Gil was intrigued enough to take a chance and meet with Mirwais.

'I'll return at nine o' clock, Mr Gil. It is not good to be out on the road after that. They will stop us at the checkpoints surely. See you then, Insha'Allah.'

Abdul Qabir spoke in an unusually quiet voice as Gil undid his seat belt and climbed from the vehicle.

He'd made the right decision in asking Abdul Qabir to drive him to Macrorayan. He was more discreet than the other drivers, and undoubtedly had his own secrets to keep. He would be reticent to reveal their destination to Jawed the house manager.

Jawed of course would then pass it on to Mike Gomez, JTD's programme manager for Afghanistan, who would quiz him to find out why he had gone anywhere near the Jalalabad road despite recent security advisories. In March a Canadian embassy vehicle had been destroyed by an IED on the road and since then any travel had to be cleared well in advance with JTD's security team.

He had simply told Jawed he was visiting a friend in Shahr-e-Naw and would be contactable by mobile. Since three international UN staff were kidnapped in October the previous year, the security situation in the city had tightened and would tighten even further with inevitable future kidnappings and bombings. With the new bollards and checkpoints around Karzai's Palace and the American embassy already in place, Kabul was creating its own Baghdad-style Green Zone.

As Abdul Qabir pulled the vehicle back towards the

Jalalabad road, Gil turned and walked into the block entrance. Edging his way up through the gloom of the narrow unlit staircase he was aware he was walking into the unknown. He had made good friends with a few Afghan colleagues, socialising and visiting restaurants together, but he'd never been inside an Afghan home. He didn't even know this Mirwais yet he was being invited into his home. Was this an honour or a mistake?

On reaching level three, the thrum of a small generator competed with the sounds of passing traffic. A sliver of light appeared under the door of apartment 32. He knocked and waited. Two deadbolts were drawn and the door was slowly opened by a young man of about seventeen years.

'Ah... you are Mr Gil? *Salaam aleikum.* My father is expecting you. Please come in.'

Gil entered the apartment, removed his shoes and turned right into the main living room. The excited chatter of women came from a room further up the narrow corridor. Enticing smells wafted from a small kitchen.

The first thing he noticed was the colour. Even in the muted generator-fed light, the living room appeared bright and warm. A beautiful old gul-patterned Andkhoy rug stretched from wall to wall, its colour still vibrant, while burgundy-coloured *toshacks*, the large floor cushions found in most Afghan homes, were laid out round the edge of the room.

In the centre stood a low intricately carved glass topped wooden table. In a corner a small television set was switched on. There was a crisp black and white picture but no sound. On a shelf in another corner sat a large vase of multi-coloured plastic flowers.

Seated on a *toshack* opposite the door was a small man wearing a white shalwar kameez and a silver-grey turban. At first glance he appeared to be sitting cross-legged, then Gil realised with a start the man had no legs. Not even stumps, only a torso and upper body sitting ramrod straight on the cushion with the bulk of his shalwar kameez bunched in front.

'*Salaam aleikum*, Mr Gil. Greetings! Welcome to my home. Please accept my apologies for not standing to greet you. You can see my condition, Mash'Allah, this is the way it is. I live with it. What else to do?' With that the man called Mirwais gave a chuckle and ushered Gil to sit next to him.

'Actually, Mr Gil, I am blessed by Allah, Peace Be Upon Him. I am still alive and can be with my wife and know my children. It is a blessing. On many occasions we were near death, Waheed and I, many times, too many to tell. You know we fought together against the Soviets?'

Gil had no idea the two men had been mujahideen during the war. Waheed always seemed a quiet unassuming man who seldom talked about his past.

'You understand we were not violent men. We did not like killing, but there was no choice, Insha'Allah; it was our duty, our destiny. And believe me, Mr Gil, we became good at it – for our country. We killed many Russians. Now the war is over it grieves me fighting between brother and brother continues. Blood feuds, of course, are constantly with us, a curse of our history. It is difficult for me to believe

113

Waheed is dead, killed like this without even a gun in his hand.'

What struck Gil was the man's apparent lack of rancour. No trace of bitterness or frustrated resignation about his condition – or Waheed's murder – was apparent in his face. The man had the most beautiful eyes, a piercing deep-set translucent green. Gil wondered what lay behind such eyes, eyes that would intuit if a person was lying. They seemed the eyes of a man at peace with himself and the world. Gil could only envy him.

'Come, Mr Gil, let us eat and then I will tell you about Waheed.'

Mirwais clapped his hands and immediately his son entered the room with a metal basin full of water, soap and a towel draped over his arm. First he lowered the basin for Gil to wash his hands before passing it to his father. A smaller boy around ten years of age then entered the room carrying a huge platter of lamb pilaf, the rice forming a dome topped with blood-red pomegranate seeds and garnished with chopped coriander leaves. Warm naan breads wrapped in a cotton cloth sat in a woven basket, so huge each could easily have soled a giant's shoe.

After eating in silence, a process that made Gil feel uneasy, Mirwais regaled him with stories of Waheed, how as young men they had become firm friends joining the same mujahideen group to fight the Soviets. Quick learners, both soon became commanders responsible for small groups sent to attack behind enemy lines. Working together, they relentlessly harried the Soviets denying them control of a strategic route through a valley to the north-east of Kabul.

After the Soviets departed, they returned to their homes laying down their weapons but keeping an AK-47 each for family protection.

Then, after more reminiscences of the war, Mirwais abruptly changed the subject. 'You know, Mr Gil, we Afghans are a lyrical people. We love music, singing, dancing. This is why the Taliban can never truly penetrate the Afghan heart. Waheed loved music, especially the voice of Ahmad Zahir, our most famous singer who died in 1979, the year before the Soviets invaded. He was only thirty-three years old. It is the only time I ever saw Waheed shed tears. He was distraught. He so loved the songs "Akhir Ay Darya" and "Hama Yaranam". After Zahir's death, tears would come whenever he heard them.'

Mirwais paused, his eyes drifting to some far-off place, before continuing.

'Soon after, he read that Zahir was known as the Afghan Elvis. "*Who is this Elvis?*" he would say. After listening to songs on the radio, "Suspicious Minds", "It's Now or Never" and "Don't Be Cruel", I remember them well, his life became transformed.

'He was obsessed and would talk about how Elvis and Zahir were brothers of the soul like Waheed and Mirwais. Somehow he managed to find copies of these songs and would listen to them whenever he could.'

Apposite songs for Afghanistan, Gil thought, as he sat mesmerised by this small gnome-like figure.

'One day about a year ago a strange thing happened. We were walking back from a restaurant in Shashdarak when Waheed spotted a small white object lying on the roadside.

115

He bent to pick it up, gave a loud cry, and shouted, "*Look, Mirwais, it is Elvis. I have found a good-luck charm!*"

'Indeed it was a small plastic doll of the singer wearing dark glasses and with a microphone stuck in one hand. It was unmistakeable. After that he hung the figure from the windscreen of whichever vehicle he was driving. "*For luck,*" he would say. Sadly, it did not bring him any in the end.'

Gil quickly realised this was the figure that was hanging from the vehicle's windscreen when he'd visited the murder scene. Was this why he'd chosen to sing 'Blue Suede Shoes' at the Hole-in-the-Wall? Had some subconscious recognition of a plastic doll led him to choose that particular song?

Mirwais continued to talk with that distant unfocused look in his eyes people have when talking about the dead they have loved.

'You know another thing happened. About eight years ago. We were returning from Logar when two young Talibs stopped us at a checkpost. There was an old pistol under the seat, otherwise we were unarmed. Next to the checkpost stood a tall pole with unspooled cassette tapes flying from it like some tattered brown flag. Tapes taken from passing vehicles. The Taliban have little tolerance for music or dancing.

'When they stopped us Waheed, who was driving, hurriedly took his Elvis tapes and stuck them in his kameez. When they spotted the cassette player – we could not hide it, of course – they became excited and one became aggressive. There was one cassette already in the player. Luckily it was Afghan music. Waheed quickly pressed the play button and when the music started the two Talibs placed their weapons on the ground, removed their turbans and began to dance. They spun round and round, ever faster as the music grew faster, their heads spinning, their long hair waving in circles in time with the music.

"*See*," Waheed whispered to me, "*they cannot help themselves. They come from a village of dancers. I know. It is in their blood. I recognised them by the way they fold their turbans. If they had found us with foreign tapes we would have been in serious trouble. Curse them, even if they are good dancers!*"

'We laughed together as we left the checkpost, our tape of Afghan music now dancing in the wind from the top of the flagpole, its empty plastic cassette lying smashed on the ground. The Elvis singer was soon blaring from our vehicle's speakers!'

As he finished his story Mirwais looked wistful.

'Mr Gil, if there is one thing I would want to remember Waheed by it is that Elvis doll.'

Gil understood. 'I'll see what I can do, Mirwais. They've removed the vehicle to a UN compound. I can check if it's still there.'

'Thank you, Mr Gil. You know they say we all die twice, once when the breath leaves our body and again when the last person we know who is still alive says our name for the last time. As long as I draw breath Waheed will never die. He would do nothing to disgrace his family. He was a good Muslim. He would not do anything wrong, but like most of us he had enemies. Kabul is a brooding city full of suspicion and enmity.'

A sad look creased Mirwais's face. He seemed to sink deeper into the *toshack*, making him appear even smaller. As

Gil witnessed this, his mobile vibrated. It was time to leave. Nine o'clock and Abdul Qabir would be waiting for him downstairs. He was always punctual.

As he carefully made his way down the stairs Gil couldn't help thinking Mirwais had no obvious source of income yet he and his family lived in a heated apartment with a TV and good quality carpets. He was proud both his boys attended a prestigious school. Where did the money come from? There was only one bank in Kabul and recently opened at that. Where did the Afghans store their money?

FOURTEEN

AT THE MINISTRY OF
WOMEN'S AFFAIRS, IN KABUL,
Sunday 30 October 2005

Despite misgivings, Mena invited Charlotte to visit her office to discuss the ministry's work. Their time together at the Hole-in-the-Wall was all too brief being sharply truncated by Gil's impromptu karaoke performance. Charlotte, although a fellow doctor and interesting woman, was a crisis junkie. At twenty-nine, she'd already worked in Rwanda, the Congo and east Timor but with only a short stay in each.

Since arriving in Kabul, Mena was surprised by how many young expats she'd met who'd worked in many of the World's disaster zones. Gil was particularly scathing about them moving from one country to another, never staying long in any one place. They would quickly be followed by entrepreneurs setting up temporary eateries and other recreational and welfare services. Many expats had arrived in Afghanistan since the fall of the Taliban to join the development caravan or engage in the commerce of war: the diplomats, aid workers, advisors and consultants, carpetbaggers, arms and gems dealers, soldiers of fortune, spies, and civilian contractors. And this without the military and its entourage.

Was it any different from Alexander the Great and his armies as they'd rampaged their way through Asia with batteries of camp followers: the cooks, carpenters, butchers, blacksmiths, farriers, entertainers, female attendants, wine merchants and hangers-on all engaged in the commerce of war?

It was mid-morning and Charlotte arrived at last, thirty minutes later than planned. Standing at the door of Mena's small office shared with Nasiba her admin assistant, she held out her hands to both women and declared in a clear if overly loud voice, 'Sorry I'm late, got stuck in traffic. Do please call me Charlie, I hate the Sunday name!'

'Come in, Charlie,' Mena quickly replied. 'It's nice to see you again. This is Nasiba.'

She was then taken aback as Charlotte launched herself into an embrace with Nasiba, holding on too tightly for too long. Certainly too long for Nasiba, who looked awkward as she re-arranged her dupatta and hurriedly left to arrange tea and biscuits, the surprise still evident on her face.

'So, what are you *doing* here?!' exclaimed Charlotte as she settled into one of the white plastic chairs clustered round the small meeting table. 'It would be wonderful if I could contribute to your work in some way, Mena. There's not much to do at the agency and Mario keeps resisting any suggestions I make.'

Mena was not so sure about Charlie contributing to their work, but she briefly recounted the history of the ministry and their current projects. How the fall of the Taliban in 2001 seemingly heralded in a new dawn for the country's women. Many girls returned to school, women to the workplace, the draconian Taliban restrictions on their lives lifted. Women's affairs took centre stage, especially for an international community who rightly made it their mission to ensure women would be a cornerstone of the country's future development.

But the initial energy and positive progress was already beginning to wane. At some point the expats would pull out and then what? Even now over eighty per cent of fifteen-year-old girls were illiterate, most women were without healthcare and husbands still held the legal right to beat their wives. Women who were raped were shunned by their families and sent to prison as the offender not the victim. Those who fled from violent fathers, husbands, in-laws and other kinfolk were guilty of so-called moral crimes and risked being sent to prison.

The Afghan women Mena had met since arriving in Kabul, while tough and resilient, were continually exhausted by their uncertain and insecure lives. Violence still stalked the streets as well as the home. Random rockets occasionally fell on Kabul. At the root what had changed?

'You know, Charlie, Shakeba the Deputy Minister keeps a small handgun in her desk drawer. She's been threatened several times and tells me, "*I am an exception, Mena. My* husband is supportive and we have some wealth, but I trust no one. You would be wise to do the same. Our cultural traditions bind the hands of women with chains."

'You'll see even here in Kabul most women, particularly the young and beautiful, still wear burqas. They're not willing to be visible in public risking kidnap and rape, or worse. This happens. Let me take you to meet Mohammad and his sister – remember I mentioned him at the Hole-in-the-Wall, the-man-with-no-mouth? They have come for help although there is little we can offer them. It will show you the type of problem we are dealing with.'

Leaving Mena's office, they walked along a featureless corridor, down a flight of steep stairs and into a small bare room where a middle-aged woman with a worn face sat on an old *toshack*, the hood of her burqa slung over her slender shoulders revealing a shock of black hair streaked with white. To her right sat a younger man rocking slowly back and forth, his head hanging low over his thin hunched body.

'This is Mohammad and his sister. Let me introduce you. I will translate.'

At the sound of his name, the man looked up into Charlotte's face. It was hard to retain her composure. She considered herself a strong woman, a young doctor who'd witnessed a share of life's brutalities, but she had never seen such a face. It was as if all the sadness in the world collected in this one face – a face that appeared to have no mouth. Where the mouth should have been was a barely visible thin pinkish line. The man had sucked his lips so far into his mouth it appeared he had no mouth at all. His whole face was a puckered frown centred down into the mouth area, his eyes marbled stone.

'Mena, what happened to this man, please tell me?'

'Well, we don't usually deal directly with men's problems in the ministry, but in this case we made an exception. His sister brought him here. There was nowhere else for her to turn. It is his family, his missing daughter. Because of this tragedy his mind is now incomplete.'

After introducing Charlotte to Mohammad and his sister Naseema and settling down with cups of green tea, Mena told Mohammad's story. It had been a Saturday and he was at work in the Ministry of Agriculture, where he was responsible for assessing applications for new farming projects in poppy cultivation areas. It was a responsible job, one he took seriously, plus it paid a good salary supplemented by the FAO.

He was sitting at his desk trying to concentrate on writing a report to support the development of saffron fields near Herat when the phone unexpectedly rang, its grating tone annoying him. Phone calls could be important, however, so he reluctantly decided to answer it. The words from the earpiece chilled him to the bone: '*Father! Father! Come quickly, they are killing us…*' Then the phone went dead.

He sat there immobile. It was impossible. He had not heard these words. Yet it had been the voice of Hamid, his twelve-year-old son. He was certain. What to do? Quickly he phoned his brother in the village. There was no answer. He must return home immediately.

Not bothering to switch off his computer or say anything to colleagues, he quickly ran out of the building and into his old Corolla. His village lay ten miles to the south-west of Kabul on the side of a low hill off the Ghazni road. Driving as fast as he could, he paid no heed to the honking horns of vehicles he passed, for his mind was blank and his heart emptying.

When he arrived at the house many people were gathered. His sister was sitting on the ground weeping and Raz Mohammad, the local policeman, an old school friend, was trying to keep people out of the house. Rushing inside he found his wife Gulmira, Hamid and his other son, seven-year-old Aman, lying on the floor, their blood pools already congealing. There was no sign of Sima, his fourteen-year-old daughter. It was a Saturday, none of the children had been at school and Sima was gone.

It transpired the killers were two brothers from another family in the village. Young men only in their mid-teens. After an earlier dispute over stolen livestock, Mohammad and his brother had reported the incident to the police and two men from the boys' family were arrested. Currently they were in jail awaiting trial for the theft. Other members of the family then came round to Mohammad's house threatening he should withdraw the case otherwise there would be more trouble.

Never in the wildest depths of his imagination did Mohammad conceive trouble would come in the form of killing his family and the kidnapping of his young daughter. Was this what trouble meant in the new Afghanistan?

After the funeral and several days of mourning, Mohammad's brother borrowed two Kalashnikovs and made ready to go to the family to exact revenge, but

124

Mohammad was able to dissuade him. Seeking revenge would only result in more hostilities and bloodshed, with further reprisals on both sides. They should leave it to the authorities to pursue the guilty men.

His brother was contemptuous at this and angry with Mohammad but eventually, after much arguing, gave in to his wishes, creating a rift between them that would be hard to heal. His brother then accused Mohammad of being frightened, of not being a man, not a true Afghan.

After this, Mohammad began to withdraw into himself more and more, his mouth becoming thinner and thinner as the days passed until other villagers began to refer to him as 'the-man-with-no-mouth'. His mouth seemed locked shut. Only Naseema was able to communicate with him, so he went to live with her in a neighbouring village. Luckily, she was able to persuade him to take some liquid sustenance, often having to gently force it into his mouth through a straw.

Three months later and there was still no sign of Sima or of the two young men with a reputation in the village for being inveterate charas smokers and alcohol drinkers. After the killings a man in the village reported seeing the men leave Mohammad's house staggering as if intoxicated, guns hanging by their sides, wisps of bluish-white smoke still unfurling from the barrels.

Mena concluded by saying Mohammad and his sister only wanted to find Sima. There was nothing else left; the police still hadn't found the killers and were less than interested in what happened to his daughter. With Mohammad in his present state, Naseema's only hope was to contact an old friend who had persuaded her to come to the Ministry.

'The problem,' Mena continued, 'is apart from supporting them there is little else we can do. We are not police; we have little power. There are many such cases as this. We don't want to speculate. The girl could already be dead, sold into prostitution or sent to the Gulf as a slave or for body parts. We do not want to say these things to them, but in their hearts they already know.'

While she could feel a tear slowly trickle down her cheek, Charlotte was seething inside. Only one word stuck in her mind: *a-l-c-o-h-o-l*. These young men would not have gone ahead with the killing if they hadn't been drinking, she was sure of that. It was an assumption born of bitter experience. She hated the stuff ever since her alcoholic father forced her to drink two large glasses of vodka when she was thirteen, at the same time mumbling over and over, '*You'll never end up like me, Charlotte… you'll never end up like me.*' She had been violently sick and never touched alcohol since.

If it had stopped there it might have been bearable. Then she began to notice the bruises on her mother's neck, barely visible above the high neckline dresses she often wore even in the summer heat. Eventually her parents divorced but her mother continued to have bouts of depression.

Then there was Douglas, her first real boyfriend, the popular student president who liked a drink and seemed fine with it until the night he had drunk too much, pinned her to the kitchen floor and raped her like a dog.

Oh yes, she knew about alcohol and its effects alright. While her rational mind understood alcohol was only a

126

trigger, an excuse for inexcusable behaviour, only pulled after the build-up of a range of aggravating factors, her heart and gut hated it with a passion beyond words. This hatred, she knew, was what started her own drug use, the occasional smoke of hashish at first, easy to find in the affluent Sydney suburbs. It helped allay her anxieties and sleep came easier.

As Shiraz an NGO worker told her: '*You westerners have your alcohol, we have our hashish – what is the difference?*' Hashish was so easy to find in Afghanistan. As Mike had said at Jenna's party when they'd all been smoking, '*It practically falls off the trees here!*'

Shiraz explained what the Prophet said about alcohol. During his lifetime there were only three intoxicants in popular use: alcohol, opium and hashish, and of these alcohol was considered the worst because it made a person lose control of their hands and mouth. She thought of her father, her ex-boyfriend and all the other men whose violence and verbal abuse were fuelled by alcohol.

Charlotte had even considered converting to Islam. Mena's story was bad enough but imagine what the country would be like if alcohol was legal! It would be even more like the anarchic Wild West than it already was and she certainly wouldn't be here. It would be Deadwood with Kalashnikovs. She shuddered at the thought and wiped another tear from her eye.

As a young graduate doctor she had moved on from hashish, quickly learning how to forge prescriptions to supply herself, and sometimes friends, with a wide range of mood-altering pharmaceutical drugs.

127

'Some more tea, Charlie?' Mena could see Mohammad's story was affecting the young woman. Tears formed in her eyes. Eyes that held the same distant haunted look Mena occasionally saw in Gil's eyes, if only for a fleeting moment.

'Oh yes… thank you, Mena. What a terrible thing to happen to anybody. It is unimaginable. Do you think there is any chance of finding his daughter?'

'It is doubtful. The longer she's gone the less likely she'll be found. We want to give them some hope.'

'Is there anything I can do to help?'

Mena looked thoughtful. 'Well, you told me at the restaurant you've trained in PTSD counselling so you could possibly work with them, although you'd need an interpreter.'

Charlotte became more animated, sitting so far forward on her chair she nearly fell off. 'That sounds excellent! I've worked with interpreters before and been involved with post-trauma counselling in east Timor.'

'So let's arrange a time, perhaps one day next week. You could begin then if you like.'

After taking one last look at Mohammad and Naseema, Charlotte said her goodbyes, threw her scarf over her shoulders with a dramatic gesture and walked out the door.

Mena couldn't help wondering if she'd made the right decision, whether Charlie was the right person to help Mohammad. Her sheer energy verging on the manic, the constant smile yet with a readiness to tears. Could this behaviour be drug-induced? Mena quickly dismissed the idea. Charlotte was a doctor, and in any case Afghanistan was full of depressant drugs not stimulants.

FIFTEEN

THE GOLDEN HOUR, IN KABUL,
Sunday 30 October 2005

Alex understood the importance of the Golden Hour. In the case of Waheed it had already passed. The first and crucial stage of any police investigation, the vital hour immediately following the discovery of a murder victim. The opportunity to preserve and collect forensic evidence from the crime scene before it becomes contaminated by increasing numbers of people, even if they are wearing protective clothing. Before strong winds, dust or the rain changes everything. Not that the Kabul police had access to protective clothing, and rain and strong winds were sparse in late October.

After dropping out of university and working as a logger in the camps up near the Arctic Circle, Alex had spent five years in the Royal Canadian Mounted Police. *'Your first real job,'* as his mother liked to remind him.

The words of the tough training sergeant at the college, a hard-bitten square headed ex-lumberjack from Quebec who'd come late to the Mounties, were still ingrained in his mind. '*Remember the crime scene assessment and your five essentials: location, victim, offender, scene forensics and post-mortem. Without these you're fucked.*'

Fucked indeed, Alex thought. They only knew the location and the victim; the rest were unknown and likely to remain so. The Afghan police had little recourse to even rudimentary forensic equipment or post-mortem facilities. The three magic bullets needed to solve any murder case were just not there in Afghanistan – DNA, ballistics and fingerprints – and Alex knew most cases not solved in forty-eight hours were never solved. Plus, there was no chance of any witnesses waiting around to talk to the police. They would as likely be arrested for the crime as the real perpetrators. Enforced false confessions were de rigueur.

Many households kept an AK-47 (what use was a handgun?) for self-protection. Searching for a murder weapon was useless; searching for those capable of such a crime impossible. There was no shortage of men in Afghanistan capable of killing. A history of serial invasions and internecine fighting enforced ample opportunities to practise the necessary skills.

The location was more interesting. Why kill someone in daylight hours in a relatively busy upmarket area of the city? It could more easily have been carried out under cover of darkness closer to Waheed's home near the old palace in the southern suburbs. More importantly, why do it at all?

The only clue they could hope to find that might help to unravel the mystery was the motive.

Alex sat in a room in the police station near his home close to Kolula Pushta Road in the Karte Parwan district of the city. A small claustrophobic room, its walls covered in a dull yellow substance that could hardly be dignified with the word paint. The battered plastic chair he squeezed his frame into faced Captain Ahmed Fayaz, currently attacking a cup of tea after stubbing out his cigarette against the side of a metal desk and throwing the butt into a basket full of wastepaper.

After another noisy slurp, the captain spoke in a booming voice. 'For us this case is not a priority, Mr de Wolfe. You realise this? We have few resources. In the last three years we have spent over eight hundred million dollars in training and have our own purpose-built police academy. It is not enough, not nearly enough. In June we lost our chief when the Qandahar mosque was bombed. An internet café was destroyed back in May less than a kilometre from here. The insurgent just walked through the door and blew himself up. Acts of such terrorism increase yet this is not our main concern. The people are more fearful of being kidnapped. It is a thriving business. They want protection for themselves, their families and property. Militias and private security companies have spread like poppies. Theft is common. The population in Kabul has more than doubled since the Taliban left. It will soon increase even more but, well… you know these things, you have lived here for some time.'

Alex did indeed know these things. He had spent the last three years living in Kabul and before that had spent considerable time in the country while managing to avoid the excesses of both the mujahideen and Taliban regimes. His formative teenage years had been spent in Kabul in the 1970s when he'd become fluent in both Pashto and Dari. His life in Canada now seemed a distant dream.

He loved this city and its people. There was nowhere else he would rather be. This was his home despite the undeniable risks. Most expats saw him as eccentric, or just plain mad, choosing to live in an unpredictable post-conflict zone – and there wasn't much post-conflict about it. He smiled. Expats were too busy promoting *qawm*, that 'us and them' environment insulating them from any community outside their own incestuous little expat bubble. How many made even one true Afghan friend or kept in touch with colleagues once they left the country?

Farooq was able to put it precisely. '*They live in glorious isolation, Alex. You are an exception. Even although our country has been ripped apart by years of conflict and war, we still have a sense of community, even as it breaks around us. You have become part of this, while others come and go so quickly. There is no time for understanding in the west.*'

Captain Fayaz shifted in his chair, slid his feet off the desk and lit another Marlboro. 'I lived in Germany and in the UK for a short time. I helped my brother run a pizza shop in Streatham. All people seemed to talk about was the lives of celebrities and movies they had seen on TV. It was strange for me. They talked about events that never happened, people they'd never met. They knew more about these celebrities than the people who lived next door. This disturbed me so I returned home.'

Alex humoured the captain while sympathising with him, and doubted whether he could be of any real help. He'd only agreed to speak to the police to help Gil and didn't want to call in favours from his few trusted government contacts.

Any police station would have done; it would enable him to find out where the authorities stood in a case like this. The UN security team had not been much help. They were too restricted, too office-bound. It was the Gurkhas who did the front work yet they had little jurisdiction on the street.

If it was an international staff member it would have been different: global headlines would have screamed and a conglomerate of agencies rapidly mobilised. Top government officials would be involved. Waheed was only a local driver, replaceable within a few days. His family would receive a one-off payment, around one thousand dollars, and that would be it – forgotten, done and dusted. One life ended. Account closed.

Alex was concerned about Gil. He didn't need another mystery in his life, yet helping Asidullah might help take his mind off Stella's disappearance. It had been nearly three years and he was still obsessed with finding her, convinced she was still alive. For Gil her shadow was always with him. Going back to Scotland and spending more time with his children seemed sensible, but it was no option as far as Gil was concerned.

'*Who would employ me back in the UK?*' he'd laughed. '*It's like a foreign country after so many years away. Right now it's best for Mhairi and Jamie. They're with my brother and his family in the Highlands so at least they're safe. And I see them every few months on break.'*

Safe was such a crucial consideration for Gil after Stella's disappearance, especially for his children if not for himself. Being absorbed in helping Waheed's family meant his own family problems had slipped to the back of his mind, albeit temporarily.

'You need to talk to Aziz,' Captain Fayaz continued. 'He has many ears on the street. I have my sources, but I am only returned since the Taliban left Kabul. He has always been here. This city is full of gossip, rumours, plots and counter-plots, false tales used to settle old scores and acquire new wealth. Only Aziz knows how to extract the truth from a nest of vipers. It is his skill. We are not steeped in our history, Mr de Wolfe, we live it daily. We are handcuffed by it!'

Captain Fayaz laughed as he gazed at the rows of old iron handcuffs and other restraints lining his office wall. 'Our history has no time for contemplation. Do not be fooled by the satellite phones, big cars and guns; underneath we have not changed for centuries. We are still a tribal people.'

With that, Captain Fayaz shouted in a loudhailer voice, 'Abdullah, get Aziz in here – *now!*'

Within seconds a well-built man emerged from the next room. He had the appearance of an old boxer down on his luck. With a stooped gait, the man's flattened nose, pugged ears and crenelated face gave testament to a fist-fighter, a man not limited to the trigger or the knife.

134

A long scar, creeping from beneath a crevassed right cheek, was from a keen blade, not shrapnel or other scrapings of war. His dark ill-fitting suit was made even darker by a faint ripple of grease stains down the jacket front. The trousers rode some inches above black boots and there was no necktie under the off-white shirt collar. This was not some Iranian whose theocratic rulers denounced the accessory as a decadent symbol of European oppression. Aziz knew the only true purpose of a necktie is to strangle its owner.

'Mr de Wolfe, this is Sergeant Aziz, the only incorruptible policeman in Kabul still alive! I will leave you in his good hands.'

Captain Fayaz produced a short chuckle, placed his right hand over his heart, gave a short bow and returned to the mound of paperwork on his desk that had not yet reached the confines of the waste basket.

'Come, Mr de Wolfe, let us go outside and talk.' With that the sergeant led Alex out of the building and into a well-tended flower garden hidden from the street by high compound walls. Lighting a cheaper brand of cigarette than his boss, Sergeant Aziz seated himself on a low wall bordering a bed of red and yellow roses, inhaled their fragrance deeply, and beckoned Alex to join him.

'I know you, Mr de Wolfe, but you do not know me.' With this opening the policeman proceeded to tell Alex where he lived and how he earned a living. Then he added, 'I also know about your friend, Mr Banjo. Do not worry, your secret will be kept with me. This garden has no ears. I am not concerned about a few small antiquities and a deserter from the American army.'

Alex was a quiet man, but one not lost for words when the need arose. This wasn't the time. Now he was shocked into silence as his mind raced trying to make sense of what he'd just heard. It was only when Sergeant Aziz produced a blurred photo of Larry Banjo that he truly assimilated the policeman's words.

While he had carefully managed to negotiate several dangerous episodes in his life, Alex suddenly felt exposed in a way he seldom had before, and in Afghanistan too.

His research work as an ethnobotanist paid little money, so buying and selling a few antiques on the side could be easily rationalised. Afghanistan, as well as the Gandhara valley all the way to Taxila in Pakistan, held limitless treasures in their soils. The area had been a crucial stage on the Silk Road, the network of trade routes stretching from China across Central Asia to the Mediterranean. Chinese, Persians, Greeks, Mesopotamians and countless other traders and invaders had trekked through these lands, the crossroads of the ancient world, their broken buildings and cultural artefacts embedded for centuries in an earthly tomb long before the Muslim Arabs arrived.

Alex never made more than a thousand dollars on any single piece and ensured he paid the seller a fair price. Farmers tilling fields, people building houses, treasure seekers, all unearthed so many antiquities they could not be housed in ten museums. There was a difference between what he was doing and the organised smuggling gangs digging out carved wall friezes and life-size Buddha statues from subterranean temples and stupas. Even the Chicken Street shops were awash with antiques, some original, some newly minted. An acquaintance in UNESCO reckoned the fakes were more expensive than the originals because they looked in better condition.

But Larry Banjo! How could Sergeant Aziz know about him? God, he even had his photo, and it looked like it was taken since Larry arrived in Kabul. Trading in small antiques was one thing; giving sanctuary to a US Army deserter on the run after killing two civilian security contractors near Qandahar was quite another. Alex had taken a huge risk when Larry arrived at his house, but he couldn't turn him in to the authorities. Debts had to be repaid, honour had to be respected.

And Larry Banjo was a victim of conscience. Observing two of his fellow countrymen enter the mud-built house in the small village near Qandahar and smacking the woman in the face then ripping the dupatta from her young daughter left him in no doubt. This was the beginning of a rape. Without thought, he simply drew his handgun and shot each man in the back of the head. Crack! Crack! The men slumped to the floor, the fat one wearing an LA Dodgers baseball cap with his trouser zip already open. Fortunately, members of Larry's platoon were fighting insurgents in another part of the village and never heard the shots. It was time for him to disappear.

'As I say, do not worry, Mr de Wolfe. Your secret is safe with me. Who knows, I may need your help one day.'

Alex kept his reply brief. 'Thank you, Sergeant Aziz, I appreciate this. Do you know anything at all that could help us find Waheed's killer?'

137

'I know Waheed was seen at the old Russian Cultural Centre a few days before he was killed. Go there and ask for Naim. Be careful, it is full of drug dealers and criminals. Foreigners are not welcome but at least you speak the language.'

'Who is Naim?'

'He was a fighter with Waheed against the Soviets. Now he is a *poderi*, he lives only for the white powder.'

'Can he tell us anything, d'you think?'

'I do not know, Mr Alex. Waheed certainly gave him money on more than one occasion. I can interrogate him if you wish, but remember we have no... how you westerners say... advanced investigative technology, so we must rely on interrogation. Police here have no training on interrogation skills, so we use what you call third-degree methods. Then we hear the Americans torture our people in their Bagram prison, so we are the same, yes?'

Leaving the question hanging, Sergeant Aziz took another long drag on his cigarette, plucked a rose head from its stem, crushed it in a huge hand and scattered the petals at his feet.

'Thank you, but I would like to talk to this man myself if it is fine with you?'

'It makes no difference to me. As you like, Mr de Wolfe. Here is my cellphone number, call me if you change your mind. Remember, I know your ABC.' Alex didn't doubt it. At least here was one policeman in Kabul who knew his alphabet, the investigating officer's mantra: Assume Nothing, Believe No One, Check Everything.

Shaking hands with Aziz, Alex quickly walked past the

two guards manning the barrier at the fortified gates of the compound, took his mobile from his jacket pocket and called Gil. They would have to pay a visit to the old Russian Centre. Better that Gil didn't go alone.

SIXTEEN

AT THE RUSSIAN
CULTURAL CENTRE, IN KABUL,
Monday 31 October 2005

I t was late morning as they climbed into Alex's Pajero
and headed towards the south-west of the city and the
remains of the Russian Cultural Centre. The area had
been one of the worst-hit during the fighting between
warring mujahideen factions in the early 1990s. Parts of it
still looked like Dresden in 1945, devastated, while other
areas of the city remained virtually untouched, although
this was seldom captured by western TV cameras trying
to substantiate a war story.

Far from the vast expanses of Kabul's north, the
centre lay on the south side of the double-peaked
Telegraph Hill that bifurcated the city, where small
houses clung precariously to the steep slopes on either
side of the valley road. There were no power cables and
water had to be carried up by hand, small recompense

for the impeccable views.

Once past the city zoo the traffic thinned and the Pajero turned left onto the wide boulevard of Darul Aman leading to the bombed-out Royal Palace and the sweep of the mountains beyond. Parking the car on a piece of wasteland, they cautiously approached the centre.

'What do you want here?' The man stood at the top of the wrecked stairwell, the spot they'd reached after jumping over a narrow chasm dropping some fifteen feet to the ground below. They looked down on piles of rubble strewn with used syringes and wads of stained cotton. Shards of old orange peel laced the grey concrete providing unexpected flecks of colour.

They had entered the once-grand Cultural Centre up its wide set of central stairs flanked by pockmarked concrete pillars holding up a semi-circular overhang. As if entering some subterranean cave, the dark interior beckoned and repulsed at the same time. Large windows with little glass refused to let in much light even in the late-morning sunshine.

Once inside, a warren of interconnecting rooms and corridors presented themselves, some without a roof, others with only the remains of window frames. Doors had long departed. Just enough light filtered through to view the scarred remains of a skeletal if not uninhabited building.

The man seemed hesitant but repeated his words several times. 'What do you want here? You are not welcome, *kharaji*.' Dressed in a pair of old Adidas trainers, faded jeans, a ragged blue windcheater and a black and white checked cotton scarf wrapped round his head, the

141

man stood barring their way up the remains of the stairs.

Gil let Alex do the talking, only picking up on the few phrases of Dari he understood. After a few minutes the man stood aside to let them pass. The bulge outlined under Alex's kameez was the deciding factor. Gil had noticed the hidden gun as they entered the building but said nothing.

As they continued up the stairs and along an open landing leading to a cluster of rooms, the foul odour of the place grew stronger. The first room was assigned as a toilet. The stench from pools of olive-brown urine and drying piles of liquid faeces lying on the bare floor wafted along on the few strands of lingering breeze.

They hurriedly moved on, checking several rooms where groups of men sat huddled in circles eagerly awaiting their turn for a loaded syringe to be passed to them. Others with desperate vacant faces milled around looking for drugs. Even in Kabul Gil had never seen such medieval squalor.

When they reached the end of the corridor, they spotted Naim amongst a group of men crouching in the corner of a large filthy room where dust motes danced in the few shafts of light coming through gaps in a boarded-up window. The man squatting next to him had recently taken a hit, the needle still stuck in his vein, the syringe leaking droplets of blood onto his forearm, its work already done.

One of his comrades stuck a cigarette in his mouth the wrong way round and tried to light the filtered end. Catching Gil's eye, the man shrugged his shoulders and grinned sheepishly, the glassy-eyed expression of the globally intoxicated.

'Naim, we are here to ask you about Waheed.' It was

easy for Alex to pick out Naim. His white plastic crutches lay behind him as he sat with his one leg stretched out in front. While his eyes appeared unfocused, there was alertness in them despite the effects of the heroin.

'Come to my room.' The invitation was abrupt and made in a clear voice as Naim raised himself on his crutches and with amazing agility hobbled off down the corridor. Following him, they soon came to a crumpled plastic sheet that hid what had once been a walk-in cupboard. Parting the curtain, Naim invited them into the fetid space he shared with another man who lay comatose on a filthy mattress.

Two small plastic bags of personal possessions hung from hooks on a corner wall. A candle stuck in a bottle standing on a small cardboard box provided the only light in the windowless space. The two UN anti-drug posters pinned to the wall added some colour to the drabness. This was the men's home.

'What are you doing here, gentlemen?' The voice was clear and held a calm, if authoritative, tone. As they turned round, Alex already had his hand inside his kameez.

Before they could respond, Naim answered the question for them: 'Mr Malik, these *kharaji* want to know about Waheed.'

The man was tall, of indeterminate age and carried a battered brown leather satchel over his shoulder. 'Why do you want to know about Waheed?' he said, introducing himself as a social worker from a drug rehabilitation centre in Karte Parwan. 'I have been working here for nearly a year now and only met Waheed once or twice. He would come to talk with some of the *poderis*, especially Naim here.'

143

After introducing themselves, Alex explained the purpose of their visit. On hearing Waheed had been killed, Naim dropped his crutches and fell to the floor, tears streaming down his cheeks. He uttered the most melancholic wail Gil had ever heard, followed by 'Waheed, a good man. Waheed, my friend.'

'You see, gentlemen,' Malik said in a matter-of-fact voice, 'most of these men are war-damaged. Many have severe mental health problems. They have no family, no home, no job, so they turn to the white *poder*. It gives them nothing. It makes them feel nothing. Please allow me to tell the other men of Waheed's death. It would be better.'

'Of course,' Alex replied. 'We understand. We are sorry we had to break the news to Naim.'

'It is fine, Mr Alex, there is no easy way to tell it. These men have so many tragedies in their life, one more will soon settle under the effect of the *poder*. I understand Waheed gave Naim and a few other men money and tried to persuade them to come for treatment. Most are not ready. You can see, can't you? We have a long waiting list for the centre. Insha'Allah we will open another one soon.'

'Where do these men go at night? It must be dangerous for them here,' Gil enquired, shocked by scenes of such degradation.

Malik gave a gentle laugh. 'Everywhere is dangerous for them in Kabul. Many die in the winter from hypothermia or starvation. Others live in holes in the riverbank. Some have their own hiding places in derelict buildings like this one. A few go home if they have one left. Nobody likes *poderis*; they are forgotten men. Those who have families

144

are usually shunned by them; they will steal anything to get drugs. They make their families poor – money for food and clothes for their children are used to buy drugs. The police even found two of them stealing shoes from outside a mosque during Jumma prayers! They beat them up, but at least were able to prevent the mullah and his followers from lynching them.'

'Do you think Naim or anyone else can give us information about Waheed and why he was killed?' Alex interrupted.

'You see the state of the man, Mr Alex, it is doubtful he can help you.'

'Perhaps we could ask him later?'

'As you like.'

Alex turned to Gil to seek agreement just as Gil's mobile rang.

'Sorry, I have to answer it.' He smiled apologetically. The other two men shrugged. Even in Kabul a ringtone was sacrosanct.

'Yes, okay, I see. I'll be there.' Gil spoke into the phone as he looked at Alex, a frown growing on his face.

'Sorry, Alex, we'll have to leave now, there is a problem at the house.'

'Okay, let's go,' Alex replied, already walking to the crumbling door arch thinking, *Bad news never has good timing*.

SEVENTEEN

BACK AT THE HOUSE, IN KABUL,
Monday 31 October 2005

On returning to the house, Gil noticed a new vehicle parked in the yard with government number plates and an armed soldier standing next to it. Then Sarah rushing out of the side entrance from the kitchen, tears welling in her eyes.

'Oh Gil, these men have arrested Brock! He's been taken to the ministry for questioning.'

'Hold on, Sarah. What's happened?' Before she could answer, a grim-faced Mike Gomez came running down the steps.

'You better come in, Gil, we're meeting in the lounge. Where the hell have you been anyway?'

Gil pointedly ignored the question and walked quickly up the steps through the kitchen and into the lounge where the residents sat stony-faced. A senior officer from one of the ministries stood on guard at the door. Gil took the only seat available, the edge of the sofa next to the still-tearful Sarah, while Mike Gomez addressed them.

'This is Colonel Mahmoud. At eleven o'clock this morning his men stopped one of our vehicles at a roadblock near the Massoud circle. Inside under a blanket were eight cases of alcohol, mostly wine. There was also several bottles of high-end whisky and vodka. These are definitely not part of JTD official supplies, so it's alleged they were intended for sale onto the local market. At this point it's difficult to refute this. It's a most serious situation.'

'What about Brock?!' Sarah exclaimed, more tears gathering in her eyes.

'He's been taken to the ministry for questioning along with Abdul Qabir.' Mike Gomez's response was peremptory. 'At this point we don't know if anybody else in the house is involved. The colonel wants to search all the rooms. Gil, I'd like you to accompany us. You're the only resident not working directly for JTD.'

'Heh, hold on a minute,' Big William interjected, 'what about our privacy? They can't just search our rooms.'

Mike Gomez looked at Big William as if he was someone who hadn't already worked in Kabul for two years.

'Of course they can, William, they can do what they fucking like. This is not an embassy compound we're in, don't be so bloody stupid.'

Looking peeved, Big William folded his arms tightly against his chest. Along with the other house residents he watched anxiously as the colonel, Mike Gomez and Gil made their way out of the lounge and headed for the stairs.

147

The house had eleven bedrooms, each with an en-suite bathroom, as would any recently built modern-styled house in Afghanistan. Three of the rooms were situated in the basement radiating out from a large communal space where a table tennis table stood, its net sagging.

One room had been modified as the house safe room where residents could hide if under attack. It kept a supply of water and non-perishable food, a large first aid kit, some reading material and a steel door that would withstand small arms fire as well as a rocket-propelled grenade – or so it was claimed. The heavy uncomfortable flak jackets recently issued to all house residents were to be kept in bedrooms until needed.

The first room they visited was Brock's. It was situated directly to the left at the bottom of the stairwell. While Gil didn't feel overly comfortable going into his colleagues' rooms, he was intrigued. If a person's home reflected their true character what about a temporary home located in a room in a guesthouse in Kabul? To what extent was the expat personality free from the veneer of the home version?

Brock's room wouldn't have been out of place in an army barracks. The place was spotless, ultra-tidy and the bed made with consummate precision. There was no sign of anything untoward and certainly no hint of alcohol present. The only article of discord was the colourful birthday card lying haphazardly on an otherwise empty dresser top. The caption on the card read '*Zen Dog*' in large italic script. Under the caption was a drawing of a happy-looking cartoon dog with sunglasses lying in a small purple boat drifting on a sun-beaten blue sea. Underneath an inscription read:

He knows not where he's going
For the ocean will decide –
It's not the destination…
It's the glory of the ride.

As the other two left the room, the colonel seemingly impressed by its sense of order and only too keen to look for potential bootleggers among the other residents, Gil couldn't help peeking inside the card to see the inscription. It read 'To the most zen guy we know, love Chas and Laura' followed by four kisses encased in what looked like a hurriedly drawn red heart.

He'll need all the zen he can muster when he's being questioned at the ministry, mused Gil, quickly following the others up the stairs.

On the landing at the top of the stairs the colonel and Mike Gomez were already squeezing their way past the house photocopier and into Mickey's room. It was the complete opposite of Brock's, an unkempt space characterised by a row of half-empty liquor bottles sitting on the window ledge, a battered old amp and two electric guitars leaning side by side against a wall. One was a replica sunburst Fender Telecaster, a testament to local ingenuity and enterprise.

The guitar had been made and purchased in a street close to the old Kharabat Quarter of the city near the Bala Hissar, an area traditionally populated by musicians who fled to Peshawar during the Taliban era. In earlier times it had been famous as a red-light district hosting mainly Indian musicians and dancers.

The other more battered guitar once belonged to Mickey's grandfather Charly, who'd played in several rock bands in Dublin of the 1950s. It was an old Gibson and looked valuable.

As they left the room, Gil couldn't help notice the bookshelf contained only two books, both well-thumbed and by the same author, Peter Guralnick. Together they comprised a comprehensive biography of the singer they called *King Creole* after the movie of the same name. They were titled *Last Train to Memphis: The Rise of Elvis Presley* and *Careless Love: The Unmaking of Elvis Presley.*

Perhaps I should read these, Gil thought. The singer seemed to be omnipresent in his life, leaving him with an uncomfortable feeling hard to pin down. Mirwais's story about Waheed and the Elvis figure still played in his mind for some reason.

The next room along the worn red-carpeted landing was Sarah's. It was, as expected, reasonably neat and tidy with various articles of clothing lying on the bed with a vivid red lacy bra draped over the armchair. Her bathroom contained more bottles of lotions and potions than any small drugstore would hold. The only disconcerting item was tucked in the back of a bedside drawer Gil opened out of curiosity, a ridged pink vibrator. He hurriedly closed the drawer in case the colonel came over to inspect its contents.

Other rooms held few surprises, although they had to wade through piles of reports and other documents scattered on the floor of Big William's room. It was fortunate the colonel was searching for cases of alcohol rather than paying attention to smaller items such as the several soft porn DVDs lying haphazardly on a shelf. Luckily all that was visible were the spines rather than the colourful covers portraying large ladies, their pendulous breasts jiggling up and down while dancing around a room where a small man lay on a red silk-covered bed, eyes popping out of his head. Innocent souvenirs from the ersatz Marks and Spencer's bazaar in Peshawar, Big William would no doubt have claimed.

The room next door belonged to Rufus. A paperback book lay half open on his bed, *The Light Garden of the Angel King: Travels in Afghanistan* by Peter Levi. Gil was familiar with the book and its account of Levi and Bruce Chatwins' travels in Afghanistan in 1970, a more peaceful era prior to the Soviet invasion.

Similar to Brock's, the room was almost institutional, reminiscent of a well-ordered public-school bedroom. Sitting at the side of the bed was an open suitcase packed with clothes and personal items as if the resident was ready to flee at a moment's notice. Although all residents were meant to have a small bag packed in case of a rapid evacuation, this seemed overkill. Nobody had heard that Rufus was leaving any time soon, but maybe he had other plans.

Certainly all the rooms were idiosyncratic, reflecting their occupants' various penchants and peccadilloes. While Cheryl's room was uncluttered and orderly as expected, three large glass jars containing loose-leaf tea sat on the dressing table next to her perfumes. She frequently lectured the other house residents about using tea bags. '*Powdered tea, probably swept off a packing house floor, shovelled into small flimsy paper bags tied with string and label attached. Then encase the bag in an individual paper wrapper before the whole lot is stuffed into a box extolling the virtues and easiness of tea bags. Who would ever think of drinking such dreadful stuff?*'

Cheryl had tried to encourage the house residents to become tea drinkers. To her chagrin, nobody was really interested; most were addicted to coffee. She wanted them to take 'proper tea' brewed in a large china teapot brought from England, but to no avail. They were either too busy gulping down coffee or getting wired into more alcoholic beverages in the evening in preference to a pot of best Assam tea.

Gil recognised his own room also held its share of personal eccentricities. The bowl of crumbs seated on the windowsill ready for the morning sparrows. An old carved wooden face mask from Liberia that looked like it was still infested with tropical woodworm hung on one wall. A small framed photograph on the shelf above his bed showing them all on holiday in Florida looking tanned and relaxed, belying the tragedy that would rip their family life apart.

The last room on the upper landing – apart from Hans', who was on mission to Herat, and Shaheen's, who was on her breather break – was set aside as the house gym. A few sets of rubber dumbbells, a rickety rowing machine, a brand-new cross trainer and the rank odour of stale sweat were all it contained. The colonel made a swift perusal, swiftly closed the door and ushered them back down the stairs to where the others sat, quiet and stony-faced.

After talking briefly with Mike Gomez, the colonel gave a curt salute then made his way out of the house and into the yard where his driver was waiting. After he was gone, Mike turned to the gathered housemates and spoke between gritted teeth.

'The colonel is more or less satisfied only Brock was involved. He's currently being questioned at the ministry, however the hell that'll turn out. The colonel thinks no further action will be taken against JDL, but this is by no means certain. We'll have to wait and see. It goes without saying you should not under any circumstance discuss this with anyone outside the house. London has been informed. No doubt they will want to send one of the directors out. That's all we bloody need. Anyway, I'll stay for dinner now I'm here. Let's have a drink first.'

It was Big William who was first to pour himself an excessively large whisky and he was soon followed by the other residents. None of them wanted tea or coffee.

An hour later a sombre and somewhat inebriated group of housemates sat around the dinner table. Despite a few initial pleasantries, there was only one topic of conversation. While they all expected Mike Gomez to start, it was inevitably Mickey that fired off first, his loquaciousness unrestrained.

'It's hardly surprising, so it is. The drug is pure anathema to the Afghans and we're flyin' it in by the bucketful. It was fucken obvious this would happen. Kabul's awash with booze. Can you imagine the opposite? Afghan advisers and consultants living in Washington bringing in planeloads of hash for themselves then selling it in big fucken warehouses the locals can't access! Then bootlegging it out to them? Yet we do the same here. Never give it a second thought. Part of the old imperial mindset, eh? Think about it. This is the most conservative Islamic country after Saudi, and we're bringing in their most reviled intoxicant. Jeezus, when the Brits first invaded Afghanistan in 1839 it took three hundred camels just to carry the officers' wine cellar. What's new, eh!'

Most of the residents were still too shell-shocked by the news about Brock and the possibility of JDL having to leave Afghanistan to stop Mickey. If only he had said it in a more diplomatic way and without the theatrical intonations of his broad Dublin brogue. But Gil knew he was right: why import so much alcohol into Afghanistan unless there was a big demand from the expat community?

'Ask any cop, the fighting, the slagging, the abuse that goes on under the influence. And them trying to get rid of the opium harvest down in Helmand!'

Mickey took a quick swig of wine, ensuring no one had a chance to interject before he continued. It was a seamless transition.

'If they hadn't given Auntie Aislin morphine when she was with the terminal cancer last year it would have been criminal. Then cousin Peadar died from it. Pulled him out of the Liffey a month ago, so they did. Just down from the Ha'Penny bridge, needle still stuck in his arm. Jeezus, the world is short of opium, countless millions dying in agony because they can't get hold of the stuff, and we ban it!

154

Doesn't make fucken sense. Why not buy it off the farmers? That would solve the problem, so it would.'

Cheryl looked at Mickey as if he was insane. 'What are you babbling about, you idiot? Opium might be made into morphine for medicine, but what about heroin and the damage it causes? You said your own cousin died from it... *schloop*. It has to be eradicated.'

'I think Mickey has a point,' Gil interjected, 'but buying it off the farmers wouldn't work. They'd all start growing it and other countries would follow, the well-known balloon effect. We'd be swamped and there'd be more leaking onto local markets. It's bad enough now. You should see the heroin addicts living like sewer rats in holes in the riverbank near the Shah-Do-Shamshira mosque—'

'Never mind all that, we could be in the shit here,' Mike Gomez interrupted Gil. 'The alcohol was found in a company vehicle and Brock must have known about it. Christ, it's an incident like this that could get JDL thrown out of Afghanistan. We're going to have to pay four thousand dollars to get the stupid bastard released from custody. Thank Christ he's being flown back to the US.'

'Good riddance,' Mickey muttered under his breath but loud enough to merit a swingeing glance from Sarah.

'Do any of you know anything at all about what Brock was up to?' questioned Mike Gomez.

'Didn't have a clue.' Big William's reply was accompanied by nods of agreement from the other house residents except Mickey.

'Youse are all blind,' he retorted. 'You need to get out around town a bit more. I've been in two restaurants in the last month where they were loading cases of booze onto the back of the old Land Cruiser Abdul Qabir drives. After dark, like. The managers buy it in the Blue PX. Unlimited amounts available if you run a restaurant.'

'Why would he do it? Surely he didn't need the money?' Sarah spluttered as she dabbed at her eyes with an already wet silk handkerchief, dejected that Brock never confided in her regarding his extra-curricular activity.

'Ah, he'd be doing it for the craic, like. Some people get bored living in Kabul. They never leave their safe little guesthouse-office-bubble.' Mickey pontificated on in his usual manner.

As the other housemates debated Brock's motivation for bootlegging, Gil sat quietly, happy that the American's baleful presence had exited his life. He had no idea he was about to meet another American who, in the most unexpected manner, would help him unlock the mystery surrounding Waheed's murder.

EIGHTEEN

A MAN CALLED BANJO, IN KABUL,
Tuesday 1 November 2005

When Larry Banjo was a young boy he attended an evangelical church where the older members handled snakes and the congregation talked in tongues. Such glossolalia was not usually understood by the speaker, but Larry understood every sound he uttered as his eyes rolled back in his head, his body vibrating as if guided by some invisible force. While this was his first introduction to the spirit world, it wasn't to be his last.

His maternal grandmother Euphemia had been fifteen in April 1954. Elvis was nineteen, not yet a star, just paying his dues touring the smaller venues south of Memphis when she had gone to see him at the Louisiana Hayride in Shreveport. He was still singing hillbilly in R&B time and dressed in the brightly coloured clothes that did not sit well with southern sensibilities.

'*Outrageous*,' declared Euphemia's mother after she

read the account of the concert in the local paper. '*He should be put down. He'll burn in hell for behaving like that!*'

Accompanied by her best friend Peggy Sue and her elder sister Maybelle, Euphemia took a bus the twenty miles from their home into Shreveport and eagerly trooped along to the concert venue with hundreds of other teenage fans.

It was wonderful abandoned mayhem, an even more ecstatic experience than going to Pastor Eli's church on a Sunday evening. They screamed their heads off at the technicoloured presence gyrating up there on stage dressed in green velvet jacket, tight black pants and pink shirt with bootlace tie, hips swinging as if they didn't belong to his body.

Then a romp of girls managed to climb on stage. They rushed at the singer who smiled and good-naturedly held up his hands as if in surrender. Before the security men could stop them, they mobbed him, tearing at his clothes, pulling his hair and wailing like banshees. Without a second thought Euphemia and the other girls crammed into the first few rows followed suit and swept up onto the stage like a tidal wave.

Afterwards she had little recollection of what happened next. She joined in with the mob and vaguely remembered trying to grab at Elvis while fending off the pushes and pulls of other girls.

Eventually she found herself, a bit battered and with a few bruises, sitting on one of the remaining chairs in the auditorium still upright. There was no sign of Peggy Sue or her sister. Most of the crowd had already left. Only a few young girls remained stretched out on chairs, some still sobbing. She was aware her right hand was tightly clenched, the knuckles white. When she slowly opened it there was a bright green velvet-covered button lying in the centre of the palm. She could have sworn it glowed in the dim lights of the auditorium.

It was this button that Larry now gazed at as it nestled in the layer of red silk that lined the small leather pillbox resting on his lap. Given to him by his grandmother as she lay on her death bed, he knew if he removed the button and held it in his hand what would happen, so resisted this.

At the same time he owed Mr de Wolfe a favour, if not his life. For an AWOL US soldier in Afghanistan wanted for killing two of his fellow countrymen there were few hiding places. However, he felt safe in this house, at least for the moment. It was a calm space with a jungle of green plants adorning the rooms, a few chickens scratching in the backyard and a duck lolling in a tub of dirty water under an almond tree in the garden.

It wasn't some common form of synaesthesia Larry inherited from his grandmother. It wasn't grapheme synaesthesia where letters or numbers are viewed as inherently coloured. It wasn't mirror-touch synaesthesia where a person experiences the same sensation another feels when touched.

His grandmother explained it on the promise that he would never tell another soul. What he was experiencing was neither a medical condition nor a neurological aberration. It was simply a gift from God and it was his duty to take responsibility to use this gift for the benefit of others. Sometimes he felt it was more a curse than a gift.

He had smelled the evil emanating from the two civilian contractors as they began the rape. It was tangible. Even now the remnants of the pungent odour lingered at the back of his throat. He knew it was no excuse for killing them, but the outcome arising when his gift manifested was not always predictable.

When he was fifteen, he sensed a child was drowning in the creek behind their house and ran down to the water. Diving in he found no sign of life. Then, under a patch of reed, his fingers touched flesh, the boy's bare arm, which he grabbed before kicking them both up to the surface. Luckily his cousin Jack followed him and was able to haul them both out of the water. Larry had never learned to swim. His was a deep fear of moving water.

The power he felt in Alex's house was different. It was calmer and more predictable. It gave him a sense of peace, clear as the blue sky edging its way through the window on the far side of the room. The button was pulsing. It was about to make a connection. Within minutes he heard the door open and Alex walked into the room accompanied by a stranger.

To Gil the man seemed young but was older than he looked; there was something ancient about him. As he sat cross-legged on the cushioned floor, his darkly handsome features turned towards them. A fine-skinned enquiring face encompassed a small once-broken nose, broad mouth and eyebrows that met in the middle, shielding eyes so black they appeared to stare from the depths of the night.

While only a pinprick of light illuminated them, they appeared to be dancing in their sockets. The man looked like he was high on some type of drug. On the other hand, Alex had already forewarned Gil about Larry's paranormal powers.

'Larry, this is Gil, an old friend of mine.' With Alex's words the man seemed to levitate from the cushion and stood in front of Gil with his right hand outstretched. Gil, his arms still hanging loosely by his sides, sensed in that movement something verging on magic – or madness. A suspension of time for those few seconds it took the young man to raise himself from floor to vertical.

On the way to the house Alex had told Gil about Larry's backstory: the Southern evangelical upbringing; the killings outside Qandahar; the flight to Kabul hidden under a pile of melons in the back of an old truck; his arrival at Alex's house; and the reason why Alex gave him sanctuary, the fulfilling of an old debt, an obligation to a colleague who once saved his life in Central America.

They were military advisors at the time working for the same unit. The colleague was Larry's father, who hadn't seen his son since separating from his wife two years after the boy's birth.

As he took the offered hand, Gil could feel something pass from the young man's hand to his own, like an electric current. It wasn't unpleasant. It felt like a display of unavoidable power, the foreknowledge of the clairvoyant.

'Hi, Larry, I'm pleased to meet you. Alex has told me all about you.' The young man simply gazed at Gil through the dark lenses of his eyes, continued to hold his hand,

and intoned in a bright steady voice, 'It's in your left-hand jacket pocket.'

For Gil, this was confirmation the man wasn't quite with it before he realised that in the pocket was the plastic figure of Elvis he'd managed to retrieve from the UN vehicle yard before the Land Cruiser went for scrapping. He hadn't bothered with the arm in the ashtray, simply snapped the string attaching the one-armed figure to the mirror and pocketed it.

Now as he slowly withdrew the figure from his pocket he was aware Larry's tightly clutched hand was pulsing, the flesh squeezing in and out in a liquid rhythmic manner. With a quick fluid movement the hand flicked open revealing an old green cloth button. The Elvis figure immediately fell into Larry's hand, landing on the button. Gil could have sworn it jumped.

Before he could be stopped, Larry wrenched the figure's arm from its socket and pulled out a small piece of paper that was tightly rolled in the body.

'This is what you've been looking for,' he exclaimed, and handed the paper to Gil. Masking his shock, Gil carefully unrolled the paper, smoothing it out before reading the line of numbers written in neat tiny script: '783-845-69247'. Looking over Gil's shoulder, Alex simply said, 'Looks like the number of a bank account to me.'

'Yes,' came Gil's reply in a still voice, 'and I know where we can find who the account belongs to.'

NINETEEN

MACRORAYAN RE-VISITED, IN KABUL,
Wednesday 2 November 2005

I t was with some trepidation that Gil, accompanied by Alex, walked up the stairs to Mirwais's apartment. No invitation this time, only a hurried request from Gil they should meet as soon as possible, but with even less idea what to expect compared to his previous visit. Gil was not to be surprised. Instead of the elder son's welcoming face at the door they were met by a tight-lipped man pointing a Kalashnikov at them.

'Enter!' was the terse statement as the door slowly opened. The man's eyes held them in his gaze as he ushered them through to the room with the *toshacks*. The barrel of the gun traced their every footstep.

'Ah, Mr Gil. Welcome to my home once again. You are most welcome.' Seating themselves opposite Mirwais, Gil introduced him to Alex.

'It is fine. I know of Mr Alex. He has a reputation

here in Kabul. He is one of the few *kharaji* who lives among us in true peace. Unfortunately since your last visit life has changed, as it must. The only constant thing in my country is change.'

Mirwais gave a shrug and paused before speaking again. 'My family have moved back to the village and, as you see, I have protection. Life is becoming harder once more. What to do?'

The gunman stood at the door cradling his weapon, face expressionless.

'Mirwais, I've brought you the Elvis figure as you requested.'

'Thank you, Mr Gil, this is appreciated. It will remind me of Waheed and the songs he would softly hum as we waited in ambush for the Soviets.'

Gil watched as Mirwais took the figure and looked at it with an almost imperceptible narrowing of his eyes as he realised it had no arms and an empty body. Looking up with the same soft eyes that held Gil on his first visit, the message was simple but blunt: 'Ah, Mr Gil, you are an astute man. I think you have something belonging to me? It should now be returned. If you please…'

As he took the small roll of paper from his jacket pocket Gil could feel himself trembling. Before he could stop, he blurted out the words he'd tried hard to restrain. 'You lied to me, Mirwais! You wanted the figure for what it contained, not because it reminded you of Waheed.'

A silence fell over the room. Calling an Afghan a liar was a risky enterprise but Gil was too upset to stop himself. Alex let his hand drift to the handgun inside his jacket, a gesture observed by the gunman, who raised his weapon pointedly and shook his head.

A momentary shadow passed across Mirwais's face before he gathered himself and smiled at Gil. 'You are a lucky man, Mr Gil. I like you and you are my guest. Please let me explain and you may begin to understand. We know who ordered Waheed killed and we will find the man who pulled the trigger. They will be dealt with, rest assured.'

Signalling to the guard to bring tea and biscuits, Mirwais looked sad. 'Do not doubt my love for my brother Waheed, but what you have belongs to me and must be returned. There was never any bag to steal. The westerners that came to Waheed's house were, thankfully, misinformed. We know who these men are. They will also be dealt with. We will not have Waheed's family threatened by such people.'

Gil regretted his outburst. He could see in the pause before Mirwais continued that he was genuine, the sadness all too apparent in his eyes.

'Waheed told me you were the only *kharaji* we could trust, so we had his son request that you visit me. Apologies for the pretence. We are used to such ploys here. I did not mean to offend you. The paper you hold contains the code for a safety deposit box held in Dubai. You must collect this box for me, Mr Gil. None of us can travel safely there. But first you and Mr Alex will accompany me out of Kabul. You will understand. Rashid, call for the car.'

'What! Wait a minute, Mirwais… this is kidnapping. We cannot go with you! I cannot just go to Dubai like that, I have work to do here.'

Gil was incensed as he looked uneasily at Alex, who shook his head slowly from side to side, the message obvious.

Alex couldn't believe Gil had spoken in such a rash manner. However, he knew Mirwais was bound by *pashtunwali*, the Pashtun tribal code where protection of a guest is sacrosanct, or the outcome could have been very different. He also knew Mirwais's apology was a sign of strength, not weakness.

'Mr Gil, do not be alarmed. No harm will come to you and Mr Alex. You are my guests for the next few days.'

'I must phone my office, a friend—'

'No. No one must know where we are going. There are no cellphone connections there. We will inform your office, do not worry.'

TWENTY

UP FLOWER STREET, IN KABUL,
Wednesday 2 November 2005

Mena regretted not having gone to the UN club with Gil after the dogfight. Since lunch at the Serena, she had been bothered with stomach cramps resulting in frequent painful trips to the bathroom. How she managed the meal at the Chinese restaurant she'd no idea but didn't want to let Gil down by not turning up. He was very keen that she should meet Charlotte.

For the past few days taking electrolytes and resting at home had helped. Now she felt much better, if still weakened. She was relieved a quick stool test at the German Clinic showed no signs of giardia or amoebic dysentery.

Eating in the most expensive hotel in the city was no guarantee some filthy faecal-feeding fly was not going to descend on your food. A few seconds was all it took. In

Kabul everybody became ill sooner or later, mostly stomach upsets or eye and throat problems due to the contaminated dust.

For expats living in Kabul there was recourse to good medical treatment. As a last resort they could be medevaced out of the country. For local people treatment cost money. If you didn't have the cash, or could beg or borrow enough from family or friends, then there was no option but to tough it out. For the fragile elderly and malnourished young this frequently resulted in death. The country already had a massive child mortality rate: twenty per cent of kids didn't even make it to their fifth birthday.

During a dinner party at Gil's House, Hans from the WHO had been very graphic as he recounted a visit to a small village in the mountains bordering Kabul one thousand metres higher than the city's already impressive altitude of eighteen hundred metres. '*It was an amazing location with a stunning view over snow-clad mountains with Kabul visible in the post-dawn distance. It was late winter, biting cold and I was sitting with the village headman outside his small house that clung to the mountainside like a limpet. We were wrapped in blankets drinking tea and warming ourselves over a wood fire.*

'*Suddenly a small child, around four years old, ran past the fire and disappeared behind another house. She only wore a thin cotton nightdress that stopped at the knees; her feet were bare. Most startlingly her skin was blue with the cold, a distinct lurid blue not the pale bluish sheen I've experienced on my own skin while mountaineering in the Alps. I asked the headman, "Are you not concerned the child will die? It looks like she's hypothermic." He gave me this look of sad acceptance and said quietly, "If it's strong it will live, if it's weak it will die."*'

Mena hadn't forgotten this story of everyday life for Afghan families living in such harsh conditions. She recognised the courage behind such a statement, the simple acknowledgement that only the fittest survived in this most impoverished of countries. It should serve as a warning to the Americans and their allies who somehow imagined they could win a war here after legions of invading armies throughout the centuries had failed. The Afghans were a tough resilient people. Their history mandated them to be survivors, if at a tragic cost. It was as if some warrior gene had coded its way into their being many eons before, a spark lying dormant waiting to be ignited when the need arose.

She smiled to herself as she remembered her colleagues from the health centre, Dr Abdullah and Dr Muhtab, the most gentle and peaceful of men, recounting their visit to London only a few months previously. Arriving a week after the 7/7 bombings they were accosted by a drunk while walking back to their hotel. The man had shouted, '*Go home, you foreign bastards!*' then staggered towards them, fists raised in challenge.

'*What did you do?*' she'd queried.

'*We crossed the street to escape from him – then he followed us.*'

'*What happened?*'

'*We fought him of course!* They laughed. *We are Afghans! We do not know how to fight but we could not run away. He was a large man. Spittle was coming out of his mouth as he shouted. He punched Dr Abdullah but it glanced off his shoulder. I grabbed the man by the collar, turned him towards me and hit him on the chin. He fell down and banged his head on the pavement. Then he lay still.*'

'*That sounds serious.*'

'*Yes, it could have been, but we are doctors. We checked his pulse and his head. There was no wound, maybe only a mild concussion. Then we walked away – we did not want to cause any trouble.*'

When she recounted this story to Gil, he'd replied that it was a salutary lesson. Afghans were a people who had been brutalised by neighbouring clans, tribes and countries for centuries and had no recourse but to fight back or flee.

He told her it was similar to the old Scottish clans, fighting each other until the English invaded then they would group together until the attack was repulsed when they would return to stealing each other's castles, cattle, lands and women. For Afghans, she'd told him, it was similar. Feuds were usually over *zar*, *zan* or *zamin* – gold, women or land.

Then he gave her a wry smile as he told a story about Tommy, his older brother. Only eighteen years at the time, Tommy was poaching salmon in a deep pool in a river a few miles from the family home near Inverness. He simply donned a wetsuit, slipped into the water and caught the fish with his bare hands.

As Tommy was coming out of a deep pool, a large salmon wriggling in his arms, the local laird appeared riding one of his Arab stallions.

'*What do you think you're doing, boy?! This is my land!*' the laird roared.

'*Oh, your land,*' retorted Tommy, throwing the salmon onto the pile he'd already caught, '*and where did you get it from, how did you come by it?*'

'*My ancestors fought for it,*' the laird blustered, his face becoming red with anger.

'*Well, get off your fucking horse and I'll fight you for it now!*'

The laird swiftly rode away.

Mena was aware she was diverting her thoughts with images of blue children, fighting doctors, dead salmon and cowardly lairds. She should be more focused on Charlotte. Already the young woman had made arrangements to visit Mohammad and his sister, and this unsettled her. There was still something about Charlotte that made her feel apprehensive.

But now Mena felt good. Walking to work was a positive step. Her work at the ministry was stressful and permitted little time for untangling unwanted thoughts and feelings. Even in the evenings she always seemed to be doing something what with meetings, visiting friends – or more likely friends visiting her because they loved coming to the old house – or going out to eat. Listening to Gil's woes, as well as his funny stories about the house, seemed to take up more and more of any spare time she had. She could feel herself becoming ever more drawn to him.

Today was a welcome break, walking slowly and enjoying the sights and sounds of the city. Shakeba had advised her to return to work only when she felt rested, advice gladly taken. As an Afghan woman with an American passport, she knew she was flouting security regulations but felt safe in such a busy part of the city as Shahr-e-Naw. From her house it only took twenty minutes to walk to the ministry and she needed the exercise.

The walk took her past the crossroads that divided Chicken Street from Flower Street on the long road passing Shahr-e-Naw Park. Down Flower Street she spied two white wedding cars decked out with plastic flowers and bunting. The grand displays of these plastic flowers outside the florists far outweighed the small bunches of drooping red and yellow flowers stuck into old oil tins with 'American aid' and 'the Stars and Stripes' printed on their sides.

Some interesting shops had recently sprung up on the road, so rather than turn into Flower Street she decided to stop and look in the window of a new clothes shop, even if the styles appeared old-fashioned. Kabul was no place for serious retail therapy unless you wanted carpets or old artefacts.

A car horn sounded, drawing her attention from the window a fraction of a second before it shattered into a million pieces. Luckily her dupatta saved her from most of the flying glass; only a few small shards hit her face. The blast was sonic, booming its way from somewhere up Chicken Street. The loudest noise she ever heard in her life. Her ears deafened; she could feel the shockwaves rippling through her body.

Without thinking, and with blood running down her face, she ran round the corner towards the source of the blast. She was a doctor. There was no thought that a second blast was likely and she should take cover before the hot rain fell. Those scorching bits of tangled metal mixed with the mangled dismembered body parts that would cascade to the ground, spewing out like some devil's vomit.

Already a crowd was gathering, oblivious to the danger

as the pall of black smoke began to drift slowly over the rooftops. Reaching the scene, she saw several people lying on the ground, some moaning, some writhing in pain, and a woman and a man not moving at all, the already dead.

Her instinct as a doctor told her to attend to the injured, those who might still be saved, but she was drawn to the small body that lay crumpled on the roadside across from the blast site. It was the little match girl. The one with the grubby smiling face and tattered dress who had taken her by the hand the first time she visited Chicken Street, walking with her the length of the street clutching at her hand as if it was a life raft.

'*Please buy matches!*' the girl had implored. '*I am hungry!*'

Simple and stark as that. Who knew what stories lay behind the myriad street children selling matches, chewing gum, maps, newspapers, any small item to eke out a living for their families?

Mena picked the girl up and carried her over to a shop doorway where the owner placed an old coat on the ground. Lowering the inert body gently onto the coat, her eyes were drawn to the piece of smooth silver-hued metal shrapnel protruding from the centre of the girl's forehead. At least it had been quick. There was only a small dribble of blood running from the wound.

Aware of the tears streaming down her cheeks, Mena reached into her shalwar, took out her mobile and called Gil. It was her first reaction, but for some reason his number was switched off. She then hurriedly phoned his office and spoke to Farhad the IT assistant.

His response rooted her to the spot, compounding her

sense of dread. 'Sorry, Dr Mena, there was a phone call from a man saying Mr Gil had to leave Kabul for a few days. Then the call abruptly ended. No one has seen Mr Gil since yesterday. We are concerned. Sorry.'

Putting away her mobile she imagined she could still feel the vibrations of the blast coursing through her body until she realised it was the cold hand of fear that gripped her.

TWENTY-ONE

AT THE HEROIN FACTORY,
IN THE HINDU KUSH,
Thursday 3 November 2005

The road was bumpier. Gone was the smooth surface they'd travelled on for some time before turning onto a jarring rutted track. This was the worst part of the journey. As far as they could gauge the jarring lasted for over an hour. Exhaustion was creeping in. Gil's limbs ached; his head throbbed. There was no way they could tell which direction they were headed, though Alex sensed from the chink of sunlight afforded by the blindfold it was east towards the mountains of Nangarhar.

When the vehicle eventually stopped, Mirwais ordered one of his gunmen to untie their blindfolds, allowing them to blink their eyes in the dazzling sunlight and take in the surroundings. High barren mountains strewn with copses of fir trees surrounded the narrow plateau on which they sat providing the merest glimpse of the distant plains. A large compound lay at the back of the plateau hidden from the track.

As his eyes adapted to the intense sunlight, Gil saw Mirwais was wearing a voluminous black shalwar kameez with a broad black turban. It was similar to the dress of the man now approaching them. He was the fiercest-looking man Gil had ever seen, tall with a regal bearing, well-built and swarthy with saturnine eyes, and a look that would pierce steel. Then as he bent down to embrace Mirwais his countenance changed completely; the smile would have melted any heart.

Who were these people? Talibs? Remaining in the vehicle while Mirwais was lifted out and placed in a wheelchair by the driver, Gil turned to Alex and whispered, 'Where do you think we are? What's going on?'

'I've no idea – we'll find out soon enough.' Alex's taut reply came as he scanned their new environment. Already there was no hope of escape in his mind.

Gil could feel his heart pounding like an overactive pump. Like the day on the beach when Stella disappeared. His thoughts were jumbled. The words of the young Pakistani engineer he'd sat next to on the plane from Dubai to Islamabad soon after he'd been given his first posting in Afghanistan came flooding back to him. *Ah yes, the Afghan. Your best friend and your worst enemy*. Which was Mirwais? This was the thought plaguing Gil.

'Can we trust Mirwais, Alex?'

'That's a diamond-splitter of a question, Gil. We'll see. Just play it by ear. Say nothing and I'll translate as best I can.'

Gil was not appeased by Alex's words. How did he appear so calm under such circumstances? For Gil this was the moment expats in Afghanistan must surely dread, the *why me?* moment when the pendulum has swung all the way to the dark end of its arc.

He remembered his words to Jackie, a young woman who had been in Kabul only a few weeks and asked him, '*How safe is it here, Gil? Be honest.*'

He gave her an immediate, if somewhat facetious, response: '*Well, Jackie, let's put it this way: there's always a slight chance of a rocket landing on your guesthouse roof. In Edinburgh there's no chance – at least for the foreseeable future!*'

She'd laughed, relief at his words slowly lifting the worried look from her face, at least for the moment.

If you were in the wrong place at the wrong time it didn't matter where you were or what you were doing: home or away, near or far, falling off a stepladder, doing home repairs, slipping on a wet floor and braining yourself on the side of the bath, an articulated lorry jackknifing towards you on an icy motorway.

It could be anything anywhere, but in Kabul the risk was more immediate, more dramatic. In this case it was being kidnapped by an apparently friendly Afghan in a wheelchair and taken blindfold into the Hindu Kush. To nowhere! No wonder his heart was exploding through his chest.

The same gunman who ushered them into Mirwais's apartment now gestured for them to get out of the vehicle, although this time his gun was lowered. Alex's handgun had been taken from him before they left Kabul.

'Gentlemen!' It was Mirwais who addressed them. 'This is my cousin Daud. He is a famous commander. He saved many lives when we fought the Soviets. This is his place of business.'

Commander Daud placed his right hand over his heart and inclined his head towards Gil and Alex in a peremptory manner as Mirwais continued. 'I apologise. This is not our Pashtun hospitality, but the blindfolds were necessary. You are standing in one of the largest heroin factories in Afghanistan. Perhaps it will be the last. Heroin production is becoming a small-scale cottage industry, the factories quick to assemble and even quicker to dismantle. Your NATO technology forces us to downsize.'

Being out of the vehicle it was easier to take in their surroundings. A machine gun nest sat higher up the hill alongside a bank of radio antennae and what resembled a light anti-aircraft gun. A large water tank perched on a raised platform lay below the nest. At the end of the compound two gunmen sat overlooking the track meandering towards the plains below.

Several buildings sat in the compound looking like misplaced Nissan huts. A group of large metal drums stacked on top of each other lay beside one of the buildings. The constant hum of a diesel generator served as an aural counterpoint to the stillness of the mountains. A pungent chemical smell hung over the whole area.

Who were Mirwais and Waheed? Heroin dealers, smugglers, traffickers?

'You are thinking Waheed and I are in the heroin business, Mr Gil? The answer is no. Before you travel to

Dubai I wanted you to see what is killing my country. You have been to the Russian Centre. It is only the beginning. This country is becoming a nation of *poderis*. Young children, even whole families, are addicted, their lives ruined. The white *poder* makes money, much money, and some men become too greedy. Waheed and I are not involved in this. You are only able to be here because Daud is my cousin. He knows I do not approve of his business, but he is family. What to do?'

Mirwais laughed. 'We are all related in Afghanistan. It is difficult for you foreigners to understand. There are only three degrees of separation here. Come, let us take a tour.'

Mirwais guided them over to one of the buildings where men, some no more than boys, boiled water and raw opium in a broad-rimmed metal drum. As Gil and Alex watched in fascination, the bubbling liquid began to cool and insoluble material, mostly straw and leaves, settled at the bottom leaving thick brown liquid opium.

'So you can see, gentlemen,' Mirwais began, 'the first stage is simple, anyone can do it. If it is sold as opium farmers and traders may increase its weight, and of course its profit, by adding black tea, gur, raisins, rice flour.'

Gil listened intently. He decided to immerse himself in the tour as the only way to divert the pervasive uneasiness that plagued him. Mirwais, meanwhile, briskly moved them on to another building where two men wearing face masks were busy attending to an even bigger drum.

'As the solution cools lime is added to the mixture and then siphoned off through a filter. Here they use burlap sacks. The mixture is then heated with ammonium chloride

179

and allowed to cool. Look over there,' Mirwais added, pointing to dirty white cloths lying on the ground covered in a light brown powder.

'So that's heroin, what the men in the Russian Centre use?' Gil asked.

'No, Mr Gil, it is only crude morphine base. To turn it into heroin you need heat and acetic anhydride. It becomes technical. After cooling, water and activated charcoal and soda ash are added then the heroin is filtered and dried. This process only produces a crude form of brown heroin. It needs to be further refined using a more sophisticated method requiring chemicals like acetone and ethanol. You smell vinegar? That is the acetic anhydride, a most pungent smell, unmistakable.'

Gil was all too aware of the noxious smell while Alex was already wrapping his scarf round his nose and mouth. Both noticed the two men who were walking across the compound towards them. They were definitely not Afghans.

'Let me introduce our colleagues from Myanmar. No names, of course.' Mirwais gave a chuckle as the two men approached and bowed towards his wheelchair, a short stretch given they were small in stature themselves.

'Without these men it would be impossible for us to produce high-grade heroin. Now we can reach over ninety per cent purity. For export only, you understand. But soon we will have learned from them and do the final cooking ourselves.'

Gil was increasingly disturbed by Mirwais's use of the words 'we' and 'us' when he claimed he had nothing to do with the drug trade. For someone not involved he seemed to know a lot about it. How far was he involved, and how did these men get to Afghanistan; how were they contacted in the first place?

Again, as if reading Gil's mind with discomfiting accuracy, Mirwais said, 'Remember, Afghanistan has a land bridge to Myanmar through the Wakhan Corridor. We are not so far apart. Another cousin has several businesses there and was able to procure the services of these men. They are chemists.'

For Alex the thought came all too quickly. It could only be a matter of time before high-grade methamphetamine produced in Myanmar and China was smuggled through the Wakhan Corridor for sale in Afghanistan. While heroin was a pacifier, a painkiller, a wrecker of souls, the amphetamines had the opposite effect: they were unpredictable stimulants.

He knew that during the Second World War methamphetamine was used extensively by the German armed forces for its performance-enhancing stimulant effects. It had aided a raving Hitler at the Nuremburg rallies as he stoked the fire of Nazi atrocities. Branded as Pervitin, it became known among the German troops as 'Tank-Chocolates'. Alex could imagine it being re-named 'AK-47-Candies' if it ever reached the hands of Afghanistan's many gunmen.

'They do not finish the packaging here,' Mirwais continued. 'This is completed in another location closer to the wholesale market. The heroin is packed in one kilo brown paper wraps then sealed in plastic before the final wrapping in cotton cloth. The heroin of Commander

181

Daud is stamped with date of manufacture and his motif, a flying hawk. He loves these birds and keeps two peregrines for hunting.'

'What happens to the heroin then?' Gil enquired, reluctantly intrigued by Mirwais's description of the factory's work.

'It is exported to your country. The heroin used here is usually of poorer quality. It is not our concern if your young people take this drug and your police and politicians are unable to stop them. Insha'Allah, I want to see our people use none of it. Anyhow, before we take tea let me show you the finished product.'

Moving over to another building they witnessed a young man repack the cloth wraps into larger bundles and stack them in the back of an old Toyota Hi-Lux truck.

'These will be taken to the drug bazaar and sold to one of the traders before it is moved out of the country.'

'The drug bazaar?' queried Gil.

'There are still a few drug bazaars left in the country, Mr Gil, but US and ISAF surveillance is rapidly forcing the business onto a smaller, less visible scale. There is a bazaar, closer than you may think, where you can buy the chemicals and other equipment necessary to produce heroin. It is where the finished article is traded along with opium. But these bazaars will soon close. The Shaddle bazaar on the Torkham road is already under tight surveillance.'

Gil could hardly believe such bazaars existed and looked to Alex for some type of confirmation it was true. Alex raised his eyebrows and shrugged his shoulders as if to say: '*This is Afghanistan, don't be surprised by anything that happens here.*'

Mirwais called a guard over and gestured for his wheelchair to be pushed to one of the huts. Turning towards Alex and Gil he said, 'Come, gentlemen, let us take tea. You have seen enough. Then tonight you will return to Kabul, Mr Gil, and prepare for your journey to Dubai. We will see you when you return on Saturday evening.'

As they reached a rickety wooden table placed outside the hut where a boy was pouring green tea into small china cups, Gil looked at Mirwais. 'What about Alex – he will be coming with us?'

'No, Mr Gil. Mr Alex will stay here with my cousin until you return safely with the package from the bank.'

'You mean he's a hostage, Mirwais, don't you?'

'You can say that if you wish. It is merely insurance. Please remember his fate is in your hands.'

Gil's exasperation was obvious as he looked towards Alex, who appeared more intent on selecting one of the biscuits lying on a cracked white plate than considering what fate might have in store for him.

TWENTY-TWO

TWILIGHT TIME, IN KABUL,
Thursday 3 November 2005

I t was the worst time of day for Olivier. What the French call *l'heure entre chien et loup*, those moments after sunset when the sky darkens, vision becomes unclear and the dimming light can make it difficult to distinguish between a dog and a wolf, between friend and foe.

As he sat in his room in the guesthouse without the burden of that interminable knocking on his office door, the meetings with staff, the stream of daily emails back and forth to Geneva, he pondered the many uncertainties he faced, most importantly whether he would even survive another day in this godforsaken country.

That morning, while taking a bite of his breakfast croissant, he had been startled by the massive thump of an IED going off somewhere in the vicinity. Not on the other side of the mountain but close, all too close. Dropping the rest of the croissant into his cup and splashing his suit trousers with hot coffee was a bad start to the day.

Now this twilight time gave him the opportunity to open a fresh bottle of Lagavulin. Downing a stiff glassful clutched in a trembling hand, he considered a current uncertainty. Where had that bloody Moncrief disappeared to? The call had come from JDL that he would be gone for a few days. They didn't even know exactly where or for how long. How incompetent. The man and the organisation were unreliable.

He urgently needed him to review and approve a new project to build a series of apartment blocks and low-cost housing to the east of Kabul – a most profitable project. Before he signed off on the contract, he'd negotiated a substantial facilitation fee for himself from the NGO contracted to do the building work. This would be paid directly into his bank account in Switzerland, the one known only to himself that contained similar fees from previous contracts signed by him. He had considered the Caymans or the British Virgin Islands, safe havens for all sorts of financial chicanery, but there was nowhere safer than with the gnomes of Zurich.

He recognised he was a man of secrets. If Monique ever knew! He didn't want to think about the consequences, better to pour another glass of whisky. Seated at the window looking out over the ever-darkening guesthouse garden, his thoughts turned to Francesca, the love of his life, and their two daughters Imelda and Pia.

Thirty-six at the time and on mission to Manila, he'd met her at an exclusive expatriate club where she worked as a receptionist. He still didn't know how it happened. It was that much-cliched 'love at first sight', a thunderbolt that seemed to strike without warning. She was twenty-five, unmarried and the most beautiful woman he'd ever seen. She was also a devout Roman Catholic who attended mass every day at the little white stuccoed chapel down the street from the club.

Married to Monique since he was twenty-four and with their two sons at private school in Geneva, his affair with Francesca began almost immediately. His six-week mission to the Philippines was soon over and when he left she was already pregnant. Eight months later he was able to arrange a follow-up mission to Manila so he could attend the birth of their first daughter Imelda.

Two more missions quickly followed, resulting in another pregnancy and the birth of Pia. Now both girls were at university, Pia in Manila studying psychology and Imelda doing a masters' degree in business studies at NYU. This cost money, unlike with the boys funded through university by the UN. It was imperative for him to provide his secret family with the support they needed, he loved them so dearly. Throughout the relationship he managed to manoeuvre a visit to see them every year, taking a week's leave while telling Monique he was on a field mission.

During all this time he never considered divorcing Monique; it would have been too expensive. Instead, they continued to live a conventional and socially convenient life in Geneva. Two years from retirement, he had no intention of spending it in some rustic farmhouse in the Dordogne with Monique settling into the life of some rural grande dame.

Such a fate might be good enough for his contemporaries, but he intended to spend his retirement in luxury. He and Francesca would live in a purpose-built villa in the countryside outside Manila, complete with stepped gardens and swimming pool.

Then he would take her to Paris, London, New York, all the places she had never been. They would stay in five-star hotels and travel business class if not first class. For all this he needed considerable cash to supplement his not inconsiderable pension and terminal lump sum from the UN. And Monique would not go cheaply, that was for sure.

After staring through the thick bottom of his empty glass at a distorted carpet, he carefully wiped the glass clean and placed it on the bedside table before reluctantly making his way down to the dining room for the evening meal. Where was Moncrief? He needed to see him right away. The man was erratic. An image appeared in his mind. *With his unkempt appearance and unruly hair he reminds me of a street dog, a mongrel. Yes, it could only be a mongrel.*

TWENTY-THREE

THE SHOPPING TRIP, IN KABUL,
Friday 4 November 2005

Returning to Kabul in the early morning after another uncomfortable journey from the heroin factory, Gil shielded his eyes from the light as the blindfold was removed. For once the sky was clear. A light wind had blown away the smoke and pollution. He marvelled at the city, so peaceful in the pre-dawn glow. A city he knew his way around better than Edinburgh or Islamabad and where he had many friends and acquaintances. His current world. If only his children could be with him. The thought only reaffirmed his failure as a father. At the moment the fleeting comfort of money was all he could provide for them.

While he remained in Kabul there was little else he could do apart from emails and regular Skype calls. It wasn't enough. Jamie was adjusting well to life back in Scotland. For Mhairi, now fifteen, it was more difficult.

She had attended secondary school in Pakistan at a sedate private English-medium academy set in the leafy suburbs of Islamabad. Now she was at a high school in the Highlands of Scotland where there was no respect shown to teachers or by boys to girls.

She found it difficult after the more formal academic education of Pakistan. And there was inevitably the introduction to smoking and drinking as well as other drugs. One of her classmates became pregnant and another was expelled for selling cannabis to other students. It was all a shock for her and naturally she still missed her mother. But he would see both children soon enough; his home leave was due soon and they would go on a short holiday together before he returned to Kabul for his last six-month contract.

Letting Gil off at the house, Mirwais returned his mobile and gave him a ticket for a Dubai flight leaving at seven o'clock the next morning. He would have gone as soon as they returned to Kabul if banks in the Emirates were not closed on Fridays.

'You will have a successful trip, Mr Gil. My car will be at the airport when you return. Do not worry about Mr Alex, he is in good hands. You must understand we have to take precautions. Goodbye. Let us go.' The instruction to the driver was curt. It came from a man with a preoccupied mind.

Mirwais promptly rolled up the window and the vehicle set off down the potholed street, leaving Gil to ring the gate bell and be ushered into the compound by one of the Gurkha guards. Looking through the window as he walked

189

up the steps to the house he could see a few of the residents already seated at the breakfast table, early for their day off.

'My God, Gil, where the hell have you been?' spluttered Big William, pushing his chair back from the table as Gil entered the dining room. 'It's good to see you. We were told you would be away for days.'

'Good to see you too.' Gil gave a faint smile as Cheryl and Sarah pulled their chairs out and came over to give him a hug.

'It was a private emergency, I'm afraid. In fact I have to go to Dubai tomorrow. I'll be back on Sunday.'

'Nothing too serious, I hope?' Big William probed, a cryptic look on his face.

'No not really. Look, it's Friday. Why don't we do the shopping as usual? We all need a breather.'

'Oh, Gil, you haven't heard, have you?' Sarah said in a strained voice. 'Brock has been flown out of the country. They wouldn't even let him clear his room. It's terrible.'

While Gil acknowledged Sarah's concern, he didn't want to articulate that Brock had only brought it on himself. He was no loss, and the words Gil overheard him say to Sarah describing Mickey as 'a waste of space' had certainly rebounded on the American.

'What about Abdul Qabir, what's happened to him?' Gil enquired.

'We don't know,' replied Big William. 'Apparently he's still at the ministry, helping with enquiries as they say and you know what that means. Mike Gomez told us someone passed on information to the authorities to look out for the number plate of the vehicle. They were targeted.'

'I wonder who the informant was? I hope Abdul Qabir will be alright, but I guess there is nothing we can do at the moment. Better let Mike Gomez take care of it. Let's get out of this bloody house! Give me half an hour and we can go.'

After taking a quick shower, eating a light breakfast and greeting the other residents who had appeared at the table, Gil checked his mobile as they left for the shopping expedition. Apart from a few text messages from the kids and the JDL office there were several missed calls from Olivier and Mena.

Mena's number was engaged, so he left a message saying he would come to her house in the early evening. Unfortunately Olivier's number was not engaged so he had to listen to a rant describing some new and, as always, urgent project Gil was meant to review. It would be difficult without seeing the relevant documents although the project sounded fine in principle if over-budgeted. Much to Olivier's annoyance, he said he would look at the paperwork when he returned from Dubai. The kids he would call around midday their time.

The others were now waiting for him on the front steps, Big William looking impatient, eager as ever to set forth in search of what Kabul could offer in the way of gourmet food. Without any more delay, Gil, Big William and Cheryl climbed into one of the house vehicles and drove to Shahr-e-Naw and Wazir Akbar Khan, the areas where most expats did their food shopping on a Friday.

The JDL house residents had their own route, buying meat, fruit, vegetables and other foodstuff from several tried and tested shops and vendors. On reaching Shahr-e-Naw Park the driver parked in the usual side street and the three house residents stepped from the vehicle.

As they set off on foot, led by Big William, they were soon followed by a small group of women swathed in blue burqas carrying babies and with several raggedy snot-nosed toddlers in tow. While being out of the vehicle didn't exactly flout the current JDL security advisory, walking round the centre of Kabul was not officially permitted given the recent IED blast in Chicken Street. Big William, however, was notorious for disregarding security advisories if they presented an obstacle to his constant search for exotic foodstuff.

The raggle-taggle group was marshalled by Malik, a slick teenage street kid dressed in denim jeans and T-shirt and wearing fake Ray Bans, who had become Big William's regular minder on these shopping trips. It was his task to make sure the women didn't bother the house shoppers as the whole entourage faithfully followed Big William down the road as if he was the Pied Piper.

When the shopping was finished, Malik would be given a handful of Afghani notes to be distributed to the women, who would wave and shout after the departing vehicle, some running after it. As a way of appreciation for small mercies or hoping for more money Gil could never work out.

Most of the shopping was completed in the Chelsea Supermarket which stocked a wide array of goods for expats and those locals that could afford them. Set among internationally branded products from Gillette, L'Oreal, Nestle and Coca-Cola, a long shelf stacked with jars of honey seemed incongruous. The honey was labelled 'Alleluya', each label displaying a black and white drawing of a man running away from a beehive chased by a swarm of bees. The man appeared to be wearing a frock coat and a wig like some eighteenth-century English beekeeper waving his broad-brimmed hat to keep the bees at bay.

It was a sign of globalisation that the honey had been harvested and packed in Argentina. How did honey from Argentina land up on the shelves of a Kabul supermarket? *Anything could be bought, sold or bartered in Afghanistan*, Gil mused.

After paying the bill to the genial store owner, they walked down to the crossroads bisecting Flower Street and Chicken Street. A police barricade still blocked off Chicken Street. Big William had already told Gil at least two people were killed in the blast.

Taking a left down Flower Street, they turned up a narrow lane where there was a small shop with the picture of a fat multi-coloured fish painted on the window. Inside the cool interior, a find. Two freezers containing a range of seafood including salmon, lobster and prawns, most likely traded from military PXs in exchange for cigarettes or other goods. Soon Malik was carrying a large plastic bag containing two frozen lobsters and a kilo of Atlantic prawns along with several other bags containing fruit and vegetables.

Gil was tired out; he could hardly keep his eyes open as they made their way back to the vehicle. At one point he staggered into a post, acquiring a graze to his forehead. It was time to go back to the house and take a nap before his evening visit with Mena.

TWENTY-FOUR

AT MENA'S HOUSE, IN KABUL,
Friday 4 November 2005

Gil was looking forward to seeing Mena, albeit with mixed feelings. He would tell her everything that had happened; she was his closest confidante in Kabul and he trusted her. Someone else had to know about Alex being held hostage, just in case. He calculated there might be some risk but knew she would understand. She was a strong woman.

The sky was darkening as the driver let him off at the compound. Old Abdul hailed him in greeting and opened the heavy metal gates. As he walked up the tree-lined path to the house Gil noticed two armed guards sitting inside the compound wall rather than the usual one.

When Mena opened the house door he could see she had been crying, the tear stains still visible on her cheeks, her eyes red and puffy. There were two stitches below her right eye, a thin strip of plaster on her forehead and pinpricks of red dotted her face. Gil looked at her in horror. As he quickly reached to hug her he could feel her body trembling.

'Mena, what's wrong, what happened to you?'

'Oh, Gil, it was terrible. Come, I'll tell you.'

Taking off his heavy leather jacket, worn to ward off the increasing evening chill, they were soon seated in the lounge clutching their whiskies with an equally disconsolate Tazi stretched out at their feet. Mena began to speak in a halting voice. As the words came pouring out, Gil could see she was still in shock.

'I'm a doctor, for God's sake. I've worked in A&E in Stanford hospitals and seen torn and maimed bodies. I never experienced anything like this, though. It was so sudden, so shocking. The noise was unearthly and then I saw that poor girl lying there on the street, a young life snuffed out. For what, Gil? And the other bodies strewn around. They are reporting two dead and many more injured with loss of limbs and eyes, body disfigurement. What future do these people have in Afghanistan?'

Gil found it hard to respond – what was there to say? He empathised as best he could but was himself shocked. After all he had been sitting drinking tea in the mountains when this happened. He stretched out his hand which she eagerly took, clutching it to her. Mena had experienced the dark side of the city. That flick of the switch where going out to restaurants, clubs, dinner parties, carpet shopping, socialising with friends could portray danger and death.

Taking a deep breath Mena continued. 'Oh, Gil, I

can't stop thinking what would have happened if I hadn't stopped to look in that shop window... what if I hadn't turned my face away just before the blast... if I'd turned into Chicken Street.'

'Don't, Mena. Don't think *what if*. You'll drive yourself insane,' he gently responded, his mind touching on the countless *what-ifs* he had considered while sitting on the beach in Goa and for a long time after. *If* was the smallest word with the biggest meaning, the architect of regret for those seeking redemption from the past.

Without warning, Mena leant forward and clutched at Gil, her tears wetting his cheeks, her body clinging to his. Before he knew it they were kissing, frantically and passionately as if they had been waiting for this moment their whole lives.

As she began to gently fondle him, Gil stammered, 'No, Mena... I can't... we shouldn't...'

'It's only love, Gil. It's only love. Let it be,' she whispered. It was a spontaneous gesture, not planned. She knew he was still in love with Stella despite the years since her disappearance She could live with that. Silently she took his hand and led him to the bedroom. Tazi opened an eye to look at them as they walked to the open door, yawned, rolled over and went back to sleep.

TWENTY-FIVE

AT THE BANK, IN DUBAI,
Saturday 5 November 2005

The flight from Kabul was uneventful. After the ancient Ariana Douglas DC-6 slowly spiralled its way up above the Kabul valley it settled onto a steady flight path to Dubai. Gil wondered whether the spiralling was due to the age of the plane or the continued threat of Taliban rocket attacks from the surrounding mountains.

The plane was certainly old. The passenger seated two rows in front of Gil kept trying to adjust his seat before he realised it wasn't properly bolted to the floor resulting in it slipping backwards and knocking into the knees of the person in the seat behind.

On arrival in Dubai, as instructed by Mirwais, Gil took a taxi directly to the EDA Bank International located next to the new Emirates Mall with its gigantic indoor ski slope and ice rink, an alien escape from the searing desert climate. The taxi driver, Rafi, came from Pakistan. Gil joked he must be one of the Peshawar mafia as each time he visited Dubai the taxi drivers he met all came from Peshawar.

When they arrived at the bank Gil instructed Rafi to wait, explaining that he wouldn't be long. Sunlight sparkled on the diamond panes of the twenty-storey glass tower as he entered the cool interior of what resembled a five-star hotel. Two healthy palm trees stood guard inside the main entrance hall and well-tended ceramic troughs of greenery were strategically placed throughout the lobby.

There was no cashier or clerk in sight, only an elegantly dressed man clutching a clipboard walking towards him over a mosaic circle etched on the marble floor. It was as if he was entering the Starship Enterprise. A circle of overhead lights illuminated the mosaic, its Arabesque design stark in their glow. Gil felt he could be beamed up at any moment.

'Good morning, sir, may I be of assistance? I am Abdul-Bari. I am here to facilitate your visit to the bank. Welcome.'

'Yes, good morning, Mr Bari. I am Mr Moncrief. I understand you are expecting me?'

'Indeed. We have instructions from our client to allow you access to his security box. May I have your passport and letter of authorisation, please?'

After handing over the necessary documents, Gil was ushered to a recessed seating area.

'Would you like some refreshment, Mr Moncrief? Tea or coffee, perhaps?'

'Yes, thank you, a coffee would be fine.'

'We will take some minutes to verify your documents, please take a seat and relax.'

Settling into a red velour chair panelled with ersatz Rococo carving, Gil gazed round at the plush interior of the bank. This was Dubai, as far from Kabul as Pluto was from planet Earth. Hard to think they were less than three hours apart, even on a rickety old Ariana plane. Gil had never taken to the place. It appeared so temporary, constructed as it was on the shifting sands of Arabia, a family corporation run through the majlis on untold oil wealth.

A land where there was little crime and what there was would be quickly and ruthlessly dealt with by the authorities. Yet Gil knew a bank like this must be full of black money from many sources: the drug trade, the arms trade, human trafficking, the many speculative land deals covering the Middle East and beyond.

It all added to his sense of distance, the deepening feeling of disorientation that had emerged during the past week. Was it paranoia? Was he in danger, some risk in coming to Dubai? Rafi had spotted a black Mercedes with darkened windows that appeared to be following them on the road in from the airport, but it veered off two streets before they arrived at the bank. It was enough to set Gil on edge and increase his sense of unease.

Recent events all too painfully resurrected his memories of Stella and her disappearance. Then he thought of Mena and their night together, which brought an unexpected lightness to his being, however temporary.

'Mr Moncrief.' Abdul-Bari's words snapped Gil out of

his reverie. 'Would you please follow my colleague Ghanim downstairs to the vault?'

Unlike the Saville Row suit worn by Abdul-Bari, Ghanim wore the traditional Emirati dress of a long white *kandoora* accompanied by a red and white *ghotra* head dress. He was twice the size of Abdul-Bari with muscles clearly defined even beneath the flowing robes.

Finishing his coffee and the last of the delicious dates accompanying it, Gil walked across the mosaic circle towards a lift flanked by two uniformed security guards. Ghanim quickly ushered him into the lift and pressed the button for a level two floors below.

Emerging in an anteroom, he was instructed to sign an official form before the heavy metal doors of a floor-to-ceiling vault swung open. Banks of numbered lockers along the walls led to a small well-lit alcove containing an ornate desk and two chairs. Ghanim quickly located the locker, opened it and removed the metal box from inside.

An armed guard carried the box to the table where Gil was already seated. Opening it with the combination number hidden inside the now armless Elvis, he stared at the contents, a heavy tightly wrapped rectangular bundle. Inside he knew there were two million dollars in new one hundred bills weighing twenty kilos, the exact luggage limit allowed on his flight back to Kabul.

Lifting the bundle he placed it inside the nondescript suitcase he'd purchased at the airport on landing and closed the lid, making sure the catches were secure and the lock fastened. Now all he had to do was return to Terminal 2 and wait for his plane to Kabul, where Mirwais had assured him he would have no problem with the customs. '*Money flows in and out of Kabul airport like water from a spring, Mr Gil. You would be surprised. Two million dollars is, how the Americans say, chicken feed. We have it arranged. There will be no problem for you.*'

Mirwais then went on to explain about the hundreds of millions of dollars taken out of the country through the airport and the ingenious methods used for smuggling it. '*Drug money, stolen aid money, bribes. Here there is nothing under the sun or moon that is not subject to corruption. When you enter our country they are only interested in finding contraband alcohol or hidden arms; they are not interested in what flows out apart from drugs.*'

Arriving at Terminal 2 and bidding goodbye to Rafi with a generous tip, Gil checked in for his flight then quickly passed through passport control and customs before making his way to the lounge area.

Inaugurated in 1998 to alleviate congestion at Terminal 1, Terminal 2 supposedly catered to scheduled, charter and special interest flights. UN staff in Afghanistan often joked this was Dubai's 'Axis of Evil' airport, where flights left for riskier destinations than New York, London or Melbourne – destinations like Tehran, Baghdad and Mogadishu as well as Kabul..

While the terminal embraced a wide range of duty-free goods including food, tobacco, luggage, electronics and music, perfumes and cosmetics, this was not on the scale of Terminal 1, which masqueraded as a grand shopping mall. Neither was it lost on Gil that passengers going to more upmarket destinations in Europe and the USA were kept well clear of Terminal 2.

Looking round at his fellow passengers, he was struck by the men in combinations of fatigues, combat boots and camouflage clothing. Small clutches of young women wearing long dresses and coloured headscarves stood around chattering with each other. Maids or desperate women making their way to lands where some form of work beckoned, or so they hoped.

Several men and couples sat around guarding substantial carry-on luggage filled to capacity with products too expensive or unavailable in their own countries. Their hold luggage would mirror their domestic consumption with boxed and plastic-wrapped televisions, video players, food mixers, microwaves and other domestic appliances. Their faces displayed the eager anticipation of returning home to unpack their wares.

As Gil's flight was called, it was with a sense of relief he walked to the departure gate. He felt more relaxed. At the same time his favourite driver in Kabul was far from relaxed. Abdul Qabir sat in a small bare room in the basement of the ministry waiting to enter a door he prayed would never open.

TWENTY-SIX

THE INTERROGATION ROOM, IN KABUL,
Saturday 5 November 2005

Ahmed had lost count of the men he'd peeled skin off, a small slice at a time. Said, his assistant, too eager and zealous by far, had urinated on the prisoner's skinned flesh until Ahmed stopped him. The man strapped to the chair screamed and wept, pled to God, to anybody or anything that would take away the agony, but nothing would. Only Ahmed held that power. He would make Said scrub the stone floor until it shone. The basement interrogation room was no charnel house.

Ahmed's great-grandfather had been chief torturer to Abdur Rahman Khan, the Iron Amir and absolute ruler of Afghanistan at the turn of the twentieth century. Not that the Amir needed a torturer; he was quite capable himself of doing whatever was necessary to retain control over his people. Over the years he had executed over one hundred thousand men as an example to others yet people still defied him and broke the law – his law.

Slitting throats and beheading was not uncommon. The *fanah* was used frequently, a crude medieval instrument in which the foot was placed between two wooden blocks and crushed, resulting in the loss of toes or even the whole foot. Skinning an inch at a time was common, as was beating with sticks until bones were broken. Death would usually follow.

Ahmed's great-grandfather had told his grandfather tales of the Amir his own father in turn recounted to him. The one that stayed uppermost in his mind, told when he was only ten years old, was of a man and woman who loved each other but were already married with families of their own. One day they ran away together. When caught and brought in front of the court, the Amir told the man that as he was so fond of the woman he could have her completely. Sbe was then thrown into a huge cauldron of scalding water and boiled down into soup. Bowls of this soup were then given to the man, who was forced to drink it. Then he was hanged.

Ahmed remembered this story. It kept him from giving in to carnal thoughts of his brother's wife, a woman he truly loved and from the looks she furtively gave him on the few occasions they had met, reciprocated his feelings. It was the cannibalism that stuck in his mind. According to the Koran a cannibal could never enter Paradise, a place Ahmed desperately wanted to reach.

Even in the early 1900s his grandfather recalled men being stoned to death or left to starve in iron cages suspended from high poles. The latter, along with heads hung by their hair from the battlements of the old city gate, were said to be most effective in making men desist from evil and breaking the law.

Then there was the ancient Dance of Death, although Ahmed had never witnessed it himself. Some said it was only a legend, a myth. It was allegedly even carried out for amusement, something he could never thole. He only interrogated to extract information and confessions, not for any sense of pleasure. He was a professional. This was his family's work, although none of his sons wanted to follow in his footsteps, they were too intent on leaving the country and building new lives elsewhere.

He knew about the dance from his cousin Kareem who had been a young commander with a particularly brutal mujahideen faction in the early 1990s. They had used it on selected prisoners from a rival faction when they battled for control of Kabul.

There was a house near the old Palace in the southwest of the city where they would take the prisoner into a room with a charcoal brazier heating a pan containing a fat sheep's tail. The prisoner would be forced to stand while the tail melted, leaving the pan full of boiling fat. His head would then be cut off with one swipe of a sword and the boiling fat immediately poured into the body through the gap where the head had been. The fat would sizzle as it drained into the body which would start to jerk and dance, arms wildly flapping, body swaying for nearly a minute before it collapsed to the ground. Sometimes only the throat would be slit and the fat poured in there. The result was much the same.

Such a barbaric act made Ahmed wince; his job was to apply the minimum of pain to effect a confession or gain information. His profession was that of interrogator not executioner, an art as well as a science. He took no joy in prolonging a prisoner's agony. The sooner it was over the better, then the law could take its course. Like the young man sitting in chains in the next room listening to the cries from the Talib Said had pissed on. Ahmed doubted whether they would even have to cut him.

The Captain had instructed Ahmed to find out what this Abdul Qabir knew about the trading of alcohol in Kabul. While Ahmed didn't imbibe, a couple of his friends would take vodka when the weather became colder, '*For medicinal purposes, Ahmed, you should try it, it would do you good.*' He never had. While he had nothing against alcohol, although it was proscribed in the Koran, peddling it for profit was anathema to him, especially if it was done in conjunction with infidels. There was no question, the young man would talk about his activities as would the American held in an upstairs room, although he would be able to trade his freedom for information and dollars.

Ignoring the twelve-volt truck battery and alligator clips standing in the corner of the cell (he was a traditionalist with little time for such modern methods), Ahmed showed the young man the implements he would use. It was not until he peeled back a few centimetres of skin from the young man's cheeks that bravado deserted him and he confessed.

He was ashamed he had been drawn into selling a substance haram in Islam but his younger brother was going to university in Delhi and needed the money for the fees…

Ahmed had heard it all before. '*My family needs the money… grandmother has to travel to Peshawar for an operation… the roof is falling down and needs repaired… I am being married in a month… I am a farmer not a Talib…*'

The lies, the rationales – for which he had some sympathy – were of no concern to him. His job was to find out what they knew and this Abdul Qabir knew a lot – where the alcohol was purchased, how it was transported, who sold it and who bought it. No doubt those involved would all be dealt with. Captain Mahmoud was unforgiving and he would be pleased with the information gained from the young man. What happened to him after he left the room was of no concern to Ahmed.

TWENTY-SEVEN

THE TITLE DEEDS, IN KABUL,
Saturday 5 November 2005

The plane from Dubai arrived on schedule as night was falling. As Mirwais predicted, there was no problem at the airport. After presenting his passport, Gil quickly passed through customs, where each passenger's baggage went through an electronic security scanner, only recently installed much to the delight of the customs officers who could now finish their work much quicker.

A young Belgian aid worker was arguing with one of the officers who opened his holdall and found two bottles of malt whisky. It was doubtful the young man would be drinking any of it this evening, or for several evenings.

As Gil made his way through the arrivals gate, he spotted Mirwais's driver among the waiting throng crowded into the dimly lit vehicle bay. The driver's wave was cursory. He was already walking back towards his car.

As they drove down the Airport Road into the city, Gil realised they were not taking the left turn leading to the Macrorayan complex and Mirwais's apartment. Instead they were driving along the riverside towards the south-west of the city.

After barely twenty minutes, for Kabul was a city that slept early with little traffic on the night roads, they turned into a darkened street off Darrulaman and stopped outside the gates of a large imposing house.

The house appeared newly built and was surrounded by a high compound wall topped with wicked-looking razor wire, a fortified home. A large white alabaster eagle with outstretched wings that looked strikingly similar to the one portrayed on the dollar bill sat impassively on an abutment protruding over the main entrance. A wide wooden door with large brass pointed studs on its raised panels presented an imposing barrier for any unwanted visitor.

Slowly the door was opened by a gunman and they drove into a compound where several other men cradling guns sat on chairs next to an outhouse. Where did they all come from, these gunmen? There was seemingly an inexhaustible supply.

Gil and the suitcase were then led up a broad winding staircase to a spacious lounge with western-style furniture, including several easy chairs and an old brown leather couch as well as a thick Afghan rug and two ornate Oriental urns. An enormous flat-screen television sat on a stand in a corner recess. The red and green patterned velvet curtains were tightly drawn, shutting out the eyes of the night.

Four men sat on the chairs. Alex, Mirwais and two

others Gil had never seen before. The men swiftly rose, apart from Mirwais, with Alex being the first to cross the carpet to greet him. They never spoke; the hug and its accompanying smile each gave the other was enough. Gil was just relieved to see Alex safely returned to Kabul. There would be enough time later to recount their experiences of the last few days.

'Ah, Mr Gil,' intoned Mirwais from his chair. '*Salaam aleikum.* You have returned to us. Welcome back. I see you have the suitcase. But let me introduce you. These are my colleagues, or should I say, fellow members of our small consortium. This is Engineer Shafeeq. He is the brains of our outfit.'

Mirwais chuckled to himself and a tall thin man dressed in a light fawn shalwar kameez stepped forward and held out his hand to Gil, who returned the strong handshake.

'And this is Dr Faizal.'

The doctor, unlike Mirwais and Shafeeq, was dressed in western attire, a light green roll-neck sweater, denim jeans and soft tan leather loafers.

'Welcome to my house, Mr Moncrief. Your friend Alex has been telling me all about you.' With that, the doctor gave Gil a warm urbane smile and a loose handshake before pointing him to an empty chair.

'Tonight we only have a short time,' Mirwais pronounced, apparently in a hurry to proceed. 'Engineer Shafeeq has to leave soon, as do I, so he will explain to you then Dr Faizal will continue. My driver will take you home later – I trust this is acceptable? Let us not delay. Open the case, please, Mr Gil.'

Gil could only nod in agreement as he placed the suitcase on top of a heavy wooden coffee table placed between the chairs. He carefully turned the key in the lock and opened its catch.

As the lid opened, the men craned forward to view its contents, Mirwais lifting himself up off his seat to get a better view, his arms trembling with the effort. The two million dollars, brand new and displaying a luminous sheen from the lights of the overhead chandelier, lay there, their journey from a bank vault in Dubai complete.

To the surprise of Gil and Alex, Engineer Shafeeq quickly removed the bundles of dollars to reveal a thin rectangular package wrapped in green oilcloth nestling in the centre of the case. The package was handed to Mirwais, who opened it and then handed its contents of frayed paper documents back to Shafeeq.

Reclining in his chair, Mirwais continued. 'Engineer Shafeeq will explain what these papers represent. The money is of little consequence. Please forgive him in advance for the long version, what you westerners call "the backstory", I believe. It is important you understand what we are doing here.'

With this introduction, Engineer Shafeeq stood as if he was a professor about to give a lecture, tugged absentmindedly at his short grey beard, adjusted his heavy horn-rimmed spectacles and began to tell them about the papers. Alex smiled to himself. Give an Afghan a public platform and it's hard stopping him speak. It was one of the things he liked most about Afghans.

'You should understand Kabul has grown at an

211

exceptionally fast rate over the last ten years, around seventeen per cent each year.'

Engineer Shafeeq began his lecture in a deep sonorous voice. He looked serious. 'We now have a population over three million and the city is still growing, mostly through the construction of informal settlements that shelter around eighty per cent of Kabul's population.

'You can see that while we're a poor nation there are no shanty towns or packed slum areas in our city unlike so many others in the developing world. I am proud to say this is due to the skills of our rural migrants in building sturdy houses out of local materials. Although we still have some tented settlements on the outskirts of the city for returning refugees, you will find few homeless families sleeping in the streets of Kabul.'

Pausing for breath, Shafeeq took a long sip of water before continuing. 'This expansion of the city has been made outside any regulatory framework. Some worthless individuals have illegally profited by selling land which does not belong to them and we pray, Insha'Allah, the households that purchased land from them will not be penalised. They bought the land in good faith. You will be aware of the Sherpur land-grab some years ago when senior government officials ordered the bulldozing of houses in the city centre to build private homes for themselves.'

Shafeeq paused again, re-adjusted the spectacles that kept slipping down his nose, and took another sip of water. This was thirsty work.

'As you will also know, Kabul has grown in two adjacent valleys separated by the mountain spine dividing the north-east from the south-west of the city. The surrounding mountains and this central spine limit expansion to the north and west, but there is still a large amount of undeveloped land to the east. These papers are valid deeds to a large tract of land in this area that we intend to build on. Unfortunately there are others who think they have title to this land and want these papers.'

'Thank you, Engineer Shafeeq. That is enough for the moment,' interjected Mirwais, leaving little doubt who was the leader of the group. 'It is time for us to leave Mr Gil and Mr Alex in the good hands of Dr Faizal. He will explain further.'

Mirwais then nodded to his gunmen, who gently placed him in his wheelchair and pushed it towards a small lift that stood at the top of the staircase.

After Mirwais and Engineer Shafeeq left, Dr Faizal stood up and moved to an intricately carved glass panelled cabinet standing behind the couch.

'Gentlemen, can I offer you a small libation? I have whisky, vodka and beer. What is a little alcohol in a world full of chaos and conflict? Indeed, you may know the word alcohol is Arabic in origin, deriving from *al-kohl*, the crushed antimony used to darken the eye lines. Wine was widely drunk during the first four Caliphates, so let us drink now!'

Giving a strained laugh, he poured whiskies for Alex and Gil and opened a can of beer for himself.

'Where did you live before coming to Kabul?' Gil enquired, sensing the good doctor was more than happy to talk about himself.

Settling into his chair, Dr Faizal replied, 'Let me give you the short version – it will also help you to understand what we are planning.'

Raising their glasses in acknowledgement, Alex and Gil sat back and gave their full attention to his words. As well as being intrigued, they were keen to learn more about Mirwais's consortium; it might prove to be useful knowledge in their quest to find Waheed's killer.

'After spending my childhood in the same village as Mirwais and Waheed – we are all from the same clan – I lived in Kabul until the end of 1979 when the Soviets invaded. My family knew there would be bitter fighting with ensuing heartache and sadness so decided to leave for Germany where I completed my medical training.'

Dr Faizal continued in a more subdued voice. 'Now I am a qualified psychiatrist, a university professor who has managed to obtain a long leave of absence. I have been back in Kabul for nearly two years. It was time for me to contribute to my country's future, yet I know some of my fellow countrymen, even in the ministry, do not want me here. Those of us who fled the war against the Soviets are referred to as "dog washers", the lowest of the low with no status even if we are doctors or work in other professions. Mirwais and Waheed stayed and fought but they understood some of us had to leave. Not everybody can kill another human being, even in self-defence. Neither did I feel I needed to discharge any religious obligation. But that's enough of my story. What do you know about drug use in Afghanistan, gentlemen?'

Gil and Alex looked at each other, momentarily puzzled

by the abrupt change of subject and still no clearer about why the deeds were so important, before Alex replied, 'We have been to Mirwais's cousin's heroin factory so have some understanding of its manufacture and trade. We also visited the addicts camped in the old Russian Cultural Centre. Heroin seems an intractable problem. From my work with hakims I know people have used hashish and opium as medicines for centuries as well as socially. One hakim told me, "*Opium is a disease, but it is a cure for all other diseases.*" This makes sense here in Afghanistan.'

'Wait, Alex, you see only part of the drug problem. It is much wider than opium and heroin. And please remember Mirwais has no interest in the heroin factory. He does not approve but Commander Daud is his cousin. What to do?'

Dr Faizal looked questioningly at Alex before continuing.

'There is a much greater drug problem here. Anxiety, depression, PTSD and sleep disorders are common in my country. I am a psychiatrist, but it doesn't take a psychiatrist to know this. What did your Bob Dylan sing, something about not needing to be a weather expert to know which way the wind blows?

'There is no Afghan who does not suffer in some way. Twenty-five years of war and conflict have taken a terrible toll. While the Soviets never fought here in Kabul, in the countryside they followed a scorched-earth policy. Villages were destroyed. Woods, crops, animals, people, everything. Over six million fled to Pakistan and Iran, a third of the pre-war population. Another two million were displaced within the country. It is hard to realise that in the 1980s, half of all refugees in the world were my fellow countrymen. The Soviets brutalised our nation. Then mujahideen groups, warlords and the Taliban have continued the process.'

Alex and Gil listened attentively to Dr Faizal, who insisted on topping up their glasses and opening another can of beer for himself before continuing.

'You know we have nearly two thousand registered pharmacies in Kabul alone, eleven thousand in the rest of the country, as well as many unlicensed shops and market stalls selling pharmaceutical drugs. This is our real drug problem, gentlemen. People here take these drugs like candies, and I am not talking about antibiotics and such medicines but psychotropics, mood-altering drugs like anti-depressants, tranquillisers and painkillers. Many people self-medicate – who can blame them? After a first trip to the doctor it is too easy to buy the drugs from a plethora of outlets in the bazaar. People need a psychic crutch just to lead any type of normal life. I have doctor colleagues in the ministry who have been on tranquillisers for years. Islam and green tea can only take a person so far.'

'Okay, I can see all that, but what has this to do with the land deeds Engineer Shafeeq showed us? Why the mystery?' exclaimed Gil, feeling too worn out by recent events to concentrate much longer on this avalanche of information.

'Put simply, we intend to build a factory to manufacture pharmaceutical drugs on the land along with housing for the workers. All psychotropic drugs sold here are imported, mainly from Pakistan, China and India, with the better-quality ones coming from Iran and sometimes Germany. Do you know that thirty-five per cent of all counterfeit pharmaceuticals worldwide are manufactured in India? Twenty-five per cent of pharmaceuticals in developing countries are counterfeit, out of date or substandard. This is a criminal enterprise no less so than heroin, only more hidden and politically acceptable, of course. We estimate most of the psychotropic drugs brought into Afghanistan are smuggled without an official government import licence. Only recently three tonnes of phenobarbital and five tonnes of diazepam were brought in illegally. This is the drug mafia. We want them stopped. Our people must have access to quality drugs prescribed and monitored through a qualified medical service. It will take time but we must start the process somewhere.'

Sitting back in his chair and taking a long draft of beer, Dr Faizal waited for a response.

'These drugs will end up on the street, surely, on the black market?' queried Gil, thinking how easy it was for Abdul Qabir to buy Valium from the pharmacy near the house.

'Some will, this is true, especially if heroin becomes unavailable or too expensive. It is in the nature of addiction that the addict will search for substitute drugs. The mental health needs of the population can best be served by a return to normal life as quickly as possible. We desperately need education, homes, jobs, increased security and stability. Until such time a psychic crutch is necessary. Apart from drugs, how else to seek solace in Afghanistan apart from Islam?'

Sitting back in his chair, Gil could only nod in agreement as Dr Faizal continued, a man who appeared uneasy in his own country.

'Do not be fooled by Mirwais. He lives a modest lifestyle and is an unassuming man. He would not tell you he and Waheed were well-respected commanders during the war against the Soviets. Even rival factions respected them. Despite his condition and simple life, he is a powerful man with many allies. He also has enemies who want the deeds to our land. We are Pashtuns, we abide by *Pashtunwali*, our code of honour. Many ignore it nowadays may Allah curse them. You may know it is based on three obligations – revenge, hospitality and forgiveness – but our first duty is *badal*, to avenge a wrong. Mirwais will not consider holding a jirga with our enemies, especially those responsible for killing Waheed. No agreement is possible. For Mirwais there is no room for consensus.'

Dr Faizal took another mouthful of beer, chuckled lightly and added, 'I hear your British army is moving to Helmand. They will soon learn the truth of *badal*!'

Alex, seeing Gil look puzzled, explained. 'You mean revenge for the trouncing Helmandis were given by General Nott and his troops when they avenged the massacre of Elphinstone's army in 1842? They must have long memories.'

'Like elephants, Alex! The villagers are already talking about avenging a defeat that took place over a century ago. This is my country, what to do! But I've said enough, gentlemen, you both look tired after your adventures. Let me call the vehicle. I will be in touch with you later.'

Dr Faizal stood up, made a brief call on his mobile, and ushered Alex and Gil down the sweeping staircase to the front door, where a new blue Mercedes SUV stood in the drive, its engine already purring.

After saying their goodbyes, the two men climbed into the rear seat, the front ones already occupied by the driver and a man dressed in a faded pinstripe suit with a black and white chequered cloth wrapped round his head and an AK-47 cradled between his legs.

They watched through the vehicle's rear window as it swept through the gates, the stone eagle quickly receding as they drove at a fast pace through the city's darkened streets.

TWENTY-EIGHT

THE HOMECOMING, IN FORT HOOD, TEXAS,
Saturday 5 November 2005

C aptain Stan Bukowski of the military police recalled two memories as he waited for the troop transporter from Kabul to land at Fort Hood. The first was the spectre of the Vietnam war and the corpses in body bags used to smuggle heroin into the States by US military personnel back in the sixties.

The second was more recent; his visit to Afghanistan as an external investigator into the alleged suicide of twenty-four-year-old US Army Specialist Diego Lopez at Bagram airbase. According to the army report, Lopez was found in a shower area with a self-inflicted gunshot wound to the head. In the few days before his death, however, he had phoned his parents and fiancée back in Dallas sounding upbeat and excited about his return after a year on duty in Afghanistan.

His father recounted how his son told him over the phone, '*Dad, there are so many drugs here. I tell my colleagues, "Don't use these drugs" but they don't listen.*' Lopez was in good health, had a new job waiting for him back in Texas and was making plans for his wedding in August. Why would he commit suicide?

Some military colleagues told his family there had been a cover-up. The army retained the suicide note allegedly found at the scene, as well as the weapon, pending completion of an investigation. The Pentagon initially told the family their son died of non-combat related injuries but released no details. A soldier who had been at Bagram reported drugs were rampant at the base. He'd witnessed drug sales taking place in a room where there were large piles of dollar bills on the table.

Stan discovered other soldiers were afraid for their lives if they talked about the incident, with witnesses ordered to burn much of Lopez's personnel belongings. There were reports of his rifle being sent to Fort Hood instead of being retained at Bagram for the inquiry.

After a month's investigation, and with little cooperation from the Bagram authorities, Stan Bukowski flew home to Texas and Fort Hood, frustrated and disillusioned by the wall of silence he'd met. It wasn't the first time. When he'd investigated a prostitution racket at Fort Hood, an army sergeant pimping cash-strapped female soldiers under his command to higher-ups, he knew the base authorities didn't want it uncovered.

Now he stood with two colleagues on the edge of Fort Hood's runway as the plane landed, disgorging its cargo of

130 soldiers who then proceeded to march across Cooper Field to the sounds of AC/DC's 'Thunderstruck'. The brigade command team then uncased the unit's colours, signifying the headquarters' return from a one-year mission in Afghanistan before unleashing the soldiers into the welcoming arms of their families.

Also standing at the side of the runway, seven-year-old Timmy Collins only had one thought in his mind. He would see his daddy after a whole year. It had seemed an eternity for such a small boy. Nobody to shoot hoops with in the yard except his younger sister Marlene and his friend Bud, who preferred playing with his Gameboy. There were fewer trips to the swimming pool, his mom worked in the base PX and didn't have the time to take him. Now it would be different. Now Daddy was home life would return to normal.

As he excitedly watched the marching soldiers, Timmy spotted his daddy on the outside left of the second row. Abruptly the soldiers stopped, a signal was given and they all rushed towards their waiting families. Joy, tears, laughter, excitement flowed. It was an emotional moment.

But Timmy's embrace with his father was to be short-lived. As the family stood hugging each other a stern voice broke up their long-awaited reunion: 'Sergeant Collins, come with me. Bring your kit bag.'

The tall MP Captain approaching them appeared unexpectedly serious on such a joyous occasion. Timmy was disappointed his daddy had to go with this man, even for a second – and his daddy looked none too pleased either.

'Is there a problem, Captain?'

'It's routine, Collins. Please follow me.'

Telling his family he would be with them soon, Frank Collins followed the captain to the MP station at the side of the airfield. As they walked, he noticed his buddy Chuck Northwood being led to a different part of the building by another MP.

'Okay, Collins, empty the kit bag on the table.' The command was brusque and without any of the bonhomie expected by a fellow soldier returning from a theatre of war. The bag was soon emptied, its contents strewn across the worn grey plastic table.

'What's this?' demanded the captain in a grim voice while holding up an object tightly wrapped in brown paper.

'Whoah! Never seen it before,' was the reply. Frank was genuinely surprised by the package the captain was holding. As the package was opened, it revealed a papier mache box with an intricately designed pattern covering the lid.

Opening the box Captain Bukowski withdrew a packet sealed in fine white cloth stamped with the emblem of a flying bird, some type of hawk. After he carefully unwrapped it, only Frank stood there in sheer amazement at its contents. The block of compressed off-white powder it revealed.

'What the fuck?!'

'Well, we know what this is, don't we, Collins? It's motherfuckers like you that give the military a bad name. Consider yourself under arrest.'

As he was led away, Frank Collins knew for sure.

Somehow it had to be that little bastard in Bagram. Who else could it have been? But how… how…? The block of heroin gave off a pinkish sheen in the light of the guard house as the MP and his prisoner exited the room.

TWENTY-NINE

THE HEARTBREAK HOTEL, IN KABUL,
Sunday 6 November 2005

'*Tri rudan a thig gun iarraidh an t-eagal, an t'-eudach 's an gaol.*'

'What are you talking about, Gil?' Alex sounded exasperated.

'It's an old Gaelic saying my grandfather used to quote. Means three things that come without asking – fear, love and jealousy. I'm wondering when the jealousy's going to kick in.'

Sitting in the coffee shop on the third floor of the newly opened Safi Landmark Hotel, they watched the cold rain battering against the picture window. The city's roads were quickly morphing into muddy tracks. Rubbish and other debris floated down the rapidly filling gullies that lined Kabul's streets.

People walked past with hunched shoulders, the bottoms of their burqas and shalwar kameez spattered with brown mud. Passing vehicles sprayed dirty water, compounding their misery. The slow descent into winter had begun.

Sipping cups of weak coffee, they took in the glitzy opulence of Kabul's latest testament to attempted modernity, an elite hotel with nine floors, a shopping mall and the city's only escalator. Three laughing youths incessantly rode up and down, wishing they were permitted to ride the see-through elevators that would whiz them up to the ninth floor with its panoramic views over the city. Gil could only think that while the hotel's expanse of windows were supposedly made of explosive-resistant glass they were unlikely to survive even a medium earthquake. Yet another heartbreak hotel in Kabul.

Perfume, Breitling watches, Apple iPods and flat-screen televisions were all for sale in the brightly lit shops. The recently opened Beko store sold imported refrigerators, dishwashers and ovens, affordable to only a few of the city's inhabitants. Most had little money and no hope of any power supply. Generators constituted a major buy for those who could afford them and a profitable business for those who sold them.

'It's been tough the last few days.' Alex broke the silence as he stretched his legs and took a bite of the soggy chocolate éclair accompanying the coffee. 'How're you feeling after your trip to Dubai, Gil?'

'A bit rough. I'm really tired out, but it was tougher for you than me. I wasn't held hostage in a heroin factory.'

'At least I didn't have to fly to Dubai!' Alex gave a grin. 'Never liked the place – too smooth, too sterile. Being in the factory wasn't so bad after the commander found I could speak Pashto. Then he became friendlier. I was given mutton stew with naan bread and slept reasonably well on an old *toshack* in one of the huts. You just never know in such circumstances how it will turn out.'

Gil sat on the edge of the chair his coffee finished. Sensing a trace of anxiety in Alex's words, he responded. 'I know. I couldn't get to sleep last night – my heart kept racing. I feel drained as well as exhilarated which is weird.'

'Danger can affect you that way.'

'Maybe, but it was too much danger for me. You seem so cool in these situations.'

Alex raised his eyebrows and popped the last bite of éclair into his mouth. 'The thread of fear is never far away, Gil.'

'You never seem to show it?'

'I feel it, don't underestimate that, but here you don't show it, you don't react. I was scared during the ride to the factory – who knows where we might have ended up when the blindfolds came off? Life in Afghanistan is never predictable. You have to be ready for anything. To show fear is to be vulnerable and we're all vulnerable enough already.'

'True, I guess.'

'The lingering apprehension that comes with anxiety, all too present here, can soon turn to fear when you're faced with a threat. That's how it was for me when we were blindfolded and bundled into the vehicle. With fear the danger is always real and immediate.'

'It's like when I was in that earthquake in Pakistan two

227

years ago,' Gil reminisced. 'There's nothing to hold on to when the earth starts shaking. No security, no insurance, no guarantee of survival. And the disturbing thing is when the earth stops shaking you're still vibrating like a half-set jelly.'

'Listen, the whole world will be shaking soon. Fear is the currency of the terrorist. Al-Qaeda did it for New York four years ago and then there was Madrid last year. Their protégés will do it for Paris, London, Rome, Brussels, Moscow, wherever. It's only a matter of time. When we fought guerrillas in South America it was called the war of the flea. This is the same. You can't stop them because you can't see them. You have to deal with the fear and not let it affect you.'

'Easy to say if it's not one of yours killed or maimed. I could only think about my kids when I was in that heroin factory. A missing mother and a father fool enough to risk getting himself killed. I've had more than enough the last few weeks. I've decided to take extended leave over the Christmas period. Except for Mena, I wouldn't bother coming back. Maybe I'll try and find a duty station where I can take the kids, but I can't leave here until I find out who killed Waheed.'

'You need to leave it, Gil, let Mirwais take care of it.'

'Problem is I'm still involved because this multi-million project Olivier has agreed to fund is on the same land where Mirwais and his consortium want to build their factory.'

'Are you sure, how did you find that out?'

'I looked at the agency proposal in more detail. When I spoke with Olivier on the phone I was in a hurry and it seemed fine without completing a proper check. Now I can't pass the project and Olivier is upset. So, I have to take this forward and help Mirwais any way I can. Dr Faizal wants me to accompany him on a visit to the land and I said I'd go. There's no problem with the agency giving permission as it's the same land this new project intends to develop.'

'You'd be better forgetting it, Gil. Mirwais doesn't need your help anymore. He's quite capable of dealing with this himself. Better just take your break as soon as you can. You need it.'

'Okay, but you've been a policeman, this is new for me. You live here. You've no family responsibilities. None of this seems to have fazed you,' Gil retorted.

Alex recognised what Gil was saying and could see the strained look on his friend's face. He made a quick decision. This was not the time to tell him that when he returned home from the heroin factory he found Larry had disappeared – and taken Alex's gun with him.

THIRTY

AT THE INDIAN RESTAURANT, IN KABUL,
Sunday 6 November 2005

The Kabul valley and the city held in its bosom had witnessed many auspicious meetings over the centuries. They could only be imagined. Alexander the Great, Tamerlane, Genghis Khan, Babar, Mullah Omar, perhaps Bin Laden himself, had all held court in the valley, planning and plotting before making peace with their enemies or unsheathing their weapons of war.

But the meeting that was about to take place in a small Indian restaurant was more than auspicious. Charlotte was fed up. She'd met with Mohammad accompanied by his sister on two occasions but had yet to elicit any response from him. Only the return of his daughter Sima would enable him to break out of such abject misery. To console herself she decided to go out for dinner.

No one was available to accompany her. She'd tried Mena and Gil but neither was answering their phone so she would go alone. She was not averse to visiting restaurants on her own, or art galleries or cinemas or theatres for that matter. An interesting book was all she needed, as well as good food, and there was always the chance she might run into someone interesting.

Tonight was going to provide that chance, although she didn't know this yet as she perused the menu and sipped at the recently delivered glass of ice-free Coca-Cola.

Looking round the restaurant, her attention was drawn to a young man sitting alone at a corner table. Wearing a dark-coloured shalwar kameez, his green woollen bobble hat was pulled down over his forehead. Way down. It was strange to be wearing a hat in a restaurant, even in Kabul. Why didn't he take it off? He obviously wasn't an Afghan.

Beneath the hat bright eyes danced briefly in her direction. Was the man high on something? He certainly looked it. Immediately this alerted her to her own presence. Having taken a moddy at lunchtime, as well as a quick drag of hashish before leaving the guesthouse, her own eyes probably appeared as unnaturally bright as his.

Remembering the first time she'd taken modafinil, she placed her hand in her jacket pocket to check the blister strip was still there. She'd brought a three-month supply from Australia, not trusting the drug would be available in a region notorious for its counterfeit pharmaceuticals.

As a responsible drug taker, she carefully checked out any drug before using it. Modafinil was a eugeroic, 'a wakefulness-promoting drug', to be technical about it, approved by the United States Food and Drug Administration for the treatment of narcolepsy, shift work and sleep disorders. However, this gave little clue to the drug's true capability, already recognised by the military.

If moddies helped her to feel alive in her own skin and cope with work better, then why not? There were no side effects, only the occasional headache and a thirst easily quenched with water. For her it was simply a cognitive enhancer, one of a rapidly growing set of new smart drugs.

Anyway, if it was good enough for the military it was good enough for her. She saw herself as part of a civilian army helping to right the wrongs of fragmented impoverished countries like Afghanistan. If moddies could be given to French troops during covert operations to counter sleep deprivation, as well as to US pilots in charge of multi-million fighter jets, they were okay by her. She was only in charge of a stethoscope and a pen, not a death-dealing machine.

Was that group of men on the far side of the room staring at her, their table strewn with empty bottles? Quickly she opened her book and began to read, now becoming self-conscious she might be drawing attention to herself, although the three other tables of diners appeared to have little interest in her or the young man's eyes.

A table of NGO workers laughed and joked their way through a meal of mutton biryani. At another table four men sat hunched together in deep conversation over a faded red and white checked tablecloth and pile of empty plates. A half-empty bottle of JW Black Label and four glasses sat on the cloth. Three fuller versions of the bottle were perched on the bare shelf above the restaurant's rickety bar.

'Excuse me, would you mind if I join you?' Charlotte found herself staring into those dancing eyes. She was mesmerised. The young man leaning over the table did not feel at all threatening; in fact she felt immediately at ease and drawn to him in some strange way.

'Eh… no… I'm just about to order. Okay, yes, do please join me. I'm Charlotte, by the way.'

'Thanks, Charlotte. Let me get my drink.'

Charlotte watched as the young man returned to his table and collected his drink, the hat still pulled tightly down over his forehead amplifying the intensity of his gaze, and walked back towards her table with a steady gait.

Drawing up the chair opposite, he sat down and introduced himself. 'I'm Larry, good to meet you. I don't know many people in Kabul, not been here that long.'

It was a great opening line, never mind an understatement for a deserter on the run from the US army, never mind someone being hunted for a double killing. But this was a secure place. US military police were unlikely to be eating in Kabul restaurants on a Sunday evening and it was even more unlikely they would recognise him if they did.

This was not the most popular Indian restaurant in Kabul, although its food was freshly prepared and usually tasty. Tablecloths displayed the stains from previous customers, the cutlery had to be cleaned on a napkin before use and the lighting was low wattage, giving the place a dingy appearance not helped by the grubby maroon flock wallpaper.

Larry, however, was oblivious to his immediate

surroundings. He liked to play the odds, even though his 'gift' sometimes made this impossible. This was how it had been with the two civilian contractors in the village outside Qandahar, an action guided by unseen forces with no thought or intent involved. All bets were off. In this respect he felt at home in Afghanistan, where spirits still roamed the land holding cultural sway over many. Sitting here with this woman he could already feel the vibrations.

'You're looking for someone, aren't you?' The question took Charlotte by surprise.

'I don't think so – I'm not expecting anyone,' she replied tersely.

'Then someone you know maybe, somebody else searching for someone?'

'Yes!' she started, a surprised look on her face. 'I do know someone. He's searching for his daughter, but he'll never find her.'

'Perhaps that's not the case.'

'Of course it is!' she replied with some exasperation. 'The girl was taken by men who killed her mother and two brothers. She could be anywhere. She's most likely dead. Her father is desolate.'

'I can imagine.' The eyes staring at her were weighted with compassion.

'How could you possibly help?'

'I have a gift, Charlotte, one passed down to me by my grandmother.'

'A gift? What do you mean, a gift?'

'It's difficult to explain – it's a type of sixth sense, that's the best way to describe it.'

Larry then confided in Charlotte in a way he'd never done with anyone before. It felt liberating, although he knew he was betraying his grandmother's trust. Certainly there was no reason why he should confide in this young woman, even if she appeared strangely familiar.

For her part, Charlotte could sympathise with the killings of the contractors and the hurried journey to Kabul, with being a fugitive in a land full of displaced people. The story of the box and the button and its connection with the Elvis figure, however, lay well outside her medically trained mind. Better to say nothing and let the young man continue. She was so fascinated by him she'd forgotten to order her food despite the waiter hovering in the background, notepad and pen at the ready.

It was only when Larry, with some reluctance it must be said, took the box out of his pocket and produced the button that an inkling of understanding appeared. She was surprised by her reaction as she stared at its faded green cloth. For some reason the button made her think of her father – in a much more vivid manner than she would have wished.

He'd known how to press her buttons more than her mother ever could, but then he had inserted them in the first place. For that she could never forgive him. She had been a daddy's girl despite his drinking and dark moods, her mother's withdrawn and depressed existence denying the development of any strong mother-daughter relationship.

Looking at the little box held in Larry's hand, she thought she could see the button pulsing. It was the weirdest thing.

'Don't let science blind you, Charlotte – scientists can't explain all the mysteries of life. They already study what is referred to as the paranormal. Many people are born with a gift, a talent, call it what you want – for music, sport, mathematics – so why not a talent for being able to access the paranormal world, other levels of reality? There are invisible currents that guide us all.' Despite her misgivings, Charlotte sat transfixed.

'When we were deployed in Helmand, two of my platoon were on night watch wearing night vision goggles when they saw what appeared to be a tall man at the perimeter fence. As they scanned him he turned to look at them. His eyes appeared so bright, like neon-red blood, they claimed their night vision started to burn out. One trained his machine gun on the man and its infra-red thermal imager also burned out, the man's body appearing black on the imager which meant the body was stone cold – dead. Then the figure turned, walked off and was gone.

'Talking with guys from other units we found they had similar experiences in different parts of the country, seeing strange dark shapes hardly visible on their goggles yet with eyes that blew out thermal imagers and bodies that showed up cold. They called them wraiths. It certainly spooked them.'

Charlotte was sceptical, finding the story hard to believe. 'It was most probably due to stress or sleep deprivation,' she retorted.

'Maybe you're right. The military would have put it down to combat fatigue so nobody even reported these sightings. Some guys rationalised them by saying it was an experimental SEAL unit testing new field equipment.'

Charlotte wanted to assuage Larry while still doubting him. 'I do know strange things happen here. A colleague in the agency told me about one of the assistants who claimed there was a spirit in their house that kept starting fires in his sister's room. They invited a mullah to come in and help them.'

Charlotte could add little else to the conversation.

'It's not uncommon here,' Larry quickly replied. 'Empyreal creatures are said to abound. Fire spirits, or djinns as they call them, are the commonest. Many Muslims believe in a world of demons, as well as saints and miracles. Sufism, the spiritual side of Islam, is suppressed by the Salafist Taliban, but there are still many Sufi shrines in Afghanistan visited for blessings and the possibility of miracles. Who can blame them in this war-torn land?'

'I believe you, Larry, but it'll take a miracle for Mohammad to ever find his daughter, assuming she's still alive, of course.'

'I'm sure she is alive, Charlotte. I can't promise you any miracles. I sense the girl is in Kabul in an area near a mosque. I can feel it.'

Charlotte didn't doubt Larry's sincerity. His eyes held the fire of conviction yet it sounded so implausible. Apart from anything else, there were too many mosques in Kabul to investigate them all.

'Look, Larry, I'm a doctor, I don't believe in angels and demons. It sounds like fantasy to me, but I'm willing to give it a try. Can we start to look for her as soon as possible, please?'

'Sure. Why don't we start tomorrow? But can we eat now, please? I'm starving.'

Sitting back, they smiled at each other and called the waiter over.

THIRTY-ONE

AT THE LANDS, IN EAST KABUL,
Monday 7 November 2005

I t was early afternoon, a quiet time on Kabul's roads. The blue SUV stopped at the house, picked up Gil, then made its way along Nangarhar Road before turning left at the exit leading to Camp Phoenix. In early 2003 the camp was nothing but a junkyard full of scrap metal left from an abandoned tractor trailer park.

When the US military arrived in Kabul they needed a large area to house their soldiers so decided it would be the perfect location and leased an old junkyard from an Afghan trucking company. Within two weeks, a record time for the engineers to set up operations, the junkyard metamorphosed into a military training camp with a dining facility, medic tent, showers, latrines and living quarters.

Soon the camp was at maximum capacity, quickly filled with more than three hundred 10th Mountain soldiers ready to train the new Afghan National Army. Thanks to Kellog, Brown and Root the new arrivals now had hot chow, hot showers and flush toilets from the first night they arrived.

Sweeping past the camp to the Russia Road leading north towards Bagram, Gil wondered if he'd made the right decision in accepting Dr Faizal's offer of a visit to the consortium's proposed factory site. He wished Alex had been able to accompany them, but he was meeting with a hakim and would join them later if time permitted.

Looking out the vehicle's window, Gil could see the area consisted mostly of old industrial sites, some evidently more industrious than others that appeared completely abandoned. In between lay clusters of small mud- and brick-built houses, smoke curling from their roofs. A few ragged children played in the street and a group of old men sat outside on a rickety bench chatting and drinking tea.

'You see, Mr Gil, how the Americans can quickly develop a piece of land if they want to – but only for military purposes. It will return to dust when they leave.' Dr Faizal sat relaxed in the back seat. Gil, sitting next to him, looked out on an area of the city he'd never visited before.

'What about your land, is it near here?'

'It is a few kilometres to the north-east, a vast area we are determined will be used productively. There are people living on it, squatters displaced from the north. They have been told it will be developed soon and can stay if they wish. They already agreed to pay a nominal rent for our new houses.'

After some time negotiating the rutted potholed streets,

they turned right past a small newly built mosque standing on its own, isolated from the rest of the world.

'Soon there will be many houses here and they will build a bigger mosque. Our workers will come for prayers. It will become a community.'

'Who built the mosque?' Gil enquired.

'Engineer Shafeeq arranged for the building, the consortium paid. It is our article of faith. Look, beyond the mosque you can see our stretch of land. We are to the east of District 9 on the outskirts of the city. We will build shops, mosques, healthcare facilities, a school, not only a factory and houses. We are making a new town here, Mr Gil.'

'This sounds very ambitious, Dr Faizal. How long will it take?'

'Mirwais is impatient and is keen to start work as soon as possible, especially after the brutal killing of Waheed. We are almost ready. We only need final approval from the ministry, now possible thanks to the title deeds you brought back from Dubai.'

'Glad to have been of help,' Gil responded, hoping he didn't sound too cynical about his own enforced contribution to the enterprise.

'You can see the extent of the land. It stretches right up to the foothills of Tur Ghunday.' Gil looked at the ragged barren hills that lay a good distance from where they were parked.

'Oh, Mr Gil, I forgot to mention, if you permit me I would like to make a detour on our return, to the wholesale pharmaceutical market in Khair Kana. You will see the extent of the trade. Mr Alex can join us if he wishes.'

'That's fine as long as I'm back at the house by early evening. We have a meeting with the JDL director – he arrived from London this morning.'

Gil was intrigued to see the more legal side of Afghanistan's drug trade and settled back in the rear seat next to Dr Faizal as the driver turned left onto the Taimani Road. There was no gunman accompanying them this time, though he suspected there would be a weapon somewhere in the vehicle. He was not to be disappointed.

Nearing a more populated area of the city where the roads were less potholed, Gil could see looming in the distance a strip of red lying stretched across the road. As they drew closer he realised it was a large carpet rolled out on the muddy surface.

'Stop!' he exclaimed. 'We're going to drive over that carpet.'

Dr Faizal laughed. 'They want us to drive over it.'

'But it's filthy, it's being destroyed.'

'Don't worry. They will wash and brush it until it looks like a hundred-year-old carpet still in good condition. Then it will be taken down to one of the antique shops in Chicken Street where it will fetch many times what it cost to weave. It was made in the nearby Turkmen area, back-breaking work for the women and children made easier by taking small balls of opium with their tea. Most will become addicted, whole families even. Do you know…'

Dr Faizal suddenly broke off his spiel and reached into the rear pocket of the front seat, his hand returning with a gun he laid in his lap. It was a SIG SAUER 1911 Stainless. While Gil knew little about guns, he recognised this one, even with a cursory glance. On his previous posting Franz, one of the German police officers sent to train the Afghan Police, was proud to show him his SIG during a tour of the new training college part-funded through the UN.

'*It is an excellent handgun, accurate and reliable, has a hand-fitted custom wood grip, holds eight rounds and one in the chamber. Beautiful gun! You want to try it?*' Franz had asked him.

While Gil hadn't handled a gun since his father's .22 rifle used to keep marauding pigeons off the garden, it was best to humour Franz, so they headed to the college range. It was the first time he'd held a handgun and could see and feel the craftsmanship invested in the weapon. He had become familiar with the SIG, firing off more than fifty rounds at cardboard cut-outs of human targets.

'Do not look round, Mr Gil, we are being followed. There is a black SUV with darkened windows three vehicles behind us. It has been tailing us since the Nangarhar Road.' The anxiety was all too apparent in Dr Faizal's voice.

Gil realised one of the two rear-view mirrors attached to the windscreen was not for the driver but positioned so the back-seat passenger could see the road behind. He gave a long sigh, his breath coming out between tightened lips, a deep sense of uneasiness re-establishing itself.

'It is moving closer to us, slowly passing each vehicle. It may just be monitoring our movements or has something else in mind. Please be ready. Crouch down on the floor when I tell you.'

Gil was instantly alert. He could already feel himself sinking deeper into the seat.

'It is speeding up and passing the car behind us. Now is the time.'

As Gil made to crouch on the floor, he heard blaring motor horns and glimpsed bright lights speeding towards them. In the next moment their vehicle swerved violently off the side of the road.

'It is an American military convoy!' Dr Faizal exclaimed. 'They move through the city at speed for fear of ambush. People hate them for it, forcing vehicles and pedestrians off the road in our city, but we are in luck.'

Barking an order to the driver to speed up once the Americans passed, he turned to Gil. 'The car behind is blocking the SUV – if we move fast we will escape the tail.'

After a few minutes Dr Faizal put the gun away and breathed deeply.

'Whatever they were after it signals bad news for us, Mr Gil. Maybe a kidnap attempt or worse. I will inform Mirwais. For now we are safe.'

For the moment, thought Gil, *but who was the intended target, the doctor or me?*

THIRTY-TWO

THE PHARMACEUTICALS MARKET, IN KABUL,
Monday 7 November 2005

The wholesale pharmaceuticals market was situated to the north of the city in the Khair Khana district with over one hundred traders housed in multi-storey blocks of shops built around small courtyards. Shops crammed with boxes full of medicines as well as a wide range of disability equipment, rows and rows of wheelchairs, crutches and prosthetic limbs of all shapes and sizes.

'We are approaching the complex. You can see the buildings.' Dr Faizal turned and smiled at Gil and Alex, who had joined them after completing his business with the hakim. They had picked him up on a street near the complex where traffic was lighter.

Until now there had been little chance for him to speak to Gil who sat staring out of the back-seat window.

It was disquieting for Alex to see him so withdrawn.

As the car drew to a halt in one of the larger courtyards Dr Faizal waved to a man walking towards them. 'It is my friend Dr Abdul – he will show us around.'

With that, Dr Faizal quickly jumped out of the vehicle, affording Alex the opportunity to ask Gil what was wrong. Something was amiss; it was all too plainly written on his friend's face.

While the two doctors were wrapped up in their greeting, Gil gave Alex a brief if rambling account of their recent encounter. 'It all happened so fast. I thought we were going to be killed… Images of Waheed and the Land Cruiser flashed through my mind. Even Dr Faizal appeared flustered. We were lucky… The American vehicles came through so fast. We got away… It's the not knowing. Were they just tailing us or were they going to attack? Jesus, Alex, were they after me or the doctor or both of us? Who the hell knows? I feel like I'm going out of my mind.'

Before Alex could reply, Dr Faizal ushered them out of the vehicle and introduced them to a small man with a beaming face who was standing almost at attention, shoulders pulled back and chest puffed out.

'This is my friend Dr Abdul. He has also returned from Germany where he owns a chain of pharmacies. Now he is a consultant to our consortium. He knows the industry here better than anybody.'

Wearing a smart grey suit with gleaming white shirt and lightly patterned blue tie, Dr Abdul's neatly trimmed beard matched carefully coiffured hair receding from a round smiling face. Dapper was the word that came into

Alex's mind as the doctor gave a small bow and introduced himself

'Welcome! Welcome! I hear you have already had a tour of one of our illegal drug factories, but we have no factory – yet – for legal drugs. Insha'Allah this will come soon thanks to Dr Faizal and his team.'

The doctor laughed. 'Mind you, many of the pharmaceutical drugs you see here are illegal. We estimate up to eighty per cent are smuggled into the country. Many are fake, adulterated, expired even, yet they are still traded. What else to do? There is little regulation. Competition between traders is fierce. The wholesalers in the compound complain smuggled tax-free drugs increase supply, push prices down and reduce their profit margin. This is a lucrative business. People battle for market share. There is good profit to be made but of course nothing to compare with the tears of the poppy and its white powder.

'Let me briefly show you the prosthetics warehouse. It is a tragedy. There are over five hundred square kilometres of our country still contaminated with millions of land mines and unexploded ordinance. We live in a big minefield. Over eighty per cent of our amputees are land mine survivors. Each will need up to twenty prosthetic limbs over their lifetime. You will see on the streets many amputees with old prosthetics and home-made crutches. We cannot meet the demand. People cannot afford modern state-of-the-art prosthetics even if they were available.'

A darker mood settled on Dr Abdul; the round face losing its smile.

'Most tragic are the children who lost hands because

the accursed Soviets dropped millions of butterfly bombs from helicopters, bombs designed to flutter to the ground without exploding so naturally our innocent children thought they were toys and picked them up. Then the wing of the butterfly filled with liquid explosive would ignite and explode, severing hands. This was cruelty beyond measure. Curse the infidel Soviets.' Dr Abdul abruptly turned and walked them further into the compound.

After perusing a stacked array of crutches, antique wheelchairs and rows of prosthetic legs made of faded plastic they came to one of the larger shops trading in pharmaceutical drugs.

Gil and Alex were met with the sight of a small boy perched on the highest rung of a tall ladder trying to extract a box from the top shelf. He remained bent over otherwise his head would have hit the ceiling. As the ladder wobbled precariously, the boy looked down and grinned at them before losing his footing and toppling onto a lower shelf crammed with boxes filled with a wide range of drugs.

'This is a good shop for you to visit,' Dr Abdul said, ignoring the boy who was still grinning, a large purple bruise already forming on his forehead that he rubbed with his one hand, 'because as you see it stocks many psychoactive drugs, the analgesics, anti-depressants and the benzodiazepine tranquilisers people want. You can see the many "pams" and "lams" in stock.'

Gil looked quizzical. Alex looked at the boxes labelled alprazolam, clonazepam, diazepam, lorazepam, oxazepam. The list was endless. He recognised the more common ones by their brand names: Valium, Librium, Ativan, Xanax.

Turning to Dr Abdul he was prompted to say, 'I've come from a meeting with a hakim friend of mine – he tells me the more unscrupulous hakims are now selling their traditional medicines in soft capsules as if they were modern drugs. He said some are increasingly adding tranquilisers and painkillers to their traditional preparations.'

Dr Abdul quickly replied, 'Yes, you are correct. Unfortunately the boundaries are blurring. Hakims have used opium and cannabis in their medicines for centuries. They recognise the healing powers of these plants if used correctly. Now anything that will increase profit is added and these pharmaceuticals are powerful drugs. The people like them but are unaware of their dangers.'

After looking round the shop for a while and then enduring yet another cup of green tea, this time with sugared almonds rather than biscuits, they said goodbye to Dr Abdul and the drug compound.

Back in the car Dr Faizal appeared happy. 'You can see, gentlemen, there is a need for a proper approach to these drugs. Our factory will be the beginning. We will legalise and regulate this trade.'

While Gil didn't doubt Dr Faizal's good intentions, he didn't want to keep talking about drugs. His only interest now was to imbibe some himself. He could still feel his heart racing. 'Thank you for the visit, Dr Faizal, it was interesting. Perhaps you could drop us near the Iranian embassy?'

Round the corner from the embassy and up a lane squashed between the Chinese embassy and the main UNDP compound lay the Elbow Room Bar and Restaurant. This was where Gil wanted to be: a friendly familiar environment. He badly needed a forbidden libation himself. A Valium from the blister pack he kept in his pocket washed down with a couple of strong cocktails. That would surely do the trick and induce some peace into his life, at least temporarily.

THIRTY-THREE

AT THE MADRASSAH, IN KABUL,
Monday 7 November 2005

The madrassah lay on a side street in the densely packed neighbourhood of Shar-e-barq a few hundred metres from the Id Gah Mosque where each year two million people offered their Eid prayers. Kabul's paramount religious mosque, the Id Gah or *Prayer Ground*, was where the faithful congregated during religious and national celebrations.

In 1919 the Emir Habibullah made a speech in the Id Gah urging Afghans to wage jihad against the British. A speech that seemed all too prescient nearly a century later: '*The treacherous and deceitful English Government... twice shamelessly attacked our beloved country and plunged their filthy claws into the region of the vital parts of our dear country which is the burial ground of our ancestors and the abode of the chastity of our mothers and sisters and intended to deprive us of very existence, of the safety of our honour and virtue, of our liberty and happiness,*

251

and of our national dignity and nobility. It became incumbent upon your King to proclaim jehad in the path of God against the perfidious English Government.'

Since that time, signs of modernity had crept in. The large expanse of open ground fronting the Id Gah now functioned as a parking lot for the colourfully decorated jingly trucks transporting goods to and from Pakistan. Opposite lay the Ghazi Stadium, home to the Afghan Football Federation and killing ground of the Taliban regime when public executions and amputations were held in front of large crowds.

Hadji Zarak had chosen the site for the madrassah with care. It provided enough space to open a state-of-the-art building with proper classrooms, library and a hostel, facilities lacking in most of the country's madrassahs. This meant the madrassah was less likely to draw attention from prying government officials. There was no better front for conducting his business than a well-run religious school in a secure location right in the heart of Kabul city.

Foreign troops often targeted madrassahs, suspicious they were supporters of extremism which meant neither the Afghan government nor local worthies wanted to be seen openly supporting them. On the surface there was nothing to hide in the hadji's madrassah, no cache of weapons, no extremist views. He had gone out of his way to ensure it was a venture in line with the latest government policy.

He knew the failing of madrassahs was not in what they taught but in what they did not. If the mullah was literate, and not many were, then learning was limited to reading and writing in the local language plus elementary Arabic necessary for basic memorisation of the Koran and Hadith. There was little room for subjects like science, mathematics or history, never mind the study of *tasawwuf*, the spiritual dimension of Islam.

The hadji's madrassah would provide a more comprehensive education for the boys, not because he cared about them but because it provided a legitimate front for his business. For it was a business after all, one he would dissolve in a few years when the foreign troops left and the country reverted to type. By then he would have made enough money to live in comfort anywhere in the world and have the necessary papers to enable this to happen. He would simply re-invent himself yet again.

Now Hadji Zarak sat in his small office located in a far corner of the madrassah's compound that was entered through a steel plated door – just in case. The small window overlooking the courtyard was double glazed. He did not want to hear the chattering and repetitive chanting of Koranic text by forty young boys in a language neither he nor they understood. A hidden door directly behind the office desk exited onto a narrow side street at the rear of the madrassah. In his line of work it was wise to cover all possible contingencies.

Despite being comfortably and securely entombed in his office the hadji's mind was far from feeling comfortable or secure. The boy Hassan had been a problem since returning from Bagram, becoming even more uncommunicative and withdrawn. How he even ended up in the American prison was still a mystery and appeared to have nothing to do with the hadji's business. There had been no comeback from the authorities.

After an argument with the boy's father over a late, indeed very late, payment, he decided to send the boy to a madrassah in the mountains far to the east of Kabul. If his father wanted to risk returning to Afghanistan to collect him that was his business.

At least that was one problem out of the way. More worrying was Commander Daud, a dangerous man at the best of times, who wanted more money than agreed for his last heroin shipment, claiming it was over ninety per cent pure. The hadji was all too aware Daud had a comparative advantage among the group of drug traffickers utilising his services – he had many guns at his disposal and much political influence.

Even this problem with Daud was solvable compared with Mirwais, his old adversary and now possessor of the deeds that threatened to jeopardise the hadji's plans for the land deal funded and legitimised through the UN, with his cousin's NGO as the primary implementing partner.

The hadji gave a satisfied smile. That he was still alive and well was down to his abilities as an economic opportunist and survival strategist. He understood the necessity of diversification and the ability to quickly change appearances in a time of *dar-ul-harb*, the house of war his country had lived in for the past quarter century. He'd made a substantial sum after the Soviets left by selling unused Stinger missiles back to the Americans who provided them to the mujahideen in the first place. It was easy money. He would surely find a way to outwit Mirwais and his remaining partners in their so-called consortium.

When the Taliban took over, Hadji Zarak had allowed his neatly trimmed beard to grow as it wished and traded his tailored shalwar kameez for flowing black robes. He started to wear a large black turban, although it took him some time to learn how to wrap it correctly.

Coming from Qandahar originally, he had enough contacts to be able to slip into the world of the Taliban with relative ease. As an educated man he was able to quickly develop a role as translator and scribe but kept a low profile. You never knew when it might be necessary to re-invent yourself. After the Taliban were removed from government he, like many others, simply trimmed his beard, took off the turban and changed into less obvious garb.

Now to the outside world he was a hawaladar, a link in the global hawala system that helped to facilitate the anonymous transfer of wealth from country to country, frequently necessitating money laundering and tax evasion. His particular speciality in the system consisted of transferring and receiving money for large international drug transactions, except that in hawala cash rarely changed hands.

Also used for legitimate purposes, hawala enabled the transfer of funds based on trust and an honour system as well as personal connections, family relations and regional affiliations. The settlement of debts between hawala dealers often came in the form of goods, services, properties and other non-monetary means.

This was at the nub of the hadji's problem with Commander Daud. The commander's last shipment of heroin was paid for by a Turkish trafficker in the form of a new-build house in Dubai. Now Daud wanted more for the heroin but the house deal had already been finalised, meaning the hadji would have to forego his considerable transaction fee, something he was not happy about. The added problem was Daud also expected a cash-in-hand supplement for the shipment and most of the hadji's money was safely tucked up in a bank vault in Dubai.

As the hadji felt a headache coming on, rubbing his temples with slow circular movements to alleviate the pain, there was a knock on the office door. Recognising the coded *tap-tap-taptaptap-tap* as one of the guards, he eased himself off his chair and opened the door. It was Majeed, a new guard, gun hanging at his side, a quizzical expression on his lined face.

'Hadji, there are two *kharaji* here. One is an American and the other a woman. They want to speak with you. What should I tell them?'

Charlotte stood nervously at the gate of the madrassah, aware the guard was staring at her. His dark kohl-lined eyes held no interest in Larry, who appeared as relaxed as he'd been the previous evening. After leaving the restaurant they had spent the night together in Charlotte's guesthouse. It was easy to smuggle him in through the back gate. She knew where the key was kept and twenty dollars to each of the guards ensured their cooperation.

Never had two people needed each other more, even if only for one night. Charlotte was experiencing a depth of feeling for Larry she'd never experienced with any other man. It was the peace he seemed to engender in her as if their hearts were merged in some mysterious way.

But now the gate was opening and the other younger guard was ushering them into the compound. A sea of boys kicked a football about in a small courtyard with a small green tree growing in its centre. It was a chaos that came to an abrupt end as the boys stood and gaped at them, recognising that one of the *kharajis* was a woman.

Shouting obscenities at the boys, who quickly moved off to their classroom, the guard led Larry and Charlotte across the yard and along a broad corridor lined with rooms on either side to an imposing door lying slightly ajar. As the door opened wider, they were confronted with one of the biggest men Charlotte had ever seen. Well over six feet, his girth was almost the same. Eyes too closely set together fitted well into a face too small for its owner's frame. Placing a bulbous hand over his heart, the man said in impeccable English, '*Salaam aleikum.* I am Hadji Zarak, welcome to my madrassah. You are most welcome.'

Seating his guests on the two comfortable armchairs facing the desk, the hadji slowly returned to his seat, an initial appraisal already formed. The woman constantly fiddled with the ends of her dupatta with a nervous, almost stupid, grin on her face, while the man was as still as the night, only his eyes moved. The hadji had seen the look before. The man reminded him of the old *malang* who told him – in no uncertain terms – he must go on the Haj to Mecca.

A young man at the time, Mohammad Zarak literally bumped into the *malang* on a street corner in Qandahar one

257

winter's day soon after returning home from his accountancy studies in India. The *malang* was dressed in rags and wore open-toed sandals, an old turban wrapped round his head. Several necklaces of what appeared to be ancient beads garlanded his neck. He leant on a long staff carved with strange symbols, none of which Zarak recognised. Such a mystical shaman figure was neither accepted nor respected in Afghan society, although *malangs* were usually left alone to live their secluded and solitary lives.

The transfixing stare the *malang* gave him as he said "You must go on the Haj" left no doubt in his mind he should travel to Mecca, in the same way the look in this young man's eyes left no doubt that what he had to say should be taken seriously.

'You have a girl here.' It was a statement not a question. The hadji was taken aback, the abruptness of the man, the coldness in the dancing eyes. Most importantly, the truth of his words. How could he possibly know? Was this man some type of *malang*! The hadji felt a shiver ripple down his back as his headache intensified. He recognised this was a man of unpredictable power despite the close proximity of the madrassah's armed guards.

There seemed no point in denying it. 'Yes, there is a girl here, you are correct. She was brought in a distressed state by a friend. She works in our kitchen.'

While this was partly true, the hadji had other plans for the girl. She was a slim fine-featured creature, if not beautiful, but too nervous and timid. With her it would take time.

'Do you know her background and the trauma she has

been through?' The *kharaji*'s words were taut, his voice calm yet menacing.

'She has spoken few words since arriving here.'

'She witnessed her mother and two brothers being killed. Her father needs her home. She should return with us.'

The hadji could see the outline of the gun under the man's kameez, although it would be of no use to him here. He knew the man recognised this. It was a situation that could be exploited.

'I cannot simply release the girl to you. She is of value to the madrassah and works hard in our kitchen.'

I bloody well bet she does, Charlotte thought. She was having difficulty in controlling herself and would kill this man herself if given a chance. It was difficult for her to hide her feelings, but Larry had stressed the need to take a calm approach during such a potentially dangerous meeting. She could still feel the eyes of the gate guard stripping her.

'Perhaps we can come to an understanding?' This was said in a placatory voice, the hadji sensing the woman was unstable and ready to flare up at any moment. Her manic grin was now a teeth-clenching grimace, her knuckles white with the tension of clawing at her dupatta.

'If you can do me a small favour you can take the girl, then we will both be happy. There is a man who has something in his possession I need or he will know where to retrieve it. His name is Mr Moncrief and I will give you his address. There should be no problem. He is a *kharaji* like you.'

Hadji Zarak knew where Gil lived; he'd had him

259

followed during the trip to Dubai when he was Mirwais's message boy and again when he returned to Kabul. He knew a lot about Mr Moncrief. What he didn't know was that Larry and Gil had already met each other.

THIRTY-FOUR

THE HOUSE MEETING, IN KABUL,
Tuesday 8 November 2005

Gil was fortunate the meeting with the director had been postponed from the previous evening. Staying too long at the Elbow Room, the three martinis and the Valium still dulled his brain. It was difficult to pay full attention to the supercilious words spilling from the mouth of JDL's principal owner, Justin Edwards.

The Justin Edwards, infamous in the development world as a rising star in the UK's Department for International Development before being poached by the UN Secretariat to take up a high-level post in New York. Then he abruptly resigned and started his own private company that now held several large development contracts in south and central Asia. He was building an empire and was already reputed to be a very rich man. Justin was renowned as a straight talker and a man who brooked no dissent. He certainly wasn't going to be letting the house residents off the hook.

'JDL has three other houses in Kabul and now they're all under suspicion by the authorities. For God's sake, you should have been more vigilant about Brock and his association with this Abdul Qabir. One of you must have noticed something, surely?' The director made it sound as if it was the Afghan to blame for the bootlegging, not the American.

Nobody responded at first. Big William was taking it personally as he had been the closest of the housemates to Brock, but as usual never spoke up. He was too concerned about his future career with JDL. Then Mickey, who knew JDL couldn't afford to lose his expertise and the lucrative IT contract with the British government that came with it, geared up.

'D'you really think Abdul Qabir was the mastermind?! You need to come out here and stay for a while. Get out of yer London office more often. This was Brock exploiting the locals and he's not the only one. There's a few of them at it, bootlegging alcohol to Muslims. Some development work, eh! Mind you, get the Afghans all hyped up on booze and they might start killing each other even more than they do already. That would solve yer problem now, so it would.'

Most of the residents sitting in the lounge lowered their heads, cringing at Mickey's words. Gil noticed Mickey had toned down his usual colourful rhetoric, but his words affected Justin nevertheless. The man looked put out, if not mortified. After all, he was the one who'd interviewed Brock for the post of advisor to the Ministry of Finance.

Sarah looked sharply at Mickey. She was livid but kept silent. Brock had been more than a friend to her, she missed him terribly.

'Look, we managed to cut a deal and get Brock out of the country as quickly – and quietly – as possible. Qabir will be lucky if he's out of jail in five years. You won't be seeing him again. I'm visiting the other JDL houses over the next few days to see if there's any tie in to this alcohol business. If there is we'll likely be asked to leave the country as an example to other agencies.'

The director looked at the glum faces surrounding him. Apart from Gil, nobody wanted to be going home soon.

'There'll still be plenty booze in Kabul,' Mickey chipped in.

'You can buy it from shops in Wazir Akbar Khan, no problem. They're bringing the stuff in from India and Pakistan. Go to Mazar, it's flooded with cheap vodka from Central Asia. What Brock was running was small-scale stuff.'

'It makes no difference, Mickey. I'm only concerned about JDL,' Justin intoned. 'I have to meet with the minister tomorrow to apologise and negotiate our way out of this mess.'

Mickey looked at the director, the contempt evident on his face. 'Ah well, better ask them how Abdul Qabir is doing, eh? We haven't heard about him since his arrest and he's a big family to support.' Mickey's words were not lost on the other house residents, but the director was already gathering his papers in preparation to leave.

Gil was glad the meeting was finishing. After dinner he

just wanted to go to bed and rest; his head still felt fuzzy and his body ached. It was the ring of his mobile that reminded him you can't always get what you want.

It was Alex. 'Gil, we have to go and see Mirwais immediately. There's been a development. Larry has returned. He's made some sort of deal with Hadji Zarak regarding the deeds you brought back from Dubai. It's urgent.'

It was the last thing Gil needed to hear, but he sensed the gravity in his friend's voice. Grabbing a sandwich and shrugging aside his fatigue he donned a jacket and walked to the gate to wait for Alex.

THIRTY-FIVE

IN MACRORAYAN AGAIN, IN KABUL,
Wednesday 9 November 2005

Arriving at Mirwais's apartment as twilight approached, Gil and Alex found it a place of hurried activity. A group of men were carrying furniture, carpets, the TV, pots and pans and other domestic goods down the narrow flight of stairs, blocking their way in the process. Two armed men stood on the small balcony smoking cigarettes. The blue smoke drifted off into the still Kabul evening.

'Ah, *salaam aleikum*, gentlemen. You have come just in time. I am departing Kabul for the village.'

Once again Mirwais welcomed them into his home.

'My health is not so good at the moment and it is too dangerous for me to continue living in this apartment. When I return to Kabul I will stay with Dr Faizal – his house is well protected. He has kindly offered me a suite of rooms and we will continue our business from there.

Now please tell me what is so urgent?'

It was Gil, resolutely sober after Alex had told him about Sima and the possible exchange for the deeds, who explained Hadji Zarak's deal with Larry. As he talked, the expression on Mirwais's face darkened, his brow deepening. There was a tense pause before he responded.

'Zarak is a man without honour. He may appear calm and even convivial, but it is well to remember those who keep themselves most under control can be the most dangerous when they lose it. Make no mistake, he is ruthless and will do anything to further his own ends. We must procure the girl's release. We will give him the deeds as he asks.'

'No, you can't do that, Mirwais!' Gil exclaimed. 'You need them to secure your project. There must be another way. Why not give him a set of fake deeds?'

'It would not work. Zarak is not a stupid man. He would know they were not the originals. Do not be concerned, I will deal with him personally. This moment has been inevitable ever since we were in Peshawar together. It is our destiny, Insha'Allah.'

'I didn't know you knew him all that well?' Gil enquired.

'We go back a long way, Mr Gil, to the 1980s and the jihad against the Soviets. I would regularly go to Peshawar with Waheed to gather weapons to take back to Afghanistan while Zarak stayed there until the Soviets left our country. He was an arms trader, small time certainly, acting as a conduit for American arms to the mujahideen. Later he sold Stinger missiles back to the Americans and made much money. Now he is a money trader here in Kabul.

Money is all he cares about. Unfortunately, even my cousin Daud uses his services.'

Before Gil could respond, Mirwais looked at him with a grim expression and added, 'There is another man who cares only about money you should know about, Mr Gil – your Mr Olivier. He will receive sixty thousand dollars for the land project Zarak is planning. The sub-contractors will receive kickbacks too. It is the way here. All these so-called development projects operate through a chain of sub-contractors. There is little left for the people on the ground. Buildings are substandard, new road surfaces little better than the mud they replace.'

Gil was shaking, anger building on his face. The news about Olivier swept away any lingering remnants of his hangover. He had never taken to the man and the way he locked himself away in his office, his patronising stance with the locals, but this was too much.

'Alex, I need to go and see Olivier, he'll be back at his guesthouse,' Gil spluttered.

'Wait, Gil, you can see him tomorrow. You need to cool down. Anyway, you know he's going to deny everything.'

'I don't care. I need to see him now.'

Mirwais looked stern. 'Mr Alex is right. Be careful, Mr Gil. You need to wait, to plan your strategy. I cannot help you with this. My sole concern is with Zarak.'

Mirwais's words seemed to settle Gil. After all, his job was in strategy development. He knew he had to think hard about how he would proceed with confronting Olivier. It would be difficult to find any concrete evidence of the bribe.

'Please take this, Mr Gil. I have no need for it now.'

Mirwais took the small armless Elvis figure from his kameez and handed it to Gil. 'Unfortunately, it is unlikely we will meet again. It will remind you of us, Mirwais and Waheed, true brothers in arms.'

Gil took the figure from Mirwais's hand as graciously as he could, although he'd come to consider the armless figure a bad omen, a talisman associated with death rather than good luck.

'Thank you, Mirwais. I'll always remember you. I wish you and your friends all the best for the project.'

After saying their farewells, Gil and Alex walked back down the stairs to the road passing the small truck now loaded with Mirwais's goods and chattels standing outside the entrance to the apartment block. As they climbed into their vehicle, Alex turned to Gil.

'Mirwais doesn't looks so well. I hope he will be able to finalise their project before he joins Waheed.'

THIRTY-SIX

THE HADJI'S LAST TRIP, IN KABUL,
Thursday 10 November 2005

D riving to the Ministry of Urban Development with the land deeds, Hadji Zarak felt more relaxed than he had been for some time. While he regretted giving up the girl Sima, he would soon find another to meet his needs, one more willing.

The exchange had been easy, almost too easy. He anticipated Mirwais would have put up more of a fight. He was not expecting him to hand over the deeds so easily or so quickly, yet here they were, safely tucked into his favourite briefcase with its brass fittings and monogram etched in gold on its burnished brown leather surface. It would help to make a good impression on the recently appointed minister, a man he knew only vaguely.

Aarash, a guard at the madrassah, came from the same village as the minister and had attended the same local school. '*Ah!*' he told the hadji. '*Last time I saw him he was working with the World Food Programme handing out sacks of flour to refugees in Balochistan. Karzai surrounds himself with relatives, friends and those he owes favours to. Our government is tribal.'*

But no matter if he didn't know the minister personally. Having the deeds would secure the land project without any problem, he was certain of that, although he might have to pay a little sweetener. In fact he would pay a large sum to secure the rights to the land if necessary.

If only Mirwais and his cohorts knew why the land was so valuable – more than anyone could have foreseen. The hadji and his partners would build the houses as per the UN-approved plan. The costs could be kept low and they would make a substantial profit, but the real value of the land came with owning the rights to the hills of Kohi Bad Asia and Tur Ghunday.

The company had approached him the previous year. Would he be interested in brokering a land project to the northeast of Kabul, it would be very lucrative for him? Their plan for building houses and blocks of apartments as a front for their real objective – gold mining in the adjacent hills – appealed to him. What did the westerners call it, a win-win situation? He had nothing to lose.

He never knew who owned the company; he didn't need to. It was always a nameless American residing in Kabul and a Pakistani geologist who flew in from Karachi that met with him to thrash out the details of the plan. He would arrange for his cousin's company to approach the UN agency with the land project and then offer the resident representative a substantial sum to secure funding from donors.

The only possible stumbling block was the deeds. They were a prerequisite for the project. The nervous UN representative, the little Frenchman, had been no problem. He was only too glad to accept the payment from Mahdi, who himself was well paid once the plan was in operation.

When the land belonged to the hadji and his cousin, they would seek permission from the Ministry of Mines and Industries to start mining. It would be a formality. The current minister owed the hadji a few favours, but they would have to hurry: government ministers could change more rapidly than boys in his madrassah.

It was common knowledge Afghanistan had a substantial mineral heritage with hundreds of minerals already recorded and mapped including copper, gold, chromium, uranium, cobalt, iron ore and zinc, as well as natural gas and oil. Precious and semiprecious stones abounded. Apart from gemstones such as rubies, garnets, sapphires, topaz and emeralds, the country was the main global source of the prized blue stone, lapis lazuli.

Given the poor security situation in the country, extracting the minerals and gemstones was the problem. What could be better than mining a rich seam of gold on the outskirts of Kabul, one of the more secure locations in the country? It was perfect.

Arriving at the ministry, the hadji passed through the security check at the fortified gate. He gave a silent laugh as the guard walked round his vehicle with a long-handled mirror checking the undercarriage for IEDs. What if one was hidden inside the vehicle? It would be too easy to

271

explode it once past the checkpoint.

After parking in the Deputy Minister's space, his briefcase was fed through a security scanner located inside the main entrance to the building. Asking a guard for directions to the minister's office, the reply was brusque. 'Upstairs, turn left, third door on the right.'

When he reached the second floor, he entered the secretary's office. The only way to access the minister's office was through the adjoining door between the two rooms. It was firmly shut. Two men sat on an old faded sofa patiently waiting their turn to see the minister, but the hadji was impatient. He had an appointment and was on time. Why should he be kept waiting? His was important business.

The secretary, an elderly man with a stooped appearance and one good eye, no doubt some relative of the minister, said in a frail voice, 'Ah, Hadji Zarak, the minister is expecting you, he will see you now.'

The men on the sofa looked at each other, their signs of displeasure obvious. The hadji stared at them and gave a self-satisfied smirk.

His conceit followed him as he waddled through the door and into the minister's office where a heavily bearded figure sat at a desk signing papers, a large pile still awaiting his signature. There was no one else in the office which surprised the hadji; he expected other ministry officials and advisors to be present.

After the formal greetings and introductions, the minister crossed to a door at the back of his office and beckoned the hadji.

'The meeting is going to be held in another room, please follow me.'

As the hadji walked into the room, he realised it was not going to be the meeting he expected. A black-robed figure stood at the window and turned towards him, a grim expression on his face. 'Hadji Zarak. How good of you to come. I believe you have something in your briefcase belonging to my cousin Mirwais. It should be returned to him. Come, let us leave quietly, it will be better for us all.'

Commander Daud cut an imposing figure as he led a shocked, and for once speechless, Hadji Zarak down a set of backstairs to a small courtyard where a large SUV with darkened windows sat, two gunmen lolling against its side. As they saw Daud they came swiftly to attention.

One opened the back door and gestured to the hadji to get in. Hesitating for a moment in the knowledge this might be the last meeting he would ever attend, he only stepped up into the SUV on hearing the rough voice behind him growl, 'Get in, Zarak!'

The vehicle drove fast out of the ministry compound, destination unknown, the hadji squashed between the gunmen in the back seat while Commander Daud sat in the front passenger seat, an ominous look on his face as he drew a pistol from the holster belted at his side.

THIRTY-SEVEN

THE FINAL MEETING, IN KABUL,
Thursday 10 November 2005

Gil's calls to Olivier to arrange a meeting were neither answered nor acknowledged. He put the mobile back in his pocket in frustration. Finally, as he was sitting down to dinner at the house, his mobile rang. It was Olivier, apologising. He had been in meetings all day but could see Gil later that evening in the office.

It was unlike Olivier to stay at the office past five o'clock. He had mumbled something about leaving for France on personal matters within a few days and being too busy to meet earlier.

Reluctantly having to opt for another driver now Abdul Qabir was no longer with the house, Gil asked to be dropped at the agency office.

'Don't wait for me, Samir. I'll take a taxi back to the house when I'm finished.'

While this wasn't officially permitted, he didn't want

the driver to be late. The man had a family and there was always the risk of being harassed at roadblocks after dark, even for an official JDL driver.

On arrival at the office, Gil was surprised to be let in to the compound by Mahdi rather than one of the guards. Once inside he noticed there seemed to be no staff apart from Mahdi, now standing beside him as immaculately groomed as ever wearing a smart pressed shalwar kameez, his beard neatly trimmed. His eyes burned like agate as they bored into Gil. 'He is waiting for you in his office.'

With a curt nod, Gil walked through to Olivier's office, knocked on the door, and entered.

'Ah, *bonsoir*, Mr Moncrief, please come in, *s'il vous plait*.'

Olivier sat at the desk looking not quite his usual sartorial self. His tie was undone, one shirt sleeve rolled up, the other down at the cuff, and his jacket draped casually over the back of a chair. Even his carefully coiffured hair appeared dishevelled. A half-empty glass sat on the desk. Its fumes pervaded the room.

'What is so urgent? Could it not have waited until I return from Paris? No matter, *d'accord*, I have a few minutes available. What is it you want?'

This was strange. Usually Olivier never injected French words into a meeting with international staff. Local staff were different; the odd barrage of French swear words often slipped in on the assumption they wouldn't understand their meaning.

'I want to discuss this land project that you asked me to countersign. I have a few reservations about it.'

'Reservations, Mr Moncrief? It is perfectly straightforward.'

Yes, like a fuckin' snake, Gil thought.

'There appears to be excess payments without any obvious beneficiaries. How are these to be explained?'

'This is not the case – all payments have been accounted for.' Olivier folded his arms behind his head and rocked back on the chair.

'In any case, the accounts are not your concern. They will be dealt with in the office.'

Gil tried to hold himself in check. He had worked out a plan for confronting Olivier but seeing him sitting there so smug and condescending he snapped.

'Olivier, I know about the bribe you took from Hadji Zarak for facilitating the project. Sixty fucking thousand US dollars to be precise.'

Before Gil could say anything else, Olivier jumped to his feet, a startled look on his paling face. It took a few seconds for Gil to realise Olivier was looking beyond him to the door. Turning round, he found himself staring into the barrel of a small black snub-nosed pistol held by Mahdi.

'Please stand still, Mr Moncrief, we do not want blood spilled in the office.'

It sounded almost comical coming from a man holding a gun, but Gil understood that blood was going to be spilled – his blood. In that cold instant he knew it was Mahdi who'd killed Waheed.

Gil had become used to guns while in Afghanistan, but he'd never looked down the barrel of one at such close range, one pointed directly at him. His eyes fixed on the

276

small metallic hole staring at him like some dark malevolent eye.

It seemed so impersonal, not like a sharpened blade. There would be no personal contact as the trigger was slowly squeezed and his life extinguished. Thoughts flashed through his mind like a high-speed movie, the shock of perceiving a threat and being too late to avoid it.

The look in Mahdi's eyes left no doubt. It was the same look he'd seen in the eyes of the self-possessed young Talib, the caricature of an English public schoolboy, tall and athletic, good-looking with fine skin and high cheekbones, and possessed of an arrogant entitled air.

It was the spring of 2000 in the Ministry of Foreign Affairs. Gil had been sent there to get an exit visa, necessary under the Taliban regime. Three older Talibs in white shalwar kameez and matching turbans sat at desks looking bored and dejected that they had pens in their hands rather than guns.

Then the door opened and a young Talib swathed in black robes with the most enormous turban Gil had ever seen entered the room, casting his eyes over all he surveyed. There was no show of emotion on the Talib's face, but Gil knew with unerring certainty that if so ordered the young man would simply cross the room, draw the pearl-handled dagger belted at his side and slit Gil's throat with nonchalant ease. One slash of the blade then he would simply stride back across the floor and finish his cup of tea, leaving Gil to gush blood until he dropped to the floor dead.

It was the same emotionless look on Mahdi's face as he

waved the pistol at Gil guiding him towards the armchair closest to the desk.

'Mahdi! You should have stayed outside. He has no proof. Put the gun away.' Olivier was shaking as he uttered the words, his aversion to witnessing violence all too apparent.

'I'll find proof you took that bribe Olivier, you can be sure of that, you greedy bastard.'

'Too late, Mr Gil, proof will not help you.' Mahdi's face was passive as he kept the gun trained on Gil.

'It was you that killed Waheed, wasn't it? Why?'

'He knew too much about our project. He could not be bought. It was unfortunate.'

Mahdi's coolness was in marked contrast to Olivier's increasingly agitated state as he stuttered, 'Mr Moncrief… I did not intend it this way… please believe me… we could have come to some agreement…'

'You were going to pay me off as well. Is that it, Olivier? Who the fuck do you think I am?' Gil spat the words out even as helplessness overwhelmed him.

'Let us not waste words, we must leave immediately.' Mahdi pointed the gun in the direction of the door. There was no cool *Goodbye, Mr Bond* from the villain. Olivier looked panic-stricken and reached for his whisky glass as Gil was steered through the door at gunpoint.

As they slowly walked across the compound yard, Gil heard the crack of the gunshot but felt no pain. He was still standing. You were meant to be dead before you heard the shot, a bullet travelling faster than sound, yet he was still alive. Turning, he saw a figure emerge from the shadow of the building holding a smoking gun by his side.

'Do not worry.' The voice was measured and in strongly accented English. It came from a heavy-set man wearing an open parka over a crumpled suit that seemed to match the man's worn face.

'No one hears another gunshot in Kabul, Mr Moncrief. It will remain behind a curtain of silence. Your friend Mr Alex is waiting for you on the road. Leave now. Quickly. Tell him the ABC always pays dividends, he will understand.'

Gil didn't understand but didn't wait. As he hurried out of the compound he could swear his fear-driven senses detected a faint smell of roses. In a paved compound with no garden?

He gave it no more thought as he quickly passed Mahdi's body lying on the ground, the blood around the head pooling, the gun still clutched in his hand.

THIRTY-EIGHT

AT THE FAREWELL GIG, IN KABUL,
Thursday 17 November 2005

I t was Mickey's first gig at the club with his new band The Frontier Five. Practising for several weeks, this was only their second public performance. As he strapped on his Fender guitar and swaggered to the microphone, the crowd cheered. He met them with his usual aplomb.

'Good evenin', ladies and gentlemen. How're ye all doing this fine Thursday evening in Kabul? Let's be having a good time tonight! This first one's dedicated to me Grandpa Charly, God bless him.'

As the first chords of Elvis's 'It's Now or Never' rang out, Mickey wondered if he could conjure up his grandfather's ghost.

Dressed in the obligatory draped velvet collared jacket and drainpipe trousers and with his greased-back black hair, Charly had played in a famous Irish showband in the early 1960s. He was given the nickname 'The Creole King' by his bandmates after he claimed he saw Elvis's ghost one night as they were returning to Dublin from a gig in Dundalk.

It was Charly who introduced Mickey and his sister Ciara to the IRA. After basic training in their teens, both had become messengers for the organisation in the early 1990s delivering instructions to units in England engaged in bombing economic targets. They both relished the work; it was the start of a lifetime commitment, Mickey's only intensifying after Ciara was killed by a UVF member while on a mission to Belfast.

Working with the British Army down in Helmand to set up their new IT system, Mickey possessed the skills and knowledge to put his commitment into practice. In his own time, in his own way, no instructions necessary. Carefully planned sabotage could be a subtle thing in the IT world, sometimes not identifiable for months, even years. There was no harm in getting paid for it by JDL, a real bonus to go along with his Kabul job. If only Justin Edwards knew who he had hired.

'He's not a bad singer, is he?' Mena murmured as she and Gil sat at a corner table with some of the other housemates.

'Sings better than he talks, that's for sure. Let's hope he keeps it shorter than one of his usual caustic monologues,' Gil replied.

'That's unfair, he's really a nice guy. He's polite when he's talking to me.'

281

'He would be. You don't have a beard.' Mena nudged Gil in the ribs, a smile playing on her face.

Gil felt better than he had for a while. At least now he knew who killed Waheed even if he would never know the exact story behind the killing. He recognised the complex machinations of life – and death – in Afghanistan precluded this. Better to trust Occam's razor – the simplest explanation is usually the best one.

As Mahdi had said, Waheed could not be bought and he knew too much about the corrupt land deal. Yet why use an AK-47 and not a handgun to kill someone in such a public place during daylight hours? Gil felt nothing for Mahdi, only relief that at Alex's request the policeman Aziz had been following him that evening.

After the shooting, the UN quickly ghosted Olivier back to Geneva 'for further investigation', although the man's state of mind meant he had to be transported in a military plane under escort. There would be no public acknowledgment of the incident, especially the bribe. The UN avoided washing its dirty laundry in public at all costs.

Charlotte was also notable by her absence. After Sima was freed from the madrassah and reunited with her father, Charlotte had told Mena it was the right time for her to move on. She had left abruptly only a few days previously, never even handed her notice in to the agency. Her final destination remained unknown. She disclosed little, only saying, '*I'm meeting with a friend in Islamabad, then I'll think about what we're going to do next.*' Mena guessed the 'friend' was Larry who seemed to have vanished into thin air.

Gil suspected, although he didn't articulate it to his housemates, that Charlotte was the one to report Brock and his bootlegging activities to the authorities. While he felt little for Brock, the fate of Abdul Qabir was another matter. The leaking of such information to the authorities had resulted in his imprisonment. Brock and Charlotte had each played a role in the driver's fate, alcohol claiming yet another victim.

'*Salaam aleikum*, Mr Gil.' The voice floated over the sound of Mickey's guitar. It came from one of the club's waiters standing at the table wearing a newly pressed white shirt and black bow tie. It took Gil a few moments to recognise the young man.

'Asidullah! What are you doing here?'

'I am working in the restaurant. It pays well and I like the work. Is it fine to speak with you?'

'Yes, of course you can speak, we are among friends.' Asidullah looked apprehensive but noticed the Afghan woman seated next to Gil smiling at him with a quick nod of approval.

'You must forgive me for lying to you. It is not in my nature. There was no choice but to assist Mirwais. He was my father's best friend. There was no bag and no money, although those men I told you about did come to our house and threaten us.'

'It's alright, Asidullah, I don't blame you. Anyway, Waheed would have approved. Mirwais is a wily old fox. It would have been hard to resist him.'

'You know he is in poor health. He is at the village with

283

his family. It is doubtful he will be returning in the near future.'

'I know. I hope he'll recover soon.'

'I do too. Already he feels better now that Hadji Zarak is no longer with us.'

'What do you mean, "no longer with us", Asidullah?'

'He went for a meeting at one of the ministries nearly two weeks ago and has not been seen since. His madrassah has been closed down by the authorities.'

'And what about the land project?'

'The members of the consortium will carry on without Mirwais if necessary. The factory and the houses will be built. I am to be given a job there when it is complete.'

'If you see Mirwais please give him my regards.'

'I will be glad to. You know he holds you in high regard.'

'Me?'

'Yes, you always treated him with respect, you and your friend Mr Alex. Not everybody does.' Asidullah glanced at his stern-faced manager standing at the bar. 'Forgive me, Mr Gill, I must return to my work. Will I see you here again?'

'You certainly will. I'm leaving for the UK soon but will return to Kabul in early January, Insha'Allah.'

After Asidullah left, Gil and Mena sat closer to each other, their hands intertwined beneath the table. Their faces betrayed an unexpected happiness. In a few weeks Gil would be returning to Scotland on extended leave to see Mhairi and Jamie while Mena would remain in Kabul. They had agreed that on his return they would decide on any future they might have together.

It was nearly midnight, time for the club to close. The band had been on form and after their last number the raucous cheers and whistles from the audience demanded an encore. Mickey strode up to the microphone and announced one final song.

'This one's dedicated to all of us living here in Kabul. It's a number by a new band I just heard. My brother sent me their promotional CD. Not much time to rehearse so it might sound a bit ropey, but here we go…'

The song was by the Willy Clay Band, a Nordic noir band steeped in country rock. The Eagles with attitude. The band came from the northern Swedish mining town of Karuna, a place of ice and snow as far from California and the Delta as Kabul.

Over the chatter of the club, Gil could just make out Mickey's voice accompanied by his plaintiff guitar riffs and the drums slow backbeat. *We keep cruising down this road trying to be Elvis, looking for mercy and a shoulder to cry on tonight.* The words seemed all too apposite, a summing up of his recent experiences. When the song finished, Gil stood and applauded, a tear forming in the corner of his eye.

THIRTY-NINE

ON THE ROADSIDE, IN KABUL,
Thursday 1 December 2005

The young man sat on a large flat rock lying abandoned on the pavement that lined the road leading to the newly built police college. He looked skywards without shielding his face from the bright winter sun. He loved the sun and its radiant heat filling the sad spaces in his mind. There were so many of them. Now it was too late, there was no going back. He knew that what had been done to him could never be undone.

If only his father had come and taken him home. More and more his thoughts turned to home. The mountains he loved to climb where wheeling eagles scanned for prey scurrying among the dun-coloured rocks below. The river that tumbled through the lush green valley high above the plains, full of fish he and his father would catch with nets. His family and school friends, his cousin Ahmed who he'd only met briefly but who had given him the one thing of worth he had brought all the way to Pakistan from his home so far away. A small plastic figure of a dead American singer.

Hassan was able to endure the prison and its deprivations, the loneliness and the fear, until the day the guard Northwood entered the cage, chained his hands together and led him along an unlit corridor to a small room marked 'LAUNDRY'. After pushing him into the darkened space full of grubby blue laundry sacks, the guard quickly turned and locked the door.

'On the floor, boy, let's see how tough you are now. It's time to open up!' The guard chuckled at his own joke. Hassan had no idea what he was laughing about. Without any warning, he was pushed onto the floor face down on a pile of old blankets smelling of urine.

Lying there, he felt the shalwar being ripped from his legs and heard the noise of a zipper being undone. As his legs were forced apart and a pain unlike any he'd ever felt jolted through his body, he could hear Northwood grunting.

'Nice and easy, boy, take it easy. You'll enjoy this. Just relax and tell me where that old bastard Zarak keeps his money.' Hassan had no answer. He didn't know where the hadji kept his money. All he knew was the agonising pain that continued to flood through him.

When the guard was finished, he kicked Hassan in the ribs so hard it knocked the breath from him. As he lay there gasping for air he was hauled to his feet, slowly becoming aware of the warmth trickling down between his trembling legs.

'Clean yourself up, boy, and put your trousers back on.'

The guard now spoke in a quieter voice, some part of him acknowledging the depths of his depravity.

Returning to his cage, through the pain and his quiet tears, Hassan could only think of the *bachi bazi* he'd heard his father talk about. The young boys corrupted by older men and taught to dance and act like girls, wearing makeup and dressed in women's clothing. The boys were often forced into sexual acts and frequently passed on or sold from one powerful man to another.

He remembered his father saying he had once been invited to a party while on a trip to Afghanistan where these *bachi bazi* were performing. *'These boys have been dishonoured and defiled. They have been shamed. They are shunned by their families and society. Pray such perversion never comes to our area.'* His father's words had stayed with him through the pain – he could never return to his family again.

A few days after his ordeal, and still feeling sore, they released him from the prison, no reason given, just opened the gates and he was back in Afghanistan. After making his way to Kabul and the madrassah, he was so exhausted he collapsed on the ground before the guard could let him into the compound.

When he came to, he was met with the sight of the hadji standing there glaring down at him. 'Where in hell's gate have you been, Hassan?'

Lying on the cot in his small room at the end of the boys' dormitory, he summoned enough energy to recount the details of his capture and captivity – apart from the final brutalisation. He was too ashamed to disclose that to anybody. He knew the hadji was not a man to confide in. He'd once overheard a visitor to the madrassah turn to his companion and say, '*Hadji Zarak is a rich man yet there is no shred of charity in him, no compassion.*'

Hassan found it difficult to fit back into the routine of the madrassah. He was given some small tasks to do but even found these difficult. His mind too unclear to focus, he became more withdrawn and kept himself to himself as much as possible.

After a week the hadji informed him that he was sending him to another madrassah closer to the Pakistan border. '*It's up in the mountains. The fresh air will clear your mind.*'

And indeed the air was fresher, and much colder, than in the Kabul valley. The madrassah, no more than two large sheds and some old huts, functioned as a camp where several other youths, some younger than him, were put through a rigorous military training programme. The camp was well equipped. Apart from heavy weapons, machine guns, handguns, rifles and ammunition, it contained an array of intelligence data including foreign passports, laptops, digital cameras and cards, documents and mobiles.

Hassan was impressed. He had little time to think even as the mental cobwebs began to disentangle. Each day started with morning prayers and a sermon on the importance of jihad, followed by physical fitness drills and operational training from a Chechen instructor. Already used to handling an AK-47, Hassan was introduced to PK machine guns, rocket-propelled grenades, tactics for attacking military convoys and instructions for planting IEDs.

In the evenings, to reinforce the cause of jihad, they were shown videos depicting western atrocities against their Muslim brothers and sisters. Not that Hassan needed any reinforcement, for he already hated the American infidels with every fibre of his being. The instructor told them the Afghan police and soldiers were friends of the Americans. They were all enemies of the jihad.

All the boys had to make the *bay'ah*, the oath of allegiance to their leader, although he was no spiritual master, no pir or sheikh where the *bay'ah* was given in exchange for spiritual knowledge. Instead, he was a man constantly on the mobile and computer. An unassuming young man of no more than thirty years, long-haired, thinly bearded and wearing steel-rimmed spectacles. He addressed them after they had given their oath: '*Now you know you all have brothers willing to carry their souls in their hands. You are pledged to the jihad.*'

It made Hassan feel better knowing he had brothers willing to die for him. This was his new family. Coming to the camp had restored some sense of the man he could never be and now his group was to be selected for a special task, one deemed a great honour.

The sky was still bright as Hassan sat with the IED strapped to him watching the passing traffic, his hand now shielding his eyes from the sun, the bomb hidden by his parka jacket. He shivered. With the cold or perhaps fear, it didn't matter. There was no going back. His home and his soul were distant places. He had been trained for this moment.

Slowly he raised himself and walked towards the bus drawing to a halt at the traffic lights. It was full of new recruits on their way to the police college up the road.

Behind the bus a white Land Cruiser with two passengers sat, its engine quietly running, waiting for the lights to change. A small somehow familiar figure was outlined against the windscreen, its white body stark in the sunlight. It was the last thing Hassan saw before he pressed the button on the body belt wrapped tightly round his shalwar kameez.

A share of the author's profits
will be donated to a charity that helps and supports
the people of Afghanistan

POSTSCRIPT

While this book is being typeset Afghanistan is experiencing yet another watershed moment in its turbulent history. This is the scheduled withdrawal of all NATO and US forces by 11 September 2021 - the abandonment of a vulnerable country in crisis. As a result, it is likely that the security situation in the country will deteriorate markedly and violence increase. 2020 emerged as the most violent year ever recorded by the UN in Afghanistan, with women and children constituting 43% of civilian casualties. In 2022 the violence and the hardships and heartbreak it brings for the Afghan people is only likely to increase. The Kabul of 2005 portrayed in the novel no longer exists. The bars and restaurants are long shut down, most internationals and expats have already left. For them, the party's over. For Afghans, the suffering will only continue.